A BLAZE OF STARS & DAWN

USA TODAY Bestselling Author

EVE L. MITCHELL

Editorial services provided by *Helayna Trask with Polished Perfection.*

Cover design provided by *EerilyFair Designs.*

A BLAZE OF STARS & DAWN

*For those who keep getting back up and fighting.
This one's for you.*

There are terms and words within this book that are not contained with the dictionary. This is a paranormal romance book—I reserve the right to make up names and words at my leisure (as my editor will attest to).

Please note that I am a British author, and although I have tried to make this as universal as I could, there will be some British spelling, phraseology, and terminology that I can't (and won't) eradicate from my writing, and I'm okay with that.

If swearing offends you, I recommend you stop reading now.

A Blaze of Stars & Dawn

The angels are falling.
They're coming and they're ready to hunt.
I never thought it would be *me* who would be their prey.

Confounded with the shock of recent revelations, I'm scared, confused, angry…
Yet again, I'm fleeing from those who seek to harm me.
With Azazel—the demon who hates me the most.
Hell must have frozen over.

With heaven falling and hell rising, all in the bid to find me, I soon have nowhere left to run and only a few allies by my side. It's time to stand and fight.
Fight for me and all that I love, or die trying…

 Character List

WATCHERS
Samyaza (Sam)
Azazel (Zel)
Chazaquel (Chaz)
Penemue (Pen)
Amaros (Ros)
Gadreel (Der)

NECROMANCERS
Cross
Star

ANGELS
Gabriel
Michael

HELLHOUNDS
Hound/Morax

PRINCES OF HELL
Asmodeous (Lust)
Satan (Wrath)
Lucifer (Pride)
Abbadon (Sloth)
Beelzebub (Envy)
Mammon (Greed)
Belphegor (Gluttony)

CHAPTER 1

I DIDN'T LOOK WHERE I WAS RUNNING OR WHERE ZEL WAS taking me. He led and I followed, with Hound bringing up the rear. How on earth was I pregnant? Why had no one noticed? Why had *I* not noticed? I mean, there was a bump.

A bump.

A baby was inside me.

Oh holy Jesus, I was going to faint.

"Zel!" I called just before I started to black out. I felt strong arms grab me, and then it was dark. When I came to, I was in familiar surroundings and immediately alarmed. Looking around the stone walls, the dirt floor, the wide-open entrance to the great beyond, I finally saw Hound sitting in the corner, facing me. "The caves?" I asked him. "I'm at Dunnottar Castle?"

You are.

"Why? Earth cannot be safe for us. Are the angels still coming?"

They have stopped their fall. But they will not stop.

"Of course, why would they?" I said bitterly as I rose to my feet, my legs feeling shaky below me. "So, I faint now. Yay. Where is he?"

Patrolling.

"Won't they sense me?" I asked Hound as I made my way to the cave entrance and looked out over the calm North Sea. Summertime in Scotland meant short nights, not always warm, but clear at least. The sea lay quiet in its rest below me, dark waters with hidden depths that housed many secrets. The sky was still light even though the sun was sitting low on the horizon. It was actually a beautiful night. Peaceful.

It was a pity it didn't reflect the turmoil within me.

Turning, I looked at Hound and waited for his answer. "Hound?"

The souls are here.

Trying to hide my surprise, I looked back outside. I couldn't see them, nor could I sense them.

"Am I broken?" I asked him cautiously as I rubbed my bump. "If *his* kid cuts off my powers, I will skin his hide."

You are not broken. The souls are here because Cross sent them.

"Oh." I thought about it. "I can't sense souls that Death sent? Seriously?"

He is the ultimate necromancer.

I snorted. Way to state the obvious. "I'm starving."

The Watcher will provide.

I looked at Hound with a raised eyebrow. "You've met Azazel, right? The man hates me."

"Demon, not man," Zel said as he sat on a rock with a bag in his hand, which he held out to me. "Eat."

"What is it?" I asked dubiously as I sat across from him and took the offered take-out bag. Opening it and peering inside, I took out two containers. One held a mixed green salad, the other a breast of chicken on crushed potatoes and a side of broccoli. "This looks…" *Healthy.* "Good," I lied.

"Eat it, the child needs nutrients." Zel handed me a bottle of prenatal vitamins and a bottle of water.

"Um. Coffee?"

"No caffeine."

"Today?" I had a horrible feeling he was about to tell me something disastrous.

"At all." Zel fixed his piercing blue eyes on me. "Caffeine is not recommended for pregnant women."

Seemed I was going to die today after all. Was he serious? He looked serious. "Are you joking?" Zel had a sense of humour, didn't he? Somewhere? Deep down. Real deep. I mean, you would need to dig. But surely…somewhere.

"No."

Arsehole.

"Zel, I need coffee to live."

"No, you need oxygen, food and water, *just* water, to live." He produced his own meal and a takeaway coffee. I knew it was coffee because I could smell it. Hound wasn't the only bloodhound in this cave.

"That's coffee."

He smirked at me. "It is."

"I hate you."

"Eat your chicken, take your vitamins." He took a long drink of his coffee. "Now."

I hesitated. I knew I couldn't argue with him, and to do so would alienate one of my few allies. I watched him take another drink and knew the bastard was laughing at me. With grim determination, I focused on my meal. It looked so wholesome and nourishing. I was back in hell.

As I started to eat, I glanced at him as he drained his coffee cup dry like it was his last drink.

"Thank you for the meal." See, I could be the bigger person.

Zel grunted and said nothing as he opened his package

and pulled out a wrap that looked packed full of tasty deliciousness.

"You're right," I acknowledged. "I don't need coffee to survive."

Another grunt.

"But you may not live if I don't get a caffeine fix." I looked up at him with a narrowed glare. "I believe they say that one cup of coffee a day is permissible during pregnancy," I said thoughtfully. I'd read that somewhere, hadn't I? "And it's not like I'm carrying the regular Joe's baby. It's Sam's. He drinks more coffee than I do."

"No one drinks coffee more than you do," Zel interrupted me.

I shovelled some potato in my mouth and fought the urge to stab him with my plastic cutlery. "So you see, since my blood type is obviously caffeine, the bump needs it."

"The bump?"

"Yeah, you know..." I looked down self-consciously. "Him...or her."

"The *child* needs sustenance. There is no sustenance in caffeine. You will eat well for this child, or you will be force fed." His smile was wicked. "I don't mind which you choose."

He wasn't even joking. Of all the demons to save me...I get this one.

"Can I have decaf?" What was I saying? *Decaf? Decaf was death.* Desperate times, I suppose.

"Maybe."

Opening my water, I avoided his stare. I felt it on me as I tried, and failed, to open the childproof lid of my vitamins. He reached out and took them off me and easily opened the bottle, shaking out one tablet and then replacing the cap.

Tightly. He handed the tablet to me, and reaching over, I took it off him. I'd admired his hands before, when he taught me how to reach my powers. He had long, supple fingers, his skin a beautiful shade of obsidian. It made sense to compare his skin tone to volcanic glass. Comparing Zel to anything relating to a volcano was, to me, the perfect description. His twin scars never detracted from his beauty but added to it. His striking blue eyes caught me off guard every time, full of ancient wisdom and stark brutality. It fascinated me that he would ever be considered gentle. Or in love. As my eyes ran over him, I knew why someone would be physically attracted to him, but as soon as he opened his mouth, it would be an instant turnoff.

Naomie must have been drunk…a lot.

"Why are you staring at me?" he barked at me, and I fought the grin.

"Just admiring your handsomeness."

Zel crushed his takeaway cup in one hand and grunted. "You've enough problems, there's no need to *admire* me."

"Why are you helping me, Zel?" I asked tiredly as I put the carton down, half eaten, and I watched him take note with narrowed eyes. "You dislike me, immensely."

"I told you before, it is not personal. I just dislike witches."

"I met Naomie," I told him softly as I watched his back straighten slightly. "She seems nice."

"A whore."

"Wow, Zel. Why not say what you really think?" I shook my head in disgust. "Are you sure you were supposed to fall? You're so very righteous and judgemental."

He gave a frustrated sigh. "She was a prostitute."

Oh. Well, now I just felt stupid. Then my eyes were

widening in surprise. "*You* had a relationship with a hooker? *You?*"

Zel huffed in what would be amusement in anyone else; in him, it was hard to say. He stood and, bending down, he picked up my half-eaten food and placed it back on my lap. Holding his hand over the food, briefly, he then nodded once. "Eat your chicken. The child needs food. You need food. And eat your vegetables. And your salad."

"Please, God, don't go all mother hen on me." I looked down at my container of food. "Did you just zap my dinner like a microwave?"

"Less radiation, but yes."

Radiation? What? "I—"

"Just eat, witch. The quicker you eat, the quicker you will sleep, and the sooner I'll have some peace."

I went to speak, but I caught Hound's eye, and even he was looking at me with reproach. "Fine, I'll eat."

I swore to God, even my parents hadn't watched me eat with such intensity when I was a child. When I attempted to leave some broccoli, I got a warning growl, and as I was looking at my food, I wasn't quite sure which one of them had made the noise. Once my chicken was done, the carton was removed, and the side salad was on my lap.

"What are these?" I picked up a hard round green…thing.

"Edamame beans."

"Uh-huh, and it's a what?"

"Soybean. Eat it, it's perfectly safe to consume during pregnancy." Zel was fixing his weapons.

"I don't like it." I put it back in the salad. "I'll eat around it."

"You *just* asked me what it was, so how do you know you don't like it?"

I was five years old again, and I wasn't appreciative of the fact that the male in front of me was a huge grumpy demon and not my dad. "I don't want it."

"Well, we don't always get what we want, witch. Eat your fucking salad."

Put it down to being pregnant, put it down to fear at being hunted by angels, put it down to irrational thought, put it down to anything that was understandable under the circumstances, but when I used my power to propel the salad container and its nasty beans right out of the cave and into the sea, I didn't even feel guilty.

He held my stare for so long I began to lose my bravado pretty quickly. When he smiled suddenly, I think I peed a little with fear.

"I'll just get you something extra *healthy* for breakfast."

"I can feed myself," I muttered as I lay down on the floor on the blankets we'd left last time we were here. Or maybe they were new, I no longer cared.

"If we leave the child's nourishment to you, you will feed it merely potato chips and sweets."

"I turned out all right," I grumbled as I laid my head on my arm.

"Debatable."

I felt Hound lie at my back, providing me with his warmth. *Thank you.*

You should not test him so. He is difficult on a normal day.

I grinned in the fading light and had to bite my lip to stop from laughing.

When I felt a blanket being draped over me, I turned to look up at the demon above me. "Thank you, Azazel. For the food, for the blankets and for helping."

Zel held my stare for a moment before he gave me a brief nod. "In the morning, we'll discuss strategy. We need a plan, and we need one fast."

"Is there anywhere that's safe?" I asked as I turned away from him again. "The angels won't care that neither of us intended this."

"No," Zel agreed. I heard his sigh as he made himself comfortable at the entrance. "They remember before. We all do."

"Was it really so bad?" I asked softly, almost afraid of the answer. But of course, I asked Zel, the most honest of them all.

He was silent for so long that I didn't think he would answer me, and my eyes closed to sleep. He startled me when he spoke, his tone low, heavy with remembrance. "The Nephilim kill the mothers during the birth. We were so ignorant we didn't know how to save them. The children are babes for mere weeks, their growth is rapid. We couldn't hide them amongst villages; they didn't go unnoticed. Their skin glows, almost as if in radiance. It doesn't fade quickly. There was little place to hide golden-skinned children that stood out so much. Their appetites rival that of a grown man who's worked hard all day in his fields. We thought of taking them to hell, but they cannot survive in the realms of the fallen."

What kind of being can't survive in hell? "Because they're half human?" I asked him in the low darkness.

"Yes, we suspected it was so." I heard him move, and I didn't dare turn to look in case he didn't continue his story. "Penemue discovered the ether. He would of course. A dimension that we could control, we could adapt. The children thrived. They grew..." He paused. "So fast, they grew."

I heard the heavy sadness in his rich deep voice, and I wanted so badly to turn to watch that I was rolling over almost silently, without making the conscious decision to do so. Zel's intensity always scared me, but of all the Watchers, it was Zel who stood out, because he was and always would be, a soldier. However, as I looked at him now, sitting with his back to the wall of the cave, his legs out in front of him, his head resting lightly against the cave as he stared out over the darkness, I felt a pang of sorrow. He looked so…tired. Not in a he-needs-a-good-sleep way, but in a heavy way. The kind that dragged you down until you were beat with exhaustion, a hollow fatigue that you felt deep within your bones.

"Once they had aged, they were no longer in our control. They soon began to travel from the ether to the human realm." His head dipped low, and I knew his eyes were closed. "They destroyed…*everything*. They knew no guilt, no sense of care, no desire to keep it…*good*." His hand rubbed over his forehead. "People, animals, infrastructure for what it was then, villages, nothing…nothing was safe." His head tilted back again as he recalled the past. "We fell because we Watched. We wanted to be part of this world, this creation that we were denied. But they…it was like they were created to destroy the very thing we fell to be part of."

Balance.

The Watchers fell to protect and live. Their children were born to destroy and ultimately…die. My hand was on my stomach as I felt the nausea rise. I had one of these growing inside me. What was I thinking protecting it? "Zel…why do you help me if you know what I carry?"

His head turned to me with his face shadowed in the low light. "We've come so far, seen so much, I refuse to believe we cannot make a difference. You are a witch, a necromancer, and you are bound to him like no other. It has to *mean* something."

"Him?" I asked. "You mean Sam?"

"Samyaza is strong. The death of his children hardened him like nothing else. He knows what you carry. He knows what happened last time."

I waited for more, and when Zel turned to look out back towards the water, I rose slightly from my position. "And what? You think he'll be different? Because it's *me?*" I asked him incredulously.

"Yes."

"Zel! How?" I asked in exasperation.

"Because he loves you, and he will watch this world burn before he loses you." Zel looked back at me. "And I'm counting on that, because you won't let anything harm your child, and he won't allow any harm to come to you."

I was dumbfounded. He was putting his faith in Sam's feelings for me? Had he lost his mind? Yet, despite my instant denial, I felt it. The small spark of hope that ignited inside me.

"Of course, we need to wait for him to calm down first." Zel's voice held a humour that I did not feel.

"I think we need a better plan," I grumbled as I lay back down. "I swear, Zel, your *Father* sends the rain again, you better build me a big fucking boat."

I heard his low chuckle, and it was one of the only times that I had made this male laugh. I closed my eyes with a small smile on my face before I realised my fate.

"I die," I whispered. "For my child to live, I die."

"I'll try to prevent that."

Try? Well, that snuffed out my little spark of hope.

"Sleep, witch, we cannot linger here much longer."

How he thought I would sleep after all those revelations was beyond me, but sleep I did, except my dreams were not empty. Even pregnant witches can't escape a Watcher when he's hunting.

CHAPTER 2

I WAS IN THE LAND of the SOULS, AND INSTANTLY I WAS ON edge. The dimension was still white to me, but again like before, trees surrounded me. Trees that moved to a wind that I could not feel. Looking down, I realised I was still in my clothes and not some stupid floor-length dress. Had I come here myself?

I felt him before I saw him. His presence was familiar, albeit currently unwelcome. Turning slowly, I took him in. Forest green eyes pulsed with power as he strode through the quiet of the land. His hand was on the pommel of his sword, his leathers moulded to his body, and I noted he wore his armoured plates.

They were fighting?

No. He was *hunting*. I had a pretty good idea who his prey was. As if I had entered his thoughts, Sam stopped suddenly, his head swivelling sharply to look in my direction.

Please don't see me.

"Witch?" His voice was low, cautious. An uncertain step forward as his eyes roamed over me and past me. "I know you're there."

Which meant he couldn't see me. He looked...perfect. Was I stupid to think that when I knew he would be hunting for me? Possibly? I watched as his eyes narrowed and his lips pressed together in frustration. I saw the faint flush of colour on his cheeks. Damn, I wanted to reach out and touch him. Quietly, I watched him take another step forward, almost willing him to reach me.

"You can't run forever," he spoke softly. I could almost hear the remorse. "Azazel knows we will find you." His hand ran through his hair with frustration. "Dammit, witch, you don't want Michael and his platoon to find you first. At least with me, you have a chance."

A chance at what? Survival? Did our child?

I startled when a cool hand clasped my wrist, and I met Cross's dark eyes. He shook his head once in warning, and I nodded my understanding. As I felt Cross pull me away, I placed my hand atop his, halting him from taking me away.

"Star, please, let me help you fix this." Sam's chin dipped low, and I heard the whisper. "Let me save you from this."

Tears ran down my cheeks as I saw how deep his anguish ran, but I knew his desire to help was not to help us both. The Watchers were tarnished, jaded from past experience. My child would not survive their aid, and I knew, I *knew* why, but still, my stupid heart held onto hope.

Softly Cross tugged at my wrist, and I turned away from the demon who broke me so easily. Zel was pacing the cave restlessly when Cross returned me, and I settled back into my body. "She is drawn to him when she sleeps," Cross explained to Zel as I sat up.

"Soul or awareness?" I asked as I yawned.

"Soul."

Zel watched me, his hard eyes unblinking.

"Before you lose it, I can't help it," I defended myself.

"I suggest you learn," he snapped in his usual fashion. "I do not risk this for you to betray me when you sleep."

Betray him? He had a cheek! "Me? Betray you? Are you serious?" I asked angrily as I stood. "Really?"

He looked at Cross without answering me. "Who was it, and did they sense her?"

"Samyaza, and yes, he did." Cross looked around the cave curiously. "This is terrible."

I tried to look at the cave as Cross would see it. Instead, I saw the time before when the Watchers had been with me, before it all went to shit. "I like it." The look Cross gave me told me he thought I was a special kind of "special," and I stuck my tongue out at him in response. "Why can't I be with you?" I asked him as I looked between the two of them.

"Because I cannot be with you all the time, and you are very popular at the moment." Cross smirked as he spoke.

"Plus, he's being watched," Zel muttered as he looked out of the mouth of the cave. "The souls won't keep us like this forever," he told me as I saw his shoulders tense, and he let out a loud exhale. "We need a plan. I was hoping to wait until morning, but if you aren't going to sleep, then we can do it now."

I was exhausted, and I was pretty sure the darkest demon had just told me he didn't intend to let me sleep now. "I *was* sleeping." I ignored Zel's snort as I looked at Cross pleadingly. "Tell him I was sleeping."

Cross hesitated and then gave a small nod. "I believe her body does rest. Even when she splits her awareness and her soul, one or the other takes its rest."

"She splits her awareness?" Zel was looking at me with interest. "I know only a few who can do that."

No one said anything, and I looked between them, yet again feeling that I was missing out on the conversation that they were having without me. "Is that a good thing?" I demanded.

"Depends," Zel grunted. "It's a nice trick, unless you don't know what you're doing, and then it's dangerous and leads to death."

"Death?" I was startled, and then I looked at Cross. *The* Death. "I think I'll be okay," I said as I shared a look with Cross and saw his lips twitch in a small smile.

"Just because you can control it, doesn't mean you should *flirt* with it," Zel grumbled.

Well, talk about awkward. "Seriously?" I hissed at him as I went back to my blanket. "I'm going back to sleep."

"Will you stay away from him?" Zel demanded.

"I'm sleeping, Zel, I have no control over what happens when I'm sleeping." I turned my back on them both.

"Why is she not trained better?" Zel demanded of Cross, and I really had to question his sanity, because Cross was *Death*. Should he really be questioned like that? I mean, I teased him, but I was never actually antagonistic towards him.

"I cannot work miracles," Cross replied with amusement, and I was going to rethink my nice, pleasant thoughts about showing Cross respect, when he continued. "I've only had Star in my tutelage for a short time, as you know."

"The fact she can split is not good news."

"I know, but in truth, I think Samyaza pulls her more than she willingly seeks him out," Cross shared with Zel.

"I said I was going to sleep, I didn't say I was asleep," I interjected. "I can hear you!" Honestly, these males needed to remember I was in the room. They always spoke about me as if I weren't there; was there any wonder that my soul split from my body as soon as possible? I sat up abruptly. "When I split, do I hurt the baby?" I asked them both.

"No," Cross answered immediately. "Your body is fine. It is in stasis."

"How did Araqiel even know how to shield the pregnancy?" I questioned as I drew my legs up and settled the blankets around me. "I thought *I* was the necromancer? Why did I not know there was a soul wrapped around me? How did a Watcher command the dead?"

Cross's eyes narrowed as he listened to my questions, and I knew it was in regards to Araqiel and not me. "He used the darkest of magic, it is forbidden, and it is that way for a reason."

Waiting patiently, I realised that neither of them were going to say anything else. "Cross! Spill," I demanded impatiently. When I saw him look at his shoes, I had to fight the eye roll. "Tell me what he did!"

"In order to command a soul, you need to make a bargain." Zel's words were tight, angry. "As you ran in the shadows and made your deal with a prince of hell, my brother made a deal with another."

"Okay, firstly, you need to let the whole I-had-a-deal-with-Satan thing go. I did what I did to survive; you *know* I did the smart thing." When he refused to acknowledge me, I turned to look at Cross. "Araqiel made a deal with you? I don't understand."

Cross looked affronted. "Me? I would have struck him down myself had he asked me such a thing."

This was getting me nowhere. Honestly, both of them had on separate occasions told me they were teachers. No wonder I learned nothing. Getting to my feet, I began to pace. "I can command the dead because I'm awesome and I'm a necromancer." I ignored Zel's huff of displeasure. "Cross can command the dead because...well"—I cast a look at Cross, who was grinning at me openly—"and Hound can collect the souls along with the other hellhounds." I paused and turned to my friend. "Should I call you Morax?"

No.

"Hmm." I turned back to the other two males. "So Araqiel didn't come to me—obviously— and he didn't go to Cross. Can another prince of hell do it?"

"No. Only the soul itself can agree to the bargain." Cross smoothed the pleat in his trousers without looking at me. "The Watcher struck a bargain with the soul itself."

"How—"

His soul is lost forever.

I whirled to Hound. "Wait, what? Araqiel's soul struck a bargain? With who?"

"We don't know."

My wide eyes met Zel's in shock. "What?"

"In order to work the magic, the asker relinquishes their soul completely."

"Relinquishes it where?"

"His soul is gone," Cross said quietly. "There is no purgatory, no afterlife, nothing."

Holy shit, that was intense. "He's gone?"

"Yes, you can rest easy, happy now?" Zel snarled.

"I wanted him dead," I admitted honestly as I sat back on my makeshift bed. "But..." My teeth worried my lower lip. "I think now I know more about what I am, what there *is* for the dead, I don't think I would wish that on anyone." As I stared at my feet, I realised something that was simply crushing. "He must have hated me so much," I whispered in the quiet. "To do that, to *lose* that." I raised my eyes to Zel's. "I never did anything to him."

The Watcher held my stare for a short time before he looked away. "When you took his life in the pit, it may be…" Zel flexed his shoulders as if he were uncomfortable before he continued. "It may be that his soul sought the ether, where your body was. It may be that he was going to strike you as you lay defenceless."

"Did you know this was a possibility?" I demanded, outraged.

"No," Zel admitted grudgingly. "We should have though."

"And when Araqiel saw you in the ether, in his state, he would have sensed that although you were absent, your body still housed a soul."

"The child's."

"Yes," Zel bit out.

"And he sought revenge by concealing my pregnancy?" I didn't understand half of what was going on. "What does the soul who made the deal with him gain?"

"Fast tracked through *processing*," Cross said with an angry glint in his eye.

"Are you shitting me?" I could feel that my mouth was hanging open. "Araqiel loses his soul, and the soul who concealed him and my baby gets *fast tracked* like he's in line for a fucking ride at a theme park?"

"It's a bit more complex, but basically," Cross replied.

"What a complete dick," I grumbled as I pulled the blankets higher. "But why conceal the pregnancy? I mean, okay, Sam won't react well, but it's my body."

Zel snorted but remained silent, while Cross watched me with humour. "Nephilim gestate at a quicker pace. There is a very small window where it is thought to be possible to extract the foetus from the womb at no harm to the mother."

"Abortion?" I asked in horror.

"Termination, yes," Cross confirmed.

I caught Zel's eye as he looked at my hand clutching my stomach. "I don't think that was an option for me."

"You would not have taken the chance to survive?" Zel asked me, disbelieving.

Looking at my bump, I thought about it. I had killed Araqiel for a chance at my survival. Would I kill my unborn baby for the same chance?

No.

I knew it in every fibre of my being. My child was innocent, and I was hoping that their father and their many uncles had evolved from their first experience of the Nephilim and that the same fate did not await my child.

Or I was going to be one very pissed off mama. And I would haunt the everlasting shit out of all of them.

"No," I finally answered Zel. "Never."

We held each other's stare for a long moment before he gave a slight bow of his head in acceptance. "You should sleep."

"I probably should," I agreed tiredly. As I lay down, my head was spinning with the information. "Wait, what was in the vial?" I asked Cross.

He had the decency to look embarrassed. "A potion, that would have, well, it would have—"

"A potion to terminate?" I asked coldly as I looked over at Hound. "You *gave* me it?"

I did. I would do it again.

"It's my body, my choice."

It's the fate of billions of people.

Although that was a sobering thought, they still had no right to make that choice for me. Men making choices about what *I* could do with *my* body could go fuck off back to the dark ages and try evolution one more time, because they had obviously failed on the first attempt.

A thought occurred to me. "Did *you* know I was pregnant?" I asked Cross suspiciously.

"No, but I knew, when you returned from your time in the ether, you had engaged in blood exchange."

"You make me sound like a fiend," I grumbled.

Cross merely shrugged.

I wasn't happy. Their conversation this evening had shocked me, but I was so tired now. However, there was one thing left to be said. "It is never *your* choice," I told them as I fixed my glare on both of them. "You had no right. You have both disappointed me."

To my surprise, Zel smiled widely at me for the first time since I had known him. "Finally, you say something worth listening to."

He was still smiling as tiredness finally took hold of me and I succumbed to sleep.

CHAPTER 3

WHEN I WOKE THE SECOND TIME, THIS TIME FROM AN uninterrupted sleep, I was in a place I didn't recognise. Hound sat close by, but other than that, we were alone. Looking down at my blanket and clothes, I wondered if I had been literally lifted up from where I lay last night, to this bed.

Whose bed, I didn't know yet, but as I willed myself to get up, I thought I better find out. Knowing Zel, he probably terrorised the occupants to give me their bed. Hound followed, but even though I was giving him curious looks, he was keeping his thoughts to himself.

I should have been more suspicious.

I had teamed up with the two most opinionated males in the history of males. One who was obviously being quiet, and it should have worried me. Cautiously, I made my way down a curved staircase. The carpets and the soft furnishings of the bedroom told me I was in a human home.

Human home?

My word, what had I become in so short a time to talk like this? I found Zel in the kitchen, which took me four attempts to find, so I decided I was in my own country, or a European one. I remembered reading that American homes were mostly open plan on the ground floor, so the wall of doors I was currently going through told me I was probably closer to home than I had been in a while.

Zel was staring out the window, and when I looked, I saw low rolling hills with a fine low mist.

"Where are we?" I asked him as he continued to stare outside.

"It matters not where we are, it only matters that we are leaving soon."

"Where are the owners?" I asked hesitantly as I examined the contents of the fully packed fridge. "They're…okay?"

"They live, if that's what you mean."

Wow. "Yeah, thanks, Mr Murder and Mayhem. Are they here?"

"No. Why would they be here?" He glanced at me, and I knew one day I would take his look of barely concealed patience and shove it up his arse.

"I don't know!" I snapped back at him. "I don't know where we are, I don't know whose house I'm in, I don't know how we do this, Zel!"

His eyes ran over me quickly, assessing. "Hormones?"

My mouth hung open. "No. This is *me*. Normal."

"There's nothing normal about you." He gave me his back, and I eyed the knife block on the kitchen counter with murderous intent. "You'd never get there in time," Zel added without looking at me, and I felt instantly guilty for being caught.

"Where are we? Where are we going?"

"We are somewhere rural and empty. We leave now you're awake and after you have broken fast."

Pulling the fridge doors open again, I considered breakfast. There was a packet of bacon, and looking around, I found the eggs. The fridge was well stocked, but the breadbin was empty. On a hunch, I opened the freezer and found a loaf of frozen bread.

Barbarians.

I never understood people freezing bread, but at the moment, I didn't mind, because I was having bacon, eggs and toast for breakfast. As I started to prepare the food, Zel turned slightly to watch me.

"You okay?" I asked carefully as I fried the bacon off in the pan.

"They have tea."

"I'll make a pot," I answered. I was not giving him the satisfaction of complaining about the lack of caffeine again, though I wanted to, but as I flicked the bacon over, I realised my hand was resting on my bump.

This kid better love me—sacrificing coffee was a huge deal for me.

I heard Hound snuff in disgust, and I stared at him. "What?"

Your kid *is going to die.* You *are going to die. There is no love in the heart of the Nephilim.*

"No bacon for you," I decided, trying to keep my mood jovial. "You're already salty." Grating the cheese for my scrambled eggs, I avoided Zel's curious stare as he looked between me and the hellhound. When breakfast was ready, I put my plate and Zel's on the table and waited for him to sit.

"You made me food?" His tone showed his surprise.

"I'm not a monster."

His mouth opened and quickly closed. I watched him pick up the crispy bacon and look at me.

"Don't judge. If it isn't burnt, it's not bacon."

Zel grunted but said nothing further. We ate in silence for a few minutes as I tried to avoid his look and braced myself for whatever he was away to throw at me.

"I'll find you some fruit for after," he eventually said.

"I'm okay for fruit," I mumbled, taking a large swallow of tea.

"You'll eat fruit."

Snapping my bacon in half, I popped a bit in my mouth. "Fine."

When he realised that I wasn't fighting him, he polished off his food, his plate clean. From his pocket, he produced the bottle of prenatal vitamins and handed me one.

"Thank you."

"Are you planning to escape?" he demanded suddenly.

Startled at his outburst, I sat there with a glass of water halfway to my mouth while the vitamin sat heavy on my tongue. "Wha—?" I mumbled around the tablet. When I realised it had a funky taste, I quickly drank it down. "What?" I repeated.

"You're being…amicable."

I met his suspicious icy blue eyes. "You've gone against your brothers to help me and my child," I replied quietly. "We don't exactly gel, Zel, so if you can make that sacrifice for me, I can eat some fruit and take a vitamin. It's called compromise. Plus, I know you're doing it for my own wellbeing."

"I don't know whether to believe you or not."

"Your trust issues are your own," I answered coolly as I stood and made my way to the sink. "They have a dishwasher," I told him as I thought about how much time we had spent here. "If I run it, can I grab a quick shower?"

Zel frowned at the delay, but he gave a quick nod. "Be quick, we already linger too long," he warned.

I was already heading to the door in search of a shower. I ended up back in the bedroom I had woken up in. Stripping off my clothes, I longed for clean clothes. Feeling really bad about it, I opened the chest of drawers until I found a clean T-shirt and sweater in the wardrobe. There were so many clothes of similar style and colour that I was sure they would never miss another dark jumper. I drew the line at taking her underwear though. Just ew.

When I was back downstairs, feeling human and my hair wet and braided, I saw that Zel was putting away the dishes. It looked like we both could learn to compromise.

"Where to?" I asked him as I took the bottle of water that he handed me.

"Hell."

"Cross?"

"Why would Cross be in hell?" Zel asked as he checked the food cupboards. "These people may have a worse diet than you," he grumbled as he closed the doors with more force than was probably necessary.

"Because he lives there?"

Zel laughed at me. "No, he doesn't."

I dimly recalled Sam saying something similar to Cross when he first came to the room above the pit. "Where does he live then?" I asked as I was handed some protein bars and, a moment later, a backpack.

I was robbing these people. I was nothing better than a burglar. My dad would not be amused.

"Why would Death *live*?" Zel asked me mockingly as he passed me to rummage through more cupboards.

"Can we stop thieving?" I demanded as he handed me a can of pears. "When am I ever going to need to sit down and eat tinned pears?"

Zel looked at me over his shoulder. "They're for me."

Oh.

When he had finished raiding the kitchen, he straightened. Without a word, he shouldered the backpack and reached out for me. "Come."

It was like he thought I had a choice. Once again, I was looking around at unfamiliar surroundings. "Where—"

He cut me off with a pinch on my arm as he raised a finger to his lips. Slowly, carefully he slipped the backpack off and settled it on the ground. Hound was on alert beside me as I looked over the landscape in front of me and saw nothing.

Sensed nothing.

Burnt ground, blackened trees and foliage, the land had seen trouble of some kind. With startling reality, I suddenly knew where I was.

"This is Asmodeous's level?" I whispered furiously.

"Was." Zel cast me a sideways look. "All is not well here."

I stepped closer to Hound, who shifted slightly so I could put my hand on his shoulder. He may be in a mood with me, but he was still offering me comfort.

"Should we leave?" I whispered to them both.

Zel's head snapped to the right, and I saw his shoulders relax slightly. Turning, I looked to see who he saw.

Cross was studying the ground before he straightened and noticed us. "Such despair here," he said by way of greeting. "How are you?" he asked me when Zel nor I spoke.

"Tired." And I was. I could quite easily have lain down and napped.

"The child consumes your energy. Come, we should move." Cross studied our surroundings. "We are not alone, and I don't want to be noticed."

His hand clasped my wrist loosely as he winked us to another place. Maybe me being exhausted had nothing to do with my child, maybe I was tired of being zapped through dimensions; had they thought of that?

Maybe you're irritable.

I chose to ignore my hellhound companion as I sat down on a tree stump. "Where are we now?"

"You need not be concerned," Cross answered smoothly. "Azazel, we should plan."

"I don't get to plan?" I asked them before they left me.

"You need a nap."

And just like that, I was dismissed as they walked off together and stood whispering out of earshot. I may have needed a nap, but this shit needed to stop. Rising to my feet, I walked over to where they were. "I like plans."

Both males looked at me, and I waited them out. Cross folded first before he nodded. "Well, I suppose it does involve you."

Zel frowned before he reached out, and his fingers swept my hair back. It was such a personal thing for him to do that I was frozen for a moment before I realised he had just hit me with his sleep spell.

Motherfucker.

WAKING on yet another bed that was not my own, in unfamiliar surroundings, had me tiredly lifting myself off a soft mattress and going in search of the demon that kept making decisions for me with my supposed ally.

Cross and Zel were an unlikely pairing, but it seemed they worked well together. Or at least they worked well against *me*. I was in a simple home this time, much like my cottage. Two bedrooms, a family room, bathroom, and a kitchen. A kitchen that led to a garden, which currently had one demon going through his training regime.

Of Cross, there was no sign.

"You have to stop spelling me," I told Zel as I watched him balance on one leg while both his arm and other leg stretched out at a flat angle. Which I think was some form of yoga pose, but considering Zel was a bulky hunk of muscle, it was impressive to see him hold such a pose with ease.

"You have to stop arguing, then I won't need to." He calmly changed legs and repeated the hold.

"I didn't have you pegged for yoga." Was my tone slightly mocking? Probably. Did I care? No. "Is that downward dog?"

"Warrior three," he answered effortlessly.

Of course it was. Figures it would sound all manly. "Where are we?"

"Where we were when you went to sleep."

Looking around, I took in the small garden, the trees, the stone dyke. It looked normal…if normal had a red sky and grass a little more black than green. "Lust?"

"It was." He frowned. "Maybe it still is, who knows."

"He replicated the buildings and things from earth?" I asked as I made my way over to the wall and sat on a smooth stone.

"He was denied roaming above, so he made do."

I watched as Zel slipped into another pose, and didn't care to ask him what. "You sound as if you're sorry for him?"

"I pity anyone whose head is taken and thrown into the pit."

My eyebrows raised in surprise as I looked away. I knew

who he meant, and it wasn't Asmodeous he was talking about. "I did what I had to, to survive."

He said nothing as he moved into another pose that made my eyes water. I didn't know it was possible to split your legs that wide at that angle. His balls must be made of steel right enough. "Doesn't it hurt your…you know?"

If anything, he pulled his leg higher as his head got nearer to the ground. "You know?"

"Your, um…bits."

Easily he was on his feet and standing upright. "You mean my balls?"

"Yup. Pretty much."

"Is this a bad time?" Cross asked smoothly as he walked out of the kitchen. "I can come back."

With flaming cheeks, I avoided both their stares. "You can both fuck off," I grumbled.

"But I just got here," Cross teased me as he joined me at the dyke. "How do you feel?" he asked more seriously.

"I'm okay." Easily my head lay on his shoulder like I had been doing it all my life.

"You will tire more easily in the early stages of the pregnancy," he told me, his voice matter-of-fact.

"Yeah, does it go quicker because of, well, you know…who the father is?"

"I wasn't here for the beginning before," Cross explained. "My involvement was more in regards to the aftermath."

"Death didn't play well with others before," Zel mocked as he rotated his arm to loosen his shoulders.

"What made you change your mind?" I asked as I straightened to look at him. His dark hair and warm chestnut brown eyes were so familiar to me now.

"Genocide makes me perk up and pay attention," he told me dryly.

Zel barked out a laugh as he pulled his legs behind him to rest on his butt. Who knew the Watcher was so flexible? "You've been with the witch too long, you've become dramatic."

Laying my head back on Cross's shoulder, I smiled. "I like that you have a flair for drama. And seriously, you wipe out all of humanity, what else do you call it? It's murder on a mass scale."

"Exactly." Cross's head lay against mine as we watched Zel finish his…routine? Training? I wasn't sure what it was, but he looked damn fine.

When he was done, he looked at us both and shook his head. "The pregnancies were quicker, six or seven months rather than nine." He rubbed his jaw as he thought about it. "Maybe six."

"And my time in the ether, since Sam and I slept together, how much did that fast forward me?" I looked down at my bump. Was I three months? Did women "show" at three months? I had no idea. I had never been around many pregnant women, as my female friends were few, and none of them had children.

"I'd say you were past three, maybe, but not four," Zel told me as all three of us looked at my belly.

"I'm halfway there," I murmured as my hand smoothed over my jumper. "That complicates things?"

"No," he said as he shook his head. "We know our time limit."

"Okay." I could feel the noose tightening around my neck as I looked between the two of them. "So…what now?"

"Now," Cross said with a wide smile as he stood, "you need to train. You still have so much to learn."

I suddenly realised Zel hadn't been *finishing* up his training, he had been *warming up*. "You can't be serious, with him?" My eyes were wide as I looked at Cross. "There's no way my legs will spread that wide."

The dead silence that met my poorly worded outburst had my cheeks flaming, and then I wanted to run when Zel burst out laughing.

"That's not what I heard," he spluttered.

When Cross chuckled beside me, I turned to Hound. "I'm surrounded by juveniles."

"Come, Star, let's teach you to be better," Cross said as he placed his arm around my shoulders.

"We don't have that long," Zel reminded him as he rolled his head on his shoulders.

"I hate you both," I grumbled as I readied myself for an afternoon of torture.

CHAPTER 4

WE SPENT THE AFTERNOON TRAINING. WELL, THE SUN DIDN'T shine, and the sky didn't get darker, but my brain wanted to put me in a timeline, so I'd opted for afternoon. Thankfully, I wasn't expected to fling my leg over my head and pirouette, but what I did do was no less strenuous. Who would have thought that standing still and concentrating was so exhausting?

Zel took me through some gentle exercise, and for him, it really was gentle. While he did, he gave me a whole lecture about eating well and exercising, but the workout was actually pleasant. I wasn't telling him that though.

Cross then took over, and we did his beloved meditation before we did some actual work with souls. When I had felt them in the garden with me, I had thought they were to shield, but they were my target practice. Okay, that wasn't true. I wasn't *hurting* them. I processed some while avoiding the terminology of *processing* in case Cross got pissed off.

I already knew how to use them to shield, but Cross taught me how to draw upon their energy without taxing them or me. I knew I could draw power from them, but I didn't know I could draw *energy* from them also.

Cross kept assuring me I didn't need to apologise to the soul or ask permission, but as I felt like I was literally feeding from them, I thought it was only fair to say thank you first. It wouldn't be fair to say that they didn't really care, since they were drawn to me no matter if I was sipping their energy. They all wanted to be close to me and what I carried inside me. At first, I was anxious. Were they going to try to hurt me? By the time we were finishing training, their hands were caressing my belly, much like a person would. I never understood the need for strangers to rub a pregnant woman's belly. I always felt sorry for the mother—it was like she was a good luck charm or something—but here, in hell, I had no complaints. It was a weird sense of normal in a very peculiar environment.

"They don't seem to think I have a monster inside me," I said without thinking as I cradled the bump.

Zel grunted but kept quiet. Cross however did not. "It is only a monster dependant on one's perception."

I had a memory of the wilds of Scotland as myself and six demons hunted for Hamish's remains. "I once had the very same conversation with Pen in regards to the devil." I glanced at Zel. "Do you remember?"

"That you thought *I* was the devil?" He nodded. "I do."

"You still could be," I teased as I nibbled on my apple slices. I was in a level of hell that was currently prince-less, and Zel had found me apple slices. I wasn't even surprised.

"I do not have the same level of power," Zel told me as he reached over and smacked Cross's hand from my apple. "This is hers."

Fighting my smile, I ate another slice. He was okay...now and again. In small doses. Very small doses. "Who is more powerful than you, mighty Azazel?" I asked him with a grin.

"Samyaza," Zel answered immediately. "Satan, maybe. Cross, of course."

He then fell silent.

I waited and, when he offered nothing further, I looked at him in astonishment. "That's *it*? Three people?"

"None of them are *people*," Zel corrected me.

I ignored his pedantic-ness. "*Three* beings? That's it?"

"Well…of the fuckers up there, possibly Michael, maybe Gabriel, and…Father."

Was he joking? "In the whole entire dimensions *everywhere*, five beings are more powerful than you, *maybe*? I'm ignoring God by the way."

"I do too," Cross murmured beside me, causing me to laugh at his humour.

"Four too many," Zel said gruffly as he stood. He went back to his weapons, and I stared after him for too long before I heard the unmistakable crunch of Cross eating my apple slices.

"Oi!" I protested as I gave him my attention. Cross gave me a cheeky wink as he licked his fingers clean and then told me my break was over.

Not aware that I had been *on* a break, I stood up to resume my learning, but Cross noticed my indecision. "You're full of questions today."

"This was Asmodeous's level." I looked at the small cottage and hesitated. "Each prince rules a level of hell. Who rules the pit?"

"That's difficult to answer without a long story, so for simplicity, I shall say no one being controls the pit."

"Then why was Chaz unable to be rescued by his brothers? How did Asmodeous hold him there?" This had bugged me for far too long, and I was finally in the right circumstances to be able to ask the question.

Cross sighed as he quite obviously thought about ignoring my question, but the thing with Cross was that he had literally lived with me as his kind-of-roommate for months, so he knew when he could avoid and when I would nag until he wished for escape. Right now? I was clearly in pre-nag mode, and he couldn't escape.

"The pit is not a domain held by any prince. Before they fell, hell was already formed. Humanity was already in place and"—he hesitated—"well, I am loath to say *evolving,* but they were prospering." Cross's forehead furrowed, and I knew he was debating internally on the whole evolution argument currently going on in his head. "Remember what I told you, balance? Where there is one, there is the other. Where there was heaven, there was hell."

I nodded. In my head, they went together like horse and carriage. Without heaven, there was no hell, and vice versa.

"When the angels fell, whether they were Watchers or not, they very quickly implemented a hierarchy." Cross's eyes flicked to Zel, who was saying nothing and pretending he wasn't listening. To be fair, it was Zel, he probably wasn't. "For angels who rebelled against the restrictions of their Father, they were very quick to implement their own regulations."

Zel snorted, and I realised he was listening after all.

"The Watchers, well, they weren't interested. But there were those who wished very quickly to be *more.*"

"The princes?"

"Yes, *prince* is such a misleading term. There is no king or emperor, so why they needed to be prince was always…interesting." Cross sat back in his seat. "They squabbled amongst themselves, and then the General and his soldiers stepped in."

The General? A chill ran over my body. "Sam? Sam did this?"

"Well, he wasn't alone." Cross looked at the silent Watcher

who was honing his knives. "They restored order, and they created the tiers of hell."

"The *Watchers* created the seven sins?" I demanded shrilly.

Cross frowned as he considered it. "Not exactly, they ensured there was no more fighting, and they monitored the restoration of a...system, would you say?" He looked over to Zel, who shrugged noncommittally. "The princes catered to their own needs and desires." Cross suddenly seemed to register the look of disbelief on my face. "You have to understand, angels, like anything else that exists, have their own individuality; the attributes of each level were very much in their character before they fell."

"The seven sins and seven circles of hell are created by angels. Do you know how insane that sounds?" I said to him as I shook my head. "Then you add in that he"—I pointed at Zel—"and the others are the *reason* they're there, *that* blows my mind."

Cross waited for me to come to terms with what he was saying before he continued. "As I was saying, the pit was already there. It was already in existence. The tiers of hell came later, so no one prince has control over the pit."

"Then how do they use it?" I asked as I looked between the two of them. "Why could only Asmodeous get to Chaz?"

"A bargain must be struck," Zel said quietly. "Unless you know the details of the bargain, you can't interfere."

"A bargain with who?" When neither of them answered, I felt more confused than ever. "What or who is it?" I looked between them, my eyes narrowing. "What's the secret?"

"No secret, we just don't have time at the moment, another day perhaps," Cross suggested as he stood. "Come, let us train."

Sensing that they weren't sharing anymore, I resumed my training. But my mind kept reverting to the revelations. The Watchers. Everything came back to the Watchers. As we trained, I continued to think of them. I had been in hell before, but I hadn't been in my body, and it wasn't until a few hours later that I realised, the other women from before the flood couldn't come here, but *I* could.

"Why am I able to exist here?" I asked as I took a drink of water. "Zel said that the women from before, they couldn't come here because they were human. I'm human."

Zel huffed, but he said nothing as he attended to his weapons.

"You are a witch, and you are mine," Cross said simply. "Your powers have adapted to your body, so you are no longer *purely* human." His head tilted slightly as he considered me. "But you know this. What are you really asking me?"

I could play it off, I could avoid his question, I could do so many things. "Do I die?" I asked him instead.

"I am not a psychic," he answered smoothly. "Wasn't that your skill?"

I let out a short humourless laugh at his teasing. "Yeah, I thought so, but no. If I was, then wouldn't I know that six demons were coming for me?" Rubbing my eyes, I thought of my shitshow life. "Or the fact three threes would kill me on a blood moon? Or that I was a necromancer?"

Cross leaned forward suddenly, his eyes alight with passion. "Yes! You *are* a necromancer. You are my disciple, and I cannot forecast, but can you?"

"I just told—"

"And you believed it to be true," Cross cut me off. "But have you tried?"

"You want me to try to predict the future?" I asked him. I knew I was slightly apprehensive, and I knew I sounded it. Hound knew too, and he was at my side in an instant.

"It would be interesting to know," Zel said from his spot. "I would very much like an advantage. It's my turn to have one, surely."

Cross gave a slight nod as if he were agreeing that Zel deserved a break, or was he thinking he deserved an advantage? Either way, I knew I was not what they needed.

"I can tell you now, without even trying, that's a *no* from me," I told them both as I stood.

"You didn't even try," Zel accused me as he watched me with narrowed eyes.

"I don't need to try," I replied. "As soon as Cross mentioned it, my entire inner self told me no."

"Your powers?" Cross asked me curiously.

I thought about it. "Yes, I think so."

He sat back as he kept his gaze locked on mine. "What I wouldn't give to talk to them as you do."

"She can take you to them," Zel told him. "I've been at her pool of tranquillity before, it's interesting."

Cross gave him his whole attention. "How?"

"She lets you in. It's like a cavern, very…rustic."

"You're both doing it again," I interrupted them sharply. "I'm right here."

"Take me to them," Cross demanded as he held his hands out.

"Not that way," Zel told him as he stood. Walking the few steps to us, he turned Cross's palm over and then tugged mine from under my thighs, where I was absolutely not hiding them. As he placed our hands together, he covered ours with one of his own large hands. "Eyes, witch."

Obediently I closed my eyes.

"Empty your mind," he barked his commands like a general of an army. I felt bad for him that his army was me. We were doomed. "Did I tell you to empty your mind?" he fired at me.

"Arsehole," I cursed quietly under my breath.

"Stop whining."

I definitely can't kill him? I asked Hound.

Not if you want to keep the child.

Ugh, you and I need to talk, and soon, we can't go on like this, I scolded Hound.

Empty your mind.

"Your hellhound is mocking me," I grumbled to Cross.

"He becomes sullen and suddenly he's my hellhound?" Cross asked in amusement.

"Yup."

"Quiet...your...mind," Zel ordered, and I could hear his teeth grinding as he clenched his jaw.

Fighting the smile, I emptied my mind and promptly entered the Void. Zel and Cross were with me, and both looked surprised. "Oh, oops?" I offered as a way of apology to Zel, but he wasn't interested, he was crossing the Void and then looking back at me.

"Why is he being weird?" I whispered to Cross.

"Because you've just done the impossible," Cross told me distractedly as he also looked around.

Having been with them both in the Void before, I too started to look around. "What are we looking for? What's going on?"

Of course, neither of them answered me, and why would they? Pains in the arse that they were. I actually missed Sam— at least when he didn't tell me anything, he was pretty to look at. The pang in my chest had me looking away from either male in case they noticed. When I looked back, they were staring at me.

"What?" I fought the urge to take a step back.

"It's why she doesn't experience it as we do," Cross told Zel in understanding.

"I don't know why I never recognised it." Zel looked pissed off. Must have been a day ending in *y*.

"It is the same?" Cross asked as he tilted his head back to look up.

My own head tilted back, *what the fuck was he staring at?*

"Witch, make it lighter," Zel commanded.

He used the tone that meant he was going to be pissed off if I didn't do what he wanted. Frowning in concentration, I thought *lighter.*

The Void lit up like a Christmas tree, and as it did, my jaw dropped.

"It's my powers?" I looked around my cavern. "How is this happening?" I asked as I turned in a circle. "I thought it was inside me?" I looked to Zel for answers. "I was here before, and it was all blue and lightning, and what is happening?"

"I don't know," he answered as he walked over to my cool calm pool of power. It was turquoise blue and looked perfectly at home in the once empty Void. "You've been shielding, I think."

"She's never actually been in the Void," Cross mused as he looked around. He caught Zel's attention with his thoughts. "She's pulled us *all* here each time."

"I never even felt it," Zel grunted as he cast a glare my way, which I took offence to.

"It's not as if I knew what I was doing!" I snapped indignantly. When I saw his flat stare, I admitted to myself that wasn't my best argument.

Hound decided to join the conversation as he morphed into his humanoid form. "She can be safe here?" he asked as he straightened.

Zel and Cross were obviously thinking about it, and while they did, I looked down at my pool. So peaceful and inviting. Stooping down, I trailed my hand over the waters.

A dark-skinned hand snatched my hand away from the water, and I met Zel's angry look with surprise. "Don't," he warned, and we both looked back as the waters moved.

"Aren't they mine?" I asked him as we straightened.

"Which is why I said no."

I saw the pool become a little more restless. "Hmm, I don't think they like you."

"I'm shocked," he answered dryly.

Cross went to speak, but he, Zel and Hound all suddenly looked behind them. Zel raised his hand in a tight fist to me, and I had watched enough TV to know I was being told to stay and be quiet.

After long tense moments, Cross reached out his hand. "Azazel," he warned softly.

"Take her," Zel snapped. "I've got this."

Cross never let me go, and I was suddenly looking at Zel as he winked to another place. I knew Cross and I never moved, but it was as if a layer of film had been placed over my eyes. I couldn't see clearly, but the place beyond me was… wild. There was no other word for it.

Objects swooped through the air, souls screamed as they raced all over, and I saw the other two hellhounds as they... patrolled? Yes, they were, they were patrolling. Stepping forward, I needed a closer look, but Cross held tight to my wrist.

I was going to protest when I suddenly saw it. A shaft of light that was advancing on the Watcher, and for the first time in my life, I was worried for Zel. The shaft wasn't light. It was soldiers. Marching. Soldiers?

As they came into focus, I pressed my hand to my mouth to stop the scream.

Angels.

There were angels in the Void, and they had Zel surrounded.

My eyes were wide with alarm as I looked at Cross, who shook his head at me in warning. Swallowing hard, I watched as the angels formed a circle around Zel, and blindly I reached out to Cross. I needed something to hold onto, and I was sure that between Cross and Hound, one of them would keep me upright.

The angel soldiers—my brain was short-circuiting—parted to let a male with shoulder-length blond hair approach the Watcher, who looked at him with absolute indifference.

"Azazel," the angel greeted.

"Fucker."

My jaw hung slack. Was he suicidal?

Michael.

I glanced at Hound after he spoke, but he was watching what was happening with interest.

Michael looked past Zel's shoulder, but his attention was soon back on the demon in front of him. "Alone?"

"What can I say, I don't play well with others."

Michael looked unimpressed, whereas I was nodding emphatically at Zel's declaration. "You are never far from your band of heathens."

"Heathens?" Zel considered the word. "Unbelievers?" His head cocked to the side. "Surely not. My certainty has never been in question, I just no longer had *faith*."

"You mock me?"

Zel snorted and looked away from the shiny golden soldier in front of him. As I looked at all of the angels, I saw rigid discipline. It was a wonder to me that Zel had left. He liked order, and he liked regulation; if anything, I thought he would've been in his glory.

"Where is the abomination?" Michael asked.

Well, that was just insulting.

"Which one are you looking for?" Zel asked curiously. "Asmodeous has been vanquished."

To my surprise, the angel turned his head and spat to the side. It was such a human thing to do that I wondered if it had only been the Watchers who coveted those on earth.

"I have seen him. He weeps," Michael said with glee.

Weren't angels soft and lovely and caring? This guy looked like a dick. I felt Cross's hand tighten on mine in warning, but he needn't have worried, I had confidence in Zel. A part of my brain registered that anomaly, but I was too busy trying to listen to the angel.

"As he should." Zel appeared bored. "Why the platoon?" he asked as he looked at his former angel…associates?

"You hide the abomination."

Zel scoffed and folded his arms across his chest. "Do I?" Again, he looked around and then back at Michael. "Where?"

Michael obviously didn't like his tone. "Your scars never fully healed." He changed the subject, and Zel bared his teeth in a semblance of a smile.

"They're a winner with the ladies," he said glibly.

Who the hell was this guy? Sassy Zel was almost fun.

"Disgusting," Michael snorted as he began to walk around Zel like he was a prisoner. I watched as Zel didn't even blink, he just looked at the angels surrounding him.

"Why so few of you?" he asked them.

Was he joking? There had to be about thirty or forty males around him.

"A platoon is enough for one female," Michael sniffed dismissively.

"And here I thought they were for me," Zel mocked.

Michael laughed. "If you hide the woman, it is. Where is she?"

"I don't know."

"Liar."

Zel leaned forward until he was literally in Michael's face. "Prove it."

I watched Michael take a tiny step back. It may have been a small step, but it was what it was, a retreat. So, Michael didn't want to throw down with Zel. Could I use that?

"We will find her," Michael said, and I could hear his frustration. "We have your General's approval."

They did?

It shouldn't have surprised me. It shouldn't have gutted me. It shouldn't have made my legs weak. It shouldn't have torn my heart out of my chest. But it did.

Zel didn't falter, I noticed. Did he already know? "No. You don't. My General will happily destroy you."

Michael shook his head, his blond hair skimming his armour. "As usual, Samyaza was preoccupied."

He was? With what?

Zel laughed. It was rich and loud and full of scathing. It suited him perfectly. "You done?" Zel asked as he drew his weapons. "Or can we finally cut the bullshit?"

Michael grinned, and I was taken aback at how savage he looked. "Soon, Azazel, soon." Michael and his angels backed away. "Gabriel sends his regards."

The angels vanished.

Zel stood for a moment longer before he went to sheath his weapons, and then I saw him still before his head lifted a fraction. Cross's hand was like a vice on my wrist in warning.

Sam stood in front of him. Full leathers, armoured breastplate and shoulder guards, hair falling over his forehead, his green eyes piercing. "Azazel."

"General."

I had never heard Zel address him so, and I saw Sam's brief surprise before he shut it down. "What did Michael want?"

Zel shoved his weapons into their holsters, his eyes hard on Sam. "Three guesses."

"Where is she?"

"I don't know."

Sam went to speak, and then he paused before a smile played around his lips. "I'll rephrase, where was she before the fucker cornered you?"

Zel drew in a breath, but I could tell by the set of his shoulders, he was relaxed. "She was with me," he said honestly.

"Why?" Sam's voice was low, but I heard the bitterness.

"Because she doesn't deserve to lose this too."

That demon knew me better than I thought.

"You know what she carries," Sam snapped angrily. "You lived through it before."

"And I will do so again," Zel snapped back. "She is not Hannah. She is not *only* a human."

Hannah? Was that the name of the woman who birthed his children before? Why had I never asked him? Why had I never given any thought to the fact that Sam lost his lover and his children before? Was I so selfish that I never paid any mind to the fact he had suffered through this before?

Cross's arm came around my waist, and I leaned into him, taking the silent support he offered. Which was needed because the next words from Sam floored me.

"I don't care. I lost my wife already. I will not lose the witch."

Wife? He was married? No. What?

"I don't know where she is," Zel said coldly. "But I will do everything, *everything*, to save her. Save them both."

"You don't even fucking like her," Sam bit out angrily.

"You need to go," Zel growled at him. "You have things to do, the revolt does not stop because Michael's prancing around like a stuffed pony."

Sam glared at Zel, but he eventually gave a small laugh. "I need you," he admitted.

"Until you take your head out of your arse, I can't be with you."

Sam shook his head in frustration. "I thought it was Chazaquel or Penemue, hell, even Amaros, that I would need to fight...never you."

"Your child is innocent."

Sam winced as Zel spoke. "Perhaps, until they grow into a monster, and death and destruction is all that they know." I watched as his hands tightened into fists at his sides. "I can't lose her, Zel."

They looked at each other in silence before Zel turned away. "It's too late," he said softly. "Araqiel concealed it for too long, the time to"—I actually heard him gulp—"the time to strike has passed."

Sam's head bowed as his shoulders slumped. "Does she know?"

"She knows," Zel confirmed.

"*Fuck!*" I watched him pace as he ran his hand through his hair in frustration. "You were too late?"

"I would never have struck," Zel corrected him quietly. "Would you?"

Sam's feet stilled, and he stood for a long moment. "I don't know." His head tipped back as he looked upwards at nothing. "I need to go." He sighed heavily.

"And your woman?"

Sam grunted. "She was never my woman," he answered. I had already been crying, but his words ignited a fire in my belly. *Bastard.* Sam turned to look at Zel. "She was my everything."

He travelled and Zel was left alone in the Void.

"Star," Cross murmured beside me. "Come, let us leave."

I registered dimly that we were in the Land of the Souls, but I was blinded by my tears. I thought he was dismissing me, but I was his *everything*? My heart was breaking all over again.

"Is she okay?"

At the sound of the female voice, I looked up to see Naomie. She looked the same as when I last saw her, only this time her skirt was dark with panels of flower print. I saw Naomie notice my pregnancy at the same time as I tried to hide it.

"Cross!" she hissed as her eyes widened in alarm.

"It's not his," I told her bitterly as I stood. "Will they find me here?" I asked Cross as I wiped my eyes.

"It's a Watcher's?" Naomie demanded.

Tiredly I looked at her. I had no fucks left to give. "Who else?" I turned my back on her. I didn't need to hear it. Looking at Cross, I pressed my lips together. "What now?"

When I felt a cool hand on my elbow, I turned ready to defend myself and my child. But Naomie was looking at me with concern.

"How can I help?" she asked me softly. "What do you need?"

What I didn't need was to bawl like a baby at her kindness, but that's exactly what I did. As I cried, *again*, Cross quickly explained the time in the Void.

"It's separate from her?" Naomie asked curiously as she looked at me. "Well, how do you do that?"

Sniffling, I shrugged. "I don't know. Zel told me to envision my powers, so I did."

Naomie nodded thoughtfully. "And in turn, your powers mimicked the Void, without you having ever seen it." Her hand clasped mine as we sat side by side, and she nudged me gently with her shoulder. "I always knew you would be fun," she whispered conspiratorially to me.

"How?" I asked as we watched Cross look out over the land.

"Well, I've been alive a long time," Naomie said conversationally. "I've been close to death for most of it." She gave a small smile to Cross, who nodded in acceptance, and I realised she meant literally *and* figuratively. "Asmodeous knew, eventually, a descendant of my bloodline would be born who could remove the spell."

"You had children?" I realised suddenly.

"Of course," she answered.

"Not Zel's?"

Naomie shook her head. "No, the Watchers put a stop to that. They learned the hard way." She glanced at my belly. "Or so I thought."

"Bloodlust," Cross informed her.

"Really?" Naomie's eyebrows rose. "Samyaza?"

"He was married," I said with more bitterness than was fair.

"Of course he was," Naomie laughed as if the rug hadn't just been pulled from under me. "They fell to be human. Love, marriage, family, they wanted it all."

When she put it like that, my resentment at Sam having had a wife dwindled. He was immortal. Was I really so arrogant to think I was his only love? I needed to grow up.

"And what a price they paid," Cross added as he walked over to me and stroked a hand over my hair. "You must be strong, Star. I need you to be the necromancer I witnessed at the pit."

"What if I want to curl up in a ball, watch romantic comedies, and eat my weight in chocolate?" I asked him as I looked up at him.

"Your child needs sustenance, not sugar," Naomie chided me, and I saw the same hard look in her eye as Zel had.

"You and Zel make sense now," I said before I shared a look with Cross and saw his lips twitch.

"Azazel will be delighted you think so," Naomie said with a grin. She turned thoughtful. "I need to fix this so no harm comes to you," she told me as her hand ran over my bump, and I didn't mind this woman touching me.

"Take your hands off of her," Azazel growled as he appeared beside us.

Naomie was on her feet, and Zel stood opposite her, with

me in the middle, like an umpire at a tennis match, my head swivelling between the two, waiting to see who would make the first move.

"Azazel," Naomie breathed his name like it was air. I watched as she greedily drank him in.

"Whore."

My eyes narrowed on him as he looked her over with contempt. "Jesus, Zel," I reprimanded him.

"How much did she hear?" Zel asked, ignoring us both as he turned to Cross.

Turning to Naomie, I rolled my eyes. "He does this, he talks like I'm not in the room. It's infuriating, but it's because he's a giant dick," I explained to her as if I were discussing the weather. "If he were to ask me, I would tell him I heard it all."

Thank goodness Naomie was as quick-witted as she was beautiful. "He thinks it makes him manly," she told me. "To ignore the obvious and pretend it hasn't happened. It's normal for him; it makes him feel valued."

"This is what you freed," Zel snapped at me as he reached for me. "Come, this is the worst place you could be."

"Because of me?" Naomie asked him with an arched eyebrow.

Zel didn't even look at her as he held his hand out impatiently. "Witch," he demanded.

"Zel, you're being a dick," I scolded. "Naomie is talking to you."

If looks could kill, I'd be dead. No question. With more stiffness than I had ever seen in him, and that was saying a lot, he turned his head to look at my ancestor. "What?"

"Are you leaving because of me?"

"No." When neither of us spoke, he gritted his teeth.

"Samyaza knows she is at peace here, he will come. Michael will check here. Souls may be commanded by Death, but they still *talk*."

Naomie flushed, and I knew I was missing something important.

"Azazel is right, Star," she said to me. "You need to go. I will work on a way to help you."

Zel snorted. "Your particular skill set is not required."

"It was a skill you had no objection to once."

It seemed that Naomie had some fire in her after all.

"I'm over it," Zel spat as he turned to Hound. "You need to come with me," Zel said to him.

"Hey, he's *my* hound," I protested.

Zel erupted. "Will you all remember that we are at fucking war! Do you want to live?" he demanded of me. When I nodded, he turned to Hound. "Do you want her to live?" Hound gave a quick dip of his head. "Then let me do my fucking job, stop complaining, shut up, and do what I fucking tell you to."

"I'll see you soon," I whispered to Naomie as I hugged her. "I'm sorry."

"I will help you," she promised me as she let me go. She watched Zel as he ignored her, and my heart broke for the pain in her eyes she didn't try to hide.

"Cross?" I asked as I stood by Zel.

"I will find you," he told me easily. "Azazel knows how to reach me."

Zel pulled me closer. "Take me to it," he commanded.

Nodding, I winked us to my version of the Void. "You were cruel," I admonished him as we arrived.

"I don't care."

"She does," I reminded him.

"She'll live."

"Isn't she already dead?" I shook my head as he produced the backpack from who knew where and started to lay food out.

"Yes. Her soul's fine."

I watched him as he opened his can of pears. "Will my soul be fine?" I saw him hesitate. "You know, after?"

"No." Zel picked a pear out of the syrup and licked his fingers as juice ran down them. "Your soul will cease to exist. You cease to exist."

Fuck. Way to sugar coat it, Zel.

"Well, sucks to be me." I tried to make my voice light, but the Watcher was not fooled.

"I will protect your child with everything I am," he told me quietly.

I said nothing as he handed me a slippery pear. After all, what was there to say?

CHAPTER 6

AFTER WE ATE A VERY QUIET DINNER, ZEL KEPT LOOKING around the Void, which wasn't the Void, it was my cave. My head was never going to wrap around all of this. This was insane.

"When you first came here, what were you thinking?" he asked me suddenly.

"Nothing," I answered immediately. "Cross told me to clear my mind and think of nothing."

He nodded thoughtfully. "When we first reached your powers, we were in a similar position."

I realised it was true, and I smiled in remembrance. "It feels like yesterday," I told him. "It was really...I don't even know how long."

"It's been almost a year, earth time."

"Damn." I leaned back, my weight resting on my hands as they propped me up. It was soothing on the back, but it did make the bump more pronounced. I saw Zel look at it and then look away. "I'm definitely fired from my job."

He snorted as he looked back at my tummy. "Think that's the least of your worries."

It was said with no sarcasm whatsoever, so sincere that it made me giggle. Which either loosened my hysteria or I was closer to losing it than I thought. As I sat there laughing my head off, Zel simply stood up and went over to the pool, leaving me alone to deal with my hysterics.

Wiping my eyes and getting myself back under control, I got to my feet and went to join him. "Are you searching for the meaning of life?" I asked him as I stood beside him. "You've been staring at the water for a long time."

Zel glanced at me and then returned his stare to the pool. "I can't see any depth."

"Zel, if this is where you tell me you think I'm shallow, I will drown you in my pool."

Surprising me, he gave a low chuckle. "The opposite, witch. The water runs deep."

Peering into the water, I felt my own surprise. "I have depth?" I asked him.

"It seems so, but I'm not sure it means anything."

Huh. "Should I go in?"

"Are you insane?" Zel asked me with wide eyes.

"Yes?" I thought about it. "Maybe?"

"Why would you go in?"

"Aren't you curious to know what it is?" I asked him. *Should I tell him I was feeling a desire to submerge myself in the water?*

"No." Zel grabbed my arm and tugged me back. "Stay away from it."

"Isn't it me?" I asked him as I looked back at the pool. "Before, you told me to only dip my toe in, why has that changed?"

"Because most witches don't have a fucking pool of tranquillity in their soul, which they then manifest to an actual fucking place in a dimension of hell."

I frowned as I thought about it. "Hmm, that does sound fucked up."

"Ya think?" he sassed at me.

"Naomie makes you sassy," I told him as he led me away from temptation.

"Does she," he said flatly as he gave me a look that dared me to ask him anything further.

"You're going to be grumpy?" I resumed my seat on the floor of my Void.

"Only if you ask me inane questions."

"Where is Hound?" I changed the subject. As my dad always said, you needed to know when to cut your losses.

"It's your domain, you tell me."

"Is it really a domain?" I asked him as I looked around. The walls were still dark, the floor dark, the pool twinkled in the light that came from nowhere. "I liked it before when the pool was turquoise, do you rem—" I stopped short. "Holy shit."

Zel looked up and followed my gaze to where the inky water was now tropical beach turquoise. He looked at me, obviously at as much of a loss as I was.

"It would be nice if it was a little warmer," I spoke in a normal voice even as I felt the air warm. "A chair would be nice."

Two armchairs appeared.

"Zel, I'm about to lose it," I told him quietly.

He was already sitting on the chair and made a face of appreciation. "It's good."

"Well, that's okay then," I snarked. "How am I doing this?"

"You're a witch," he started and then paused. "Conjuring? Usually needs more practice, more *ingredients*, but with you, I ran out of ideas to explain you a long time ago."

Asswipe.

"Maybe the souls are fetching things?" I guessed. "Like invisible butlers."

"As I said, I gave up a long time ago."

I maybe deserved that. "Do you need to sleep?" I asked Zel,

and a bed appeared. "This is beyond freaky now. Why am I doing this all of a sudden?"

Zel was staring at my bump. "This place is all you," he said thoughtfully. "I think you are stronger when it's effortless. When you *try* to do what we want, then you struggle."

Looking down, I stared at my bump. "I'm easier to work with when I'm not thinking about it?"

"I don't know," Zel admitted. "You have powers that you haven't even begun to test, I think, but this"—he gestured to the chairs and the bed—"this doesn't seem like something you would master without thought."

As I thought about it, I tried to swallow past the sudden dryness in my throat. "Zel…"

"I don't know," he answered without me having to finish. "I can't answer your question. I wasn't expecting it, so I don't know if it is the child. Last time, they were older. They were walking before they started to use their powers. But with you?" His look was thoughtful. "Well, I never know what to expect with you."

"Of course I'd have to be carrying little miss or mister overachiever," I tried to joke, but it fell flat.

"Try to sleep," Zel told me gently. "You need to rest."

I didn't argue, and the bed that had appeared for Zel was the one I climbed into, fully clothed. I could conjure furniture, but clothing still escaped me. Ros was right, it was a skill I needed more training for.

"You've come so far," Zel spoke in the quiet. "You're so much more than the scared child clinging to the railings of a cemetery." I lay in silence as he considered his next words. "This is not the end for you, Star Elizabeth Archer. You have overcome so much. We will succeed."

I felt the tear slip out and run down into my blonde hair. "Succeed or die trying," I whispered in the quiet.

He was silent, and I turned onto my side. "Or die trying." His words carried over the stillness of my Void.

Closing my eyes, I willed sleep to come. I needed to rest and not to think.

WHEN I WOKE, I was alone. Panic gripped me, thinking Zel had left me, until I calmed down and thought about it. He had left, but he would come back. Something I never thought I would hope for.

While Zel was gone, the pull to the water was strong, and I found myself at the edge of it with no clear memory of walking over to the pool. The colour was back to inky black. "Still waters run deep," I murmured as I edged closer. "What are you hiding?" I asked the water as I pulled my sneaker off, then my sock. Standing, I looked at my bare foot and then the water. "I swear to whoever the creator is, you have a shark in there and I'm going to scream."

I dipped my toe in the water, one eye squeezed shut as I held my breath. Nothing. Except wet water.

Pulling my foot back, I studied it. "Hmm." Making the decision, I kicked off my other sneaker and sock. "This is a leap of faith," I told the waters. Rolling my leggings up, I waded into the water.

Which is exactly when Zel returned.

"Get out of there right now!" he yelled at me as he raced towards me. I turned to do as I was told just as something grabbed my hand and pulled.

"Zel!" I cried out as I started to fall backwards.

Had I not been falling into the water, I may not have witnessed the sheer phenomenon that was Zel leaping through the air to catch me as the water rose up to claim me. He grabbed me around the waist and winked us both to the far side of the cavern, where he pushed away from me angrily.

"Are you out of your mind?" he demanded as he looked back at the water, which looked rather choppy.

"Yes?" I had my hand over my heart as I felt it racing, and I was sure I was going to pass out. What had I been thinking? Had I been thinking at all?

"Why the fuck am I trying to save you if you're fucking suicidal?" Zel snarled at me as he turned to me, his eyes livid with fury.

"I fucked up; there's no need to be a bastard," I snapped at him. I looked at my wet legs and feet, and my socks and shoes sitting innocently by the water's edge. There was absolutely no way he was going to let me get them, and if I was honest, I didn't want to go over there. "What do you think it was?"

"I don't know, but if we don't know, then we don't *walk* into it!"

Dammit, I was never going to hear the end of this. "Yup, got it."

Zel threw a bundle on the bed. "Get dressed." He turned his back before I even had to ask, and quickly I pulled clothes off and just as quickly tugged the fresh ones on. Zel had brought me underwear. Even if he was a cantankerous dickhead, he brought me clean underwear and I wanted to hug him for it.

I didn't. Despite what he accused me of, I wasn't *actually* suicidal. Not consciously anyway, and I knew me trying to hug Zel…yeah, that wouldn't end well for me. Before I asked, he tossed my sneakers at me, and I bit my tongue as I put them on.

Do not poke the demon, Star, when this one bites, it's not as much fun. When I was ready, I went to tell him he could turn around, but Zel was focused on the other side.

"Witch," he called, and immediately I walked to him. "I need to see." Together we walked to the other side.

I saw flickers of light across the wall of my Void. Cross had made it appear like we were looking through a window, a really dirty one, but a window, nevertheless. As Cross had done, I tried to pull up that murky layer between me and the actual Void. I beamed at Zel when I managed to do it, I didn't tell him I merely thought "see" and the layer was there. Unlike Cross, Zel did not offer me support as we watched Sam and the others meet the angels.

"Zel," I whispered in fear.

"Shh," he cautioned.

Michael looked even more irritating than before. He also looked smug. I knew Sam—smug wouldn't work on him.

"Why are you here?" Pen asked the angels.

"Hunting abominations," Michael sneered. "You?"

"Scouting for pricks," Ros taunted them.

"Where is your…woman?" Michael asked Sam, ignoring Ros completely.

"Which one?" Sam asked casually.

Oh no he didn't.

Michael didn't react. Unlike me, he merely smiled. "Azazel is absent," he commented.

"Your observation skills have improved," Der muttered.

Michael was unimpressed by any of their comments. He

looked them all over, and I felt myself bristling on their behalf. "You are no better than you were all those years ago." He shook his head in disgust as he looked over his shoulder at his men before turning back to them. "You have learned nothing."

"That's not true," Chaz said as he stepped forward. "We have learned so much here."

"Like what? How to rut and fornicate with women who think you could love them?"

Ouch.

"What causes you more jealousy?" Ros asked him. "The fact we can *rut* and *fornicate* with women, or the fact we can actually love them?"

"I care not who any of you animals lie with," Michael spat before he turned his attention back to Sam. "Well, except you."

"He's always hated Samyaza," Zel murmured beside me.

"So." Michael looked Sam over. "Where is she? You cannot hide her, and even if you could before she births it, you will not be able to hide the Nephilim."

"What do you plan to do to her?" Sam asked him, and I looked at Sam with outrage. If he thought for one minute I was being handed over to these golden-suited wankers, he had another thing coming.

"She dies."

Sam nodded and then he was drawing his swords. "Yeah, that's not going to work for me."

Yes! Thank you.

The rest of the Watchers had their weapons drawn too.

"You would fight us? Here?" another angel queried. He sounded surprised. Had he not met my Watchers? They excelled at violence.

"You want to make a date of it?" Der asked him as he hefted his axe.

Zel was grinning, and it was my turn to question his sanity.

"You cannot fight here."

Who the fuck was this? I looked at the male who strode towards them before I realised Zel's smile was gone, and anger had replaced it.

"Oh goody, it's the superior fuckhead," Ros said sourly.

The new one was also blond but burnt golden rather than the sandy beach tones Michael had. He was also ridiculously handsome. God made man in his image? Well, if you asked me, he kept all the hotties with him and gave earth the guys who didn't measure up. Out of all the ones gathered, only Michael was what would be considered plain to look at, and in my normal world, Michael would be a catch, but amongst all the holy hotness that was the Watchers, he looked…drab in comparison.

"Gaby, you look"—Sam looked him over—"like a dick."

"Fuck you too," the newcomer said before he turned to Michael. "You cannot engage in the Void, you know this; they have the advantage. You are the Angel of War, stop being rash."

Glancing at Zel with confusion, I wondered if it was normal for an angel to reprimand another in front of their enemies. But then, in reality, who was fighting with the angels?

The newcomer frowned as he looked around suddenly. "Where is Azazel?"

Zel stiffened beside me even further.

"We saw him earlier," Michael informed him. "She was not with him."

"No?" New guy looked around again. "She is now," he told them as he walked forward.

His advance stopped with Sam's hand on his chest. "One more move, Gabriel, and I'll send you back in pieces."

"I doubt it," he sneered. "Platoon, fall back. She is with Azazel. Our time with *these* Watchers is done."

The angels dispersed, and Sam turned to the others. He spoke to us though. "Zel, you may run with her, brother, but you cannot hide her from both us *and* Gabriel's soldiers."

Zel's lips pressed tightly together, but I saw him nod. He agreed? Well, that gave me a fifty-fifty chance of being screwed.

The Watchers slowly winked out, and Zel turned to me. "We have few places left to hide."

"I know a place," I said to him as I shared a look with Hound. "But you won't like it."

"Try me."

"It's a prince of hell."

"Forget it, I'm not taking you to Satan," Zel snapped.

"Not Satan." I bit my lip. "Another."

He turned to look at me, eyes narrowing as he thought about it. "Who?"

"Mammon."

"Mammon's dead." He walked away from me.

"Where do you think Cross got the vial?" I asked him, my voice low.

Zel whipped around to look at me. "Are you sure?"

Nodding, I stepped forward. "I'm sure."

We held each other's stare for a long moment. "You must be mistaken."

"Why?" I hadn't been expecting him to not believe me.

"It's complicated."

"Make it simple." I sounded like a brat.

"Many of the fallen hate Watchers."

"Why? Your customer care skills lacking?" I mocked him.

"Because we are the ones who kill them."

"Ohh-kay. I was joking." I rubbed my forehead tiredly. "So…what are you saying?" I asked him.

"Mammon is dead."

"You killed Mammon?" My eyes were wide.

"Yes."

CHAPTER 7

I STARED AT ZEL IN COMPLETE AND TOTAL SILENCE. WAS HE joking? How could they possibly have killed Mammon? Didn't he believe that I had *just* seen her? Didn't he trust me enough yet to know that when I said that I had seen her with my own eyes, it meant I had *seen* her? "What do you mean you killed Mammon? Are you serious right now?"

Zel looked at me and shrugged. "Why would I lie? You have no idea what this prince of hell was like. Mammon was a poison even for the princes; he had to be stopped. We were the only ones who would be able to do that, so we did."

"Zel, I can't believe this," I told him. "I *know* I saw Mammon because Cross took me to her!"

Zel's look was sharp. "*Her?*" He stared at me as I nodded, and then his expression became thoughtful. "We didn't check then for the soul, did we..." He took a few steps away from me, and I could tell that he was thinking it over. His mind was in the past, remembering what had once been. "I can't remember," he said tiredly. "I can't remember who went to check or if we did it at all."

"It doesn't matter who went to check," I said. "What matters is that I know that Mammon is alive and well...or at least their soul is, and they're hidden." I took a step closer to the dark demon. "Zel," I whispered. "Zel, she is *hidden.*"

I watched him as he considered my words, watched him as he strategised it all in his head. "It's too risky," he finally declared.

"No, it isn't," I counterargued.

"I'm not taking you there," Zel said firmly.

"Well, you wouldn't be able to," I snarked at him. "You don't know where she is."

Zel was only giving me half of his attention, I knew he was, which is why I got away with my sarcasm and didn't have to worry about his sharp tongue. Plus, he had a remarkable propensity for violence, and I had no doubt that the demon beside me would show no hesitation when he cut me down with his swords should he need. My concern was that Zel may not *need* a reason to cut me down.

"And what you saw was female?" Zel asked me suddenly, snapping me out of my thoughts.

"*She* was, yes. She was beautiful."

Zel huffed with derision. "They're all *beautiful*," he said scathingly as he began to pace. "Cross took you?"

I felt slightly guilty for admitting this, because it was obvious to me that Zel was not impressed. "Yes."

He stilled suddenly, and then to my amazement, Cross was in front of me. "Azazel, I do not appreciate the call," he said coolly. His trousers were black formal, his shirt a dark slate grey half unbuttoned, and his feet bare. He looked like he should be on the cover of something, maybe a romance book, which was not the first time I had thought about Death this way.

"Were you getting busy with a woman?" I asked suspiciously when I noticed the faint red lines on his chest. This was not the time to be thinking about Death and him getting some action. I mean, I could see it; he had the sexy charisma. I wondered if he was good? I felt my face heat and wasn't sure I had been shielding my thoughts. Ah damn, and now I was blushing.

Cross looked at me and gave me a very self-satisfied smirk.

Scrambling to cover my lurid thoughts, I decided to object to his actions. "Ew, you can't come here when you've been getting jiggy with it."

"Says the woman who stands before me, pregnant after turning up at my rooms literally having been fucked for days."

Zel tried and failed to smother his laugh, while I stood with my mouth hanging open. "Cross!" I protested as I finally found my voice.

"What? Don't be a hypocrite, Star, it doesn't suit you." He glanced down at his chest and lazily redid some buttons. "Your naïve honesty is one of your most appealing characteristics, don't ruin it now."

"But does the woman with you know who you are?" I asked, ignoring his backhanded compliment.

"Well, she isn't drugged or incapacitated. Despite *who* I am, I do prefer a living being."

"I feel…icky," I told him as I looked at Zel. "Did you know he was getting down and dirty when you called him? Also, how did you call him? Can I call you?" I asked as I turned back to look at Cross, who was running his hands through his hair like a model on a photo shoot, going through the poses. Cross being in a sexy state of…whatever this was, was doing weird things to me. I was paying far too much attention to the way he looked and not to one word of what Zel was saying.

"What's happening to me?" I blurted out as I trailed my gaze over Cross again. "Why am I looking at you like you're my new favourite snack?"

Cross's eyes widened briefly in surprise before he laughed. "Hormones?" he suggested lightly. "But honestly, I think you always liked to look at me. Sometimes more than look." He gave me a teasing wink, and I knew I was blushing again.

Turning away, I rubbed my hand over my slightly swollen belly. *Telling you right now, kid, you make me a salivating idiot around these demons and I'm going to make sure you're grounded on day one. I have enough problems with this lot and Cross; I don't need to be drooling over them too.*

"Is she done?" Zel snapped at Cross as he glared at us both.

"I don't know. Star? Are you done?" Cross asked me casually as he put his hands in his pockets and just looked like goddamn perfection.

"I'm done." *Yup, totally done.*

"Mammon?" Zel demanded of Cross impatiently, like it was Cross's fault that Zel had been waiting on an answer to a question he hadn't yet asked him.

Cross's gaze flicked to mine briefly, and had I not spent months with the guy, I wouldn't have picked up on his displeasure. "What about Mammon?"

"Apart from him being alive?" Zel drawled, and I could hear the sarcasm in his voice. "Or the fact Mammon is now apparently female."

"Maybe Mammon always identified as a female and has now rectified that in the body she's in?" When they both stopped their glare-off to look at me, both in annoyance, I bit my lip. "Or I can shut up?" I looked to Hound, whose mouth was open but not in shock or anything, more like he was laughing at me, and when I opened our link, sure enough, my hellhound was flat out hysterical. *Asshat.*

Zel recovered first. "We killed him."

"Did you? She seems perfectly content where *she* is." Cross looked up at the Void. "Why are you here again? This is reckless."

"Sam just met with the platoon hunting her." Zel avoided looking at me as he spoke.

"You're concerned he will join with them?" Cross asked with a frown. "Do they share a common enemy?" He also looked at me, but at least I could take comfort in the fact his eyes held sympathy.

"Samyaza would never join with Gabriel. He hates him for what he did to me, to the others."

"I think I would be safe with Mammon?" I suggested to Cross. "She is hidden, the Watchers think she's dead, maybe the angels do too?"

"There is some merit in your plan," Cross said as he considered it. "The difficulty with the Prince of Greed is that they will want something, and then they will want more."

"How much more?" I asked him fearfully as I wrapped my arms around myself.

"I don't know, but you need to know what you are willing to give." Cross ran his eyes over me. "What are you willing to give, Star?"

"She's already giving her life, more than her life, she has nothing left," Zel snapped impatiently.

"Then I think Mammon may be a stretch too far," Cross told him.

"It's a fucking terrible idea," Zel growled. "Sam will string me up by my innards if I let her go there."

"*Let* me?" It was my turn to glare. "That demon doesn't *let* me do anything."

"Nor should he," Zel said with firm agreement. "You're a

fucking liability at the best of times, and you need constant supervision."

The rush of outrage that surged through me almost made me speechless until I stopped myself from biting his head off. I had bigger problems. "I'm ignoring you. I can't deal with you when you're being a wanker."

Cross laughed but quickly smothered it when Zel's furious gaze landed on him. "Mammon has remained hidden from you all for centuries. It's not a bad idea to take our fugitive to her." Cross became thoughtful. "The positive is that if Mammon asks for too much, we simply leave."

Zel looked around the Void. "I cannot follow you," he said tersely. "I am duty bound to my brothers to put Mammon down. If I go, I betray them."

"Again," Cross added lightly with a devious smirk, and I almost applauded the balls it took to provoke Zel. I mean, I provoked Zel on a daily basis, merely by breathing most days, but to actually *poke* him when he was pissed off already…well, Cross was braver than me.

"Come, Star, I'll take you." Cross held his hand out, and as I reached to take it, Zel caught my hand.

"Zel?"

His blue eyes were fierce as he studied me. "You agree to *nothing* without Cross by your side. He may be a giant prick, but Cross will look after you. If he has to leave you for any reason and that slippery fucker tries to start a new deal or suggest an amendment—and he will—you agree to nothing. *Nothing*, Star. Promise me."

Holy shit, Zel was actually worried for me. He may be angry and sullen most of the time, but I could see the genuine concern in his eyes. Okay, it was mixed with the usual rage and impatience, but it was definitely there.

"I won't be stupid."

He actually rolled his eyes as he stepped back. "I said don't be reckless, I didn't expect miracles." With a look like it actually pained him, he handed me over to Cross. "I do not like this," he told Cross gruffly.

"We'll be fine," I assured him. "Hound," I called.

I cannot come.

"Why can't Hound come?" I asked the others, alarmed. My confidence that this was a good idea was waning fast.

"Mammon has a bad history with the hellhounds. We want the prince to take you in, not alert the angels where you are," Cross explained.

"Why is she against the hellhounds but you're okay?" I asked suspiciously.

Cross tried to look innocent, but when my eyes narrowed on him, he looked over to Hound. "Morax had an altercation with Mammon when Dagon refused to collect the souls that Mammon fed on."

"Dagon?" I asked as my stomach turned at the thought of anything feeding on the souls of the dead.

"There are three hellhounds, Star. Did you think they were all called Hound?" Cross was mocking me, but I ignored it as I looked at Hound.

"I never even thought of the other two having names. Are they mad at me?" I asked him.

No. They no longer answer to their fallen names.

But you do? I asked him.

Only for you, Star.

My throat closed with emotion, and I reached out for my Hound. "I love that you let me in," I whispered to him as I circled my arms around his neck and hugged him. When I pulled back, I fixed Cross with a hard look. "You gave her five souls when you took that vial. You sacrificed them for nothing!"

"I gave five souls of human beings so corrupt and vile they deserve no afterlife. I would have given ten to rid you of that danger inside you," he snapped back with such vehemence that I took a step back.

"You don't approve?" I asked him. That genuinely surprised me, but then why would it? Cross had procured a vial to rid me of my child without my consent. Of course he didn't support my decision to keep it.

"Now do you see why you are in danger?" Zel asked me quietly. "You trust too easily."

"You're letting me go there," I protested weakly.

Zel's lips pressed together in a tight line as he obviously bit back what he was going to say. "Just go. If it's too much, link with Morax, and he will come for you."

"And you'll bring Zel?" I asked Hound.

I will.

"Can we go now?" Cross asked with amusement. "Your protectors have given you their instructions."

Reaching for his outstretched hand, I stuck my tongue out at Cross. "I thought you were one of my protectors."

"I am your teacher, your master and your saviour," Cross answered solemnly.

"Master?" I laughed as he pulled me close to him. "You're no Jedi, and slavery was abolished a long time ago. Plus, you're taking me to a cannibal, and it was my idea, so who exactly do you think you're saving?"

"Shush," Cross admonished me.

We winked.

I was back in the eighties video, looking around, and when the male in the sharp black suit with a black shirt open at the throat and shiny polished black shoes walked towards me, I pressed into Cross's side. Hair so black it was almost blue, almond shaped eyes with dark irises, and an olive complexion. His looks would make any woman's—and a fair few men's—jaw drop.

"You come again, with the same morsel, but no token for me?"

Cross ignored everything he had just said. "Mammon, you look well."

"I thought you were a woman?" I blurted and felt Cross stiffen beside me.

"I thought you were human?" Mammon walked around us both. "What is she, and why is she here, again?" The male leaned forward and sniffed. "What are you, little one?"

"You saw them fall?" Cross asked once again, ignoring the questions, and had I not been staring at the prince of hell, I would have missed the brief flash of fear.

"For me?" he asked.

"For her."

Mammon looked me over again and once again circled me as Cross stepped away. "Why? She smells delicious, her soul" —he stopped and inhaled—"so innocent. I hunger."

White teeth flashed at me in a smile, and I was three seconds from screaming for Hound or Zel…or both.

"You harm her, Samyaza will not be stopped from his revenge. This time."

Mammon spat to the side when Cross mentioned Sam.

"Maybe one of the golden will finally rid us of his self-righteous stench."

So Mammon and Sam had a history. Great. Just what I needed, to be placed with Sam's enemy. Who thought *Sam* was self-righteous, which was ludicrous but did tell me how morally corrupt this demon was.

"What's in it for me?" Mammon asked Cross as he watched me. Was I sweating? I felt like I was sweating.

"Life?" Cross offered lightly.

Mammon huffed out a laugh. "I'm done with life. I like it here." His eyes dropped to my feet and slowly made their way back up my body. I felt violated. "I want her."

"No."

"No deal." Mammon turned around and made to walk away.

"She is mine," Cross explained. "Can you sense it not?"

Mammon hesitated and then looked back over his shoulder. Turning slowly as he kept his eyes on Cross, he leaned into me again and inhaled. "She reeks of Watcher..." His eyes closed as I saw the slight frown. "Something else, something...delicious."

I didn't give a flying monkey's who this creep was; he sniffed me like that again and I was leaving. "Back up, sniffy, I'm not on the menu."

Holy shit, were his eyes glowing? Yup, the demon of greed had red burning in his black eyes. Why was I here again?

"A slice or...no dice." He turned to Cross and waited.

A slice? A slice of what? Me?

"No."

Mammon's right hand ran over his jaw before he pinched

his lips between his index finger and thumb as he thought about it. "A sliver."

Oh my Jesus Lord, was he drooling? Is that why he was forcing his mouth closed?

"No, no no no." I backed away. "You aren't eating me, pal. No fucking way."

Cross snapped his hand out, catching my arm as I retreated. "Thirty souls."

"No!" I protested as I wrenched free of him. "You are not giving away souls for that greedy salivating motherfucker to eat. No."

Rich laughter sounded behind me. "You could offer a hundred, a thousand, I would refuse them all. One sliver of her or nothing at all."

Cross held my gaze, and I knew how scared I was, and I knew how easily he could read me, and I really wanted to be able to read him, but at the moment he was blank.

"I will give you the soul of a Watcher."

I never understood the expression "knock me over with a feather" but in this moment, I would topple over at the slightest puff of air, never mind a feather.

As Cross ignored my horror, Mammon looked ready to cream his suit. "Who?" His voice was breathless. "The General?"

"A deceased Watcher," Cross answered with exasperation.

Mammon thought about it. I could see him weighing my worth up against that of a Watcher. "Araqiel."

"No." Cross was firm.

"I hold all the power here," Mammon snapped at him. "You need me."

"I don't," I spoke before Cross did. "I have options."

"Like who?" Mammon asked me, and I didn't need the patronising tone to accompany his look of pity.

"Satan." What the hell was I doing? "You're scary, don't get me wrong. The whole cannibalism thing you have going, honestly, you're making me sick. But Satan? Satan terrifies me."

"Satan?" Mammon looked positively affronted. "That snake?"

"Yup." I nodded. "And he likes me." Lies. "And he would hide me, but you know, Cross suggested here." I was trying for nonchalant, I think I achieved awkward.

"Because my brother is a fool and wants what the Watchers will not allow."

"Wha—"

"Enough," Cross snapped. "The soul of a Watcher for harbouring my ward."

Mammon looked between us. "Fine. I'll take those thirty until you bring me my treat."

Cross was frustrated, I could tell, but he smiled. "Ten, and you'll make sure not one whiff of her scent leaves this place, or I'll bring a platoon of angels and an army of Watchers here, just for you."

His olive complexion paled, but he jerked his head in a nod. "She's safe with me."

No, I wasn't. I knew it with Cross standing there, and I knew it even more as soon as Cross left, when Mammon grinned at me.

I was in shit, and I didn't know how to get out of it.

CHAPTER 8

"So," I began as I looked at the Prince of Greed and worried how the hell I was going to stop him from eating my soul. "Sex change?"

Thankfully, he laughed, because Jesus Christ, my mouth would get me in trouble one of these days.

"Something like that." Mammon gestured to the double doors at the end of the room. "Shall we?"

"Shall we..." I hesitated when he walked forward, and flinched when he looked over his shoulder back at me as he stopped walking.

"Dine."

My feet were backpedalling in haste before I noticed the prick was laughing at me. "You're fucking with me?" I demanded incredulously. "What is wrong with you?"

Mammon chose not to answer as he resumed his stroll across the checkered floor. Reluctantly, I began to follow him when my feet slowed to a stop. Right in front of me, the suit morphed into a long black backless ball gown with appliqué flowers. Thick dark hair that was short and fashionable for a man grew out into locks of rich red hair that reached the waist. Bulky shoulders that had strength and power slimmed down to a delicate frame, and when Mammon looked back at me this time, her eyelashes were thick with mascara, and her ruby-stained lips smirked at my disbelief.

"I am a prince of hell, little morsel, appearances can be deceiving." She turned fully and waited patiently for me to reach her. "You shed your humanity, and I can teach you how."

I couldn't form words because my throat and mouth were so dry; I was sure that I had swallowed sandpaper. As I tried to speak, I coughed, and when I was finished with my coughing fit, I finally rasped out a refusal. "No, I'm happy in this body, thanks."

Mammon looked me over and grimaced. "Really? Your tits could be bigger, your hips slimmer, and your stomach could be flatter."

Seems like Mammon as a woman was a bitch. I almost snarked at her that pregnant women didn't have flat stomachs when I realised what I'd missed earlier.

Mammon couldn't sense my baby. Or see it apparently. How was that possible?

I had no one to ask. But my fear for the safety of my child ratcheted up severely. How, in the name of whoever was up there, was I going to hide this? More importantly, how was my child hidden now? Was this Cross? Zel? Me?

I knew so little. I needed my lessons. I needed more training. I was so out of my depth I wanted Sam. My heart gave a squeeze, and I sympathised with it. I missed my demon. I needed him so much right now. I was scared. Alone. And fucking hell, I was drowning here; I needed Sam to help me stay adrift.

"I don't sleep," Mammon declared as she pushed open the double doors, and we entered an elaborate hall with chandeliers and twin curved staircases. "Do you?"

"Yes," I answered quietly as I looked around. Was that a footman? And a butler? "You know we're in the twenty-first century now," I told her as the two males bowed as she passed.

"Hmm, disgusting age, I don't like it. The technology ages. Repulsive."

"I would think demons would thrive when there is so much temptation everywhere."

Mammon sniffed in repulsion. "You know what I love. Want."

"Hunger?" I asked her in confusion.

"No, child. Need. The desire to have more, the yearning to be filled, complete. The yearning for more, never having enough, always wanting more."

"In that case, I am surprised you find the twenty-first century so repulsive. All humans want up there is more. More land, more possessions, more power."

Mammon tilted her head as she looked at me. "But there is no deep gut-churning need to have it. In your world, you want a new toothbrush, it's at your door within twenty-four hours. You want food in your fridge, home delivery within forty-eight hours. There is no struggle. It's not real, the desire for more, it's as superficial as hair weaves, fake tans, fake tits and veneers."

My head was struggling to understand her complaints. "Aren't you the prince"—I paused as I took in the beautiful gown—"princess, whatever, aren't you the level of hell that's for greed? Shouldn't the fact that we can get those things exactly as you state, without actually needing them, factor in the greed? We're purchasing for the sake of possession, not a need of things. Isn't that greed?" I watched as she gave a small smile. "If anything, your level of hell must be overrun. Humans? Greedy bastards."

"Define greed," she snapped at me as she ascended the staircase, and I followed dutifully behind.

"Um," I faltered. "Hunger. No not hunger, hunger isn't greed, it's a result of shortage. Hang on, let me think," I said as I thought about it. "It's want." I came back to her earlier comment. "A desire for something more, something else."

A few steps above me, Mammon whirled around to face me. "It's more than desire, it's an insatiable *need*. A deep-rooted hunger driving you forward to consume, to hoard, to take, to gather, to have something that you do not *need*, that accumulates far more than you will ever have use of, but still you want *more*." When Mammon was satisfied that I was listening to her lecture, she continued up the stairs. "The impulse to have more than you need, more than is considered socially acceptable, but the urge to have is never satisfied." She turned to the left of the stairs, and we walked down a wide hallway with doors on either side. "Those humans, who get their deliveries on a whim, that man who has his new toothbrush the next day, he has one toothbrush. Two if he thinks he needs a backup. That's not greed. That's normality."

"I don't think I understand," I admitted quietly.

She turned to look me over before I got a condescending smile. "I'm a man, and my toothbrush broke. I need a new one. I go onto one of the fast delivery sites to order my toothbrush. Before I check out, I think to myself, what if this one breaks? I'll be in the same position. I'll buy another." Mammon pushed open a door to a bedroom. "Within twenty-four hours, the man has two toothbrushes. Big deal. That isn't greed, that's shopping." Mammon made a sweeping motion with her hand. "Will this do?" When I nodded, she continued. "If I were the man, and I was ordering the toothbrush, I'd order them *all*. Not because I need them, not because I would use them eventually, but because *I want it all*."

"That's stupid."

"Toothbrushes may be a weak example. I'm a CEO of an oil company. My oil rigs only work one quadrant of the ocean. I want more. I'm wealthy, my children will have more money than I will, but I want more. So I expand, I now have oil rigs in two more quadrants. It's not enough. There is still more out there that I don't have. I need to expand again. Until I have it all."

"That's…"

"Greed."

"Indecent," I countered. "That isn't greed, that's ego."

Mammon laughed out loud. "My dear morsel, to be bigger, to be better, to be the best? It's all fucking ego."

"Is that why you're male *and* female?" I challenged her. "You wanted both because being just one wasn't enough?"

Mammon leaned in and kissed me once on both cheeks. "Goodnight, morsel."

I was still standing in the same spot about five minutes later before I forced myself to move. Mammon was…a lot. More than my simple brain could comprehend. Moving slowly, I walked to the bed. It was soft, looked inviting, and I realised I was absolutely exhausted.

Suddenly in a rush to sleep, I stripped my clothes off, and without any care to investigate the adjoining bathroom, I climbed under the covers in just my T-shirt and underwear. I was exhausted and scared. If I could sleep, it would be the best thing for me, and I closed my eyes, not caring under whose roof I slept.

I knew he was beside me the moment my eyes opened. We were back in the strange land that I now doubted was the

Land of the Souls. Sam lay staring at the sky, which showed a million stars in a velvety black sky.

The trees still swayed gently to a beat that no wind sang. The grass below me was damp but not uncomfortably so, and the ground was not as hard as I would have thought.

One of his arms was tucked behind his head as he lay looking upwards, the other rested across his chest. His legs crossed one over the other, and he looked at peace.

"Gabriel is with the angels now," he spoke quietly, gently. As if he had been waiting for me to stop studying him and this place. "I really fucking hate Michael, but Gabriel, he's a whole other level of asshole."

"I'm sorry," I whispered as I turned my back on the trees, turned away from the stars and looked at the only thing that mattered to me. Sam.

His hair had fallen back slightly with the angle that he was lying, and I liked that I could see his forehead. What a weird thing to like or notice at a time like this, but I did.

"I can feel you close to me, but I cannot see you nor hear you." His eyes closed briefly before opening again, showing a faint pulse of power. "That moment in the pit, when you tossed my brother's head into the hellfire like it was yesterday's leftovers, haunts me."

I was too scared to move, to speak. I knew he couldn't hear my voice, but as he stared blankly above, I was scared to break the spell.

"I knew it was goodbye. I knew Satan made you strike, knowing it would strike in each of our hearts. Knowing it would sever bonds far more than just yours and mine, witch." Sam gave a wry smile. "But Satan—and I—are both forgetful of one thing."

"What's that?" I whispered.

"How much my brothers love you," he answered as if he had heard me speak. "Chazaquel and Amaros, they would have walked through the hellfire to take you to safety there and then. They had no love for Araqiel and all the love for you."

I wet my lips as I listened to him, tears pooling in my eyes as I heard the hurt in his heart.

"*I* would have walked through hellfire, and I think I would have made it too," he said lightly, his eyes crinkling at the corners as he joked. "I would have spanked your arse red raw for that stunt, witch, but you would have loved it."

"I beg to differ," I objected quietly.

"You would have begged for more. And I would have given you anything you wanted. I *will* give you anything you want. Always." He hesitated. "But this? I cannot give you this, my little witch. You do not know. You cannot begin to know what destruction the Nephilim cause." I watched as his jaw tightened and his hand fell from his chest to his side.

"It could be different," I said to him, the plea in my voice. "You're not who you were all those centuries ago, Sam."

"It's not different from before," he spoke. It really was eerie how he answered me without hearing me. "I am a fallen one. A demon. A Watcher, yes. From where we fell, we were favoured, and now I am an outcast. And my Father gave me what I wanted, but he did not and would *not* give me everything. *Man* will inherit the earth. Not the Watchers. Not the fallen. Not the demons. I cannot propagate in this world, in any world or dimension. I cannot be allowed children. My Father will not permit it. He may have gifted me you, witch, but he would not gift us this."

The tears fell softly as I listened to him speak, his eyes still fixed on the stars above, his words full of remorse but heavy with truth.

"You deserve so much more, little witch. My fiery, stubborn, beautiful heart. You deserve a hundred children to call your own and a male who will love them as much as he does you. But you will never have that chance, because you gave *me* your heart. As I gave you mine. And I will not share you with another. Even when I know I should."

Sam raised his hand to cover his eyes for a moment before placing it back on the grass. "Father, I am a selfish fucker, you always knew I was. She is everything I ever wanted and a whole fucking lot more than I ever knew I needed, but you go too far with this."

Turning my head, I looked to the sky. Sam had said *Father*, and I realised in a moment of clarity that he was praying.

"You cannot take her from me. You cannot take her from this world; she is not ready. She is so young, so fucking innocent. The—" He stopped to draw in a breath. "*My* child, I will not let it live, I promise you. What came before will not happen again, I swear. And you know I am steadfast in my stubbornness. But not her, you cannot take her." His eyes glowed brighter with his power. "I will rip your heaven to this earth, and I will raise every level of hell to meet it. She *will* live, or by your grace, Father, I will destroy it all."

I jumped in shock when a flash of lightning lit up the sky.

"You're angry?" Sam laughed as he stood, his head still tilted upwards. "You haven't seen angry, but you will. She dies, your world dies. I will burn them all and you with it."

More lightning flashed, followed by crashes of thunder. The trees were now bowing at the force of the wind that whipped my hair into my eyes, blinding me from the male in front of me. As I ripped my hair away from my face, I took him in: Samyaza, the leader of the Watchers. The General.

He was magnificent.

He stood tall and proud, his mouth twisted upwards in that arrogant smirk I knew so well and loved so much, his shoulders broad and straight despite the burden I knew he carried.

Who in their right mind told God—my brain shut that down immediately—told their *maker* that they would burn the world down for a woman?

For me.

"You really love me," I said in wonder.

Sam looked down at me, one eyebrow lifting in surprise as our eyes met. "Witch."

"Demon."

"You look like shit."

"You look amazing," I countered easily. "And I've been running from Watchers and angels. There's been no time to get my nails done."

"There must be time at least to brush your hair, no?"

Bastard. I take it all back.

Sam turned his back on the light show he had been watching courtesy of dear old dad. "I suggest you stop running." He looked down at my stomach, his lips thinning in displeasure. "We can help you."

"You want to kill our child, how is that helping me?"

"By killing the thing that's slowly killing you."

I felt more tears rush down my cheeks. "That you say it so easily," I whispered as I stood. "It breaks my heart."

"It will break your body when it eats its way out of your womb," Sam told me callously.

"It may be different," I protested loudly. "I'm not human, I'm not your wife!"

Sam looked like I had struck him before his eyes narrowed, even as they flared green with his power. "No, you are not Hannah, she knew her place."

"Oh, you absolute hypocritical, chauvinistic, vile, misogyn—"

He crushed me in his arms as he kissed me. I felt it all the way to my toes, and as my hands curled into his thick hair to pull him closer, I didn't care that we were angry at each other.

Here, in his hold, was where I was meant to be.

Slowly, nipping my bottom lip as he drew away, Sam stared down at me. "Let me help you," he spoke softly as he cradled me gently to his chest, as if I would suddenly disappear.

I saw her out of the corner of my eye, Naomie, waiting at the line of trees. She gestured for me to come, and I knew my time was up.

"I love you," I told Sam as I looked up at him and slowly backed away. "You don't deserve it, you're a really shitty boyfriend, and you have really bad communication skills, but I love you with all that I am. Don't let the angels get me."

"Witch," Sam began as he reached for me. "Don't..." I was beside Naomie, and I knew he could no longer see me. "Go." Sam looked around wildly and then swore loudly. "Fuck, witch, I will wring your neck, I promise you!" he called out as he turned once more in a circle.

"Come." Naomie tugged my hand, and I nodded to let her

know I was ready to leave, I just wasn't ready to take my eyes off of Sam.

As I turned away, his voice stopped me.

"Star."

I turned back, pulling Naomie to a stop.

"I love you too, little witch." He didn't even give me the chance to savour it before he ruined it. "I promise you, if they kill you, I'll burn it all. Every last one of them. Heaven, hell, earth, I will burn it all, and I will spare nothing." His words rang of truth as his eyes lit with power, the glow lighting the clearing. "You know I will. Can you live with that, knowing you caused it all?"

Sneaky bastard, always knowing exactly which buttons to push.

CHAPTER 9

"How did you know where I was?" I asked Naomie as she led me through the trees.

"I'm a witch," she answered as she pulled me along behind her.

Guessed I asked for that. "Where are we going?"

"Away from here. I get that you love your man, but you're so reckless and stupid."

"Gee, thanks, Naomie."

"I was like that once. My head spun for Azazel and only Azazel. Over time, you grow out of it." I felt her squeeze my hand as if she were consoling me. She wasn't.

"He's going to do something stupid," I confided in her as we walked.

"He is the General, he won't." She turned to look at me and smiled sadly. "His words will speak louder than his actions, Star. Trust me."

"Maybe," I conceded, and in truth, I hoped they would, but this woman didn't know him. "But in all honesty, Naomie, you don't know Sam. I do."

She held my stare for a long moment before she dipped her head in acknowledgment. "My apologies."

"No need." I waved it off, suddenly feeling embarrassed. "I'm just feeling possessive."

"Samyaza is a male to feel possessive over," Naomie teased as we resumed walking. When we cleared the trees, I looked out over the sprawling hills.

"Where are we?" I took as much in as I could, but I could

have been in the middle of the Scottish Highlands for all the good it did me. Green hills, green trees, green grass. All tinted in darkness as we walked under a starry sky.

"The Watchers have a dimension that is not in hell," Naomie told me. "It's called the—"

"The ether, I know, I've been there," I told her impatiently. "This isn't there, this smells different."

"You've been in the ether?"

Was that jealousy? "Yes, is that a problem?"

Why was I being so defensive?

Naomie smiled widely at me, and I felt at ease. "No, of course not. I have never been. Is it beautiful?"

I thought of the windy old castle and the empty rooms. "It would benefit from some soft furnishings," I told her honestly as I shrugged.

"Ha, I bet it would." Naomie chuckled before she looked up at the sky. "This is not that dimension. This is *our* dimension."

"Ours?"

"The witches'."

It was empty. "Trees and hills?"

"Nature," Naomie corrected me.

"Is it safe here?" I asked. Sam was here, and last time I looked, he wasn't a witch.

"No, the others of the supernatural world can come here, but you, you are here."

"How?"

"Your soul knows it needs to learn, so you come here, and Samyaza is old and wise, so he knows what you need."

Hot memories of Sam moving over my body flashed through my mind, and my mouth watered. Yup, that demon usually did know what I needed. And I was pretty sure the porn show my mind was currently reliving, was not what Naomie meant. "Hmm."

It was the best answer I had.

"While you are safe, wherever your body is at the moment, if you can, come here. Not to the General, but to me. Here I can teach you how to be a better witch."

"Or just a basic one would be good too," I said honestly.

"You have so much power, you are more than basic purely by default."

"Sounds like I cheated," I mumbled as I avoided looking at her.

"You're so humble," Naomie told me with a smile. "You must go now, back to your sleep. But next time, come to me, and we can train."

"I'll try," I promised as I hugged her goodbye and then somehow woke up in my body and immediately screamed at the top of my lungs when I saw Satan standing at the foot of my bed. "What the fuck!" I yelled as I scrambled out from under the covers, not caring I was only in a T-shirt. "Why are you here?"

Satan beamed at me. "It's how am I here, not why. We both know why, but do we both know how?"

"Riddles? You're going to talk to me in mumbo jumbo?" I looked for my jeans and blanched when Satan held them in his hands. "Really? Do I need to worry about my underwear too?"

"Only if you make them wet first."

I stared at him dumbfounded. "You're… That's… Shut up."

His laugh was maniacal as he tossed me my jeans and then perched on the end of the bed. I didn't utter a word as I pulled on jeans that were not mine. These were designer, better and so out of my pay grade I wasn't giving him the satisfaction of being appreciative.

"Wow, mama, you look the shit with them on."

I didn't need to tell the lunatic he was insane, because I was confident that he already knew, and then I realised what he said. "Satan?"

"Yes, girl?" His eyes twinkled with laughter, and I wondered if anyone would heed my call if I killed the irritating fucker.

"Why are you here?"

He sighed dramatically as he fluttered his eyelashes at me. "I can't stop thinking about you."

"You're an arsehole. And a wanker."

Satan made several lewd hand gestures over his groin as he leaned back. "I do like being a wanker."

Yup. I was going to kill him. He was on his feet in a flash, and I hadn't hidden my reaction of fear from him as I scrambled backwards.

"Speaking of those that are wankers, where is the little wiener? Or is he currently she? I know he gets confused. I've tried so hard to support his choices, but it gets…so…hard." Satan was laughing at me, and I didn't like it. "Know what I mean?"

"I know you're wasting my time," I snapped at him. "Why?"

"The question to me isn't why, my dear stupid ignorant witch, the question is how?"

"How?"

"Well done, that's what I said. How does dear old Satan get you, a stupid knocked up witch, out of Greed's hungry clutches?"

I was in trouble.

"I'll tell you how," he continued as he spun to face me. "You get to come live with me, and when the golden nuggets from above come knocking, you hold my hand while I cut their heads off. What do you say?"

"You really are insane."

"Nuh-uh. No, that is not the answer I was looking for." Satan performed another pirouette on the bedroom floor. "But, Star, I like you, you make good business choices. You get another try."

"Satan, I—"

The doors flew open like a hurricane had come. And in a way it had. Mammon was back in his male appearance, and he was striding to Satan with no shock in his face that he was here.

"Scum!" Mammon yelled.

"Brother!" Satan held his arms wide, his whole posture a mockery to the furious demon advancing on him. "How nice to see you with a penis again."

"Oh shit," I cried as Mammon punched Satan in the face. And then they brawled. What the hell was this?

As I pressed myself against the wall, the two of them kicked the shit out of each other. Not playful brothers tussling, this was out and out thrashing of each other. I felt their powers being used as the punches had more impact. When Satan stood with Mammon on his knees in front of him, wild eyes fixed on me as Satan's hand tightened on his throat and the other fisted his hair, bringing Mammon's head to an uncomfortable angle.

"Now, where was I?" Satan asked me conversationally.

"I don't know," I told him as I stared at the pressure of his hand against Mammon's throat.

"Tut tut, Star, you really need to pay more attention to your surroundings," Satan scolded. "I was telling you that this piece of shit will not help you."

"And you will?" I asked him sceptically.

Satan rolled his eyes as if I just told him shit stank. "Obviously, and I would gladly help you." He smiled, and I knew the shiver running through me was fear not cold. "What did you get promised, little brother, to come out of hiding?"

Mammon's eyes were full of fury as his head was jerked back. His own hands were clawing at Satan's as he fought the powerful hold the Prince of Wrath held him in.

"Cat's got his tongue." Satan winked at me as he spoke. "What did you offer this fool?"

"Nothing."

Satan's head tilted to the side as he looked me over. "I advise against lying," he warned me.

"I offered him nothing," I repeated clearly and saw his sudden understanding as he shook his head slightly.

"Cross?"

I said nothing as Satan bent low to whisper in Mammon's ear. "Are you so gullible? Has your greedy nature overcome your fucking common sense?" Satan's mouth was twisted with hate as he spoke. "He offered you a soul? Whose?"

Satan kept his eyes on me as he loosened his hold slightly on Mammon's throat. When Mammon croaked out *Watcher*, Satan laughed and then wrenched his brother's head back until he was looking at him.

"You deserved to die the first time," Satan told him coldly. "This time, even the Watchers will thank me."

The sharp scream that pierced the air was mine, I knew it was, but the horror of seeing Satan's hand punch through

Mammon's chest, holding a black heart in his hand, was too much for me. Black blood dripped in thick drops onto the white wooden floors, and the slow dripping sound was loud in the quiet of the room. Satan withdrew his hand from Mammon's chest, and I felt my stomach churn as he took a huge bite out of the heart in his hand.

Brown eyes met mine as he smiled, and the black blood stained his lips and his chin as he took another bite. "Chewy," he said conversationally as he kicked the body over. With another bite, he dropped the heart onto the body and then bending down—I watched frozen—he literally tore the head from Mammon's body.

Spinning, I emptied my stomach on the floor as I gasped for breath. I would never unsee that, and I knew no matter how long I lived, I would see that image in my head forever.

"You need to have a stronger stomach," Satan chided me as I panted for breath.

Turning my head slightly, I watched him wipe his hands on a white handkerchief. "Why?"

"Because you're in hell, witch, and you need to be stronger, or you'll die."

"No," I spat. Straightening, I wiped my mouth with the back of my hand. "*Why* did you kill him?"

"I thought he was dead. The Watchers were supposed to remove this"—he kicked the dead body—"thing centuries ago. But still it lived."

Walking to the bed on unsteady legs, I sat down. "Didn't you want him alive?"

Satan laughed. "No. He hindered me."

"How?" Rubbing my eyes, I kept my face hidden in my hands. I was in danger of hyperventilating.

"Curbed my plans for expansion."

What the fuck? I looked at him in confusion as he playfully flopped onto the bed beside me. "Think of me in real estate."

Was I supposed to know what this sociopath was talking about? I was going to ask when I realised. "You want their levels. That's why you killed Asmodeous."

Satan grinned at me. "You gave me Lust, I just took Greed, Gluttony was gone a long time ago. I'm moving on up." He frowned. "Well, down. But three down is better than none, wouldn't you agree?"

"You're trying to take over hell?" I asked him in disbelief.

Satan lay back on the bed and stared at the ceiling. "I am. I think *King* of Hell is so much better than prince, don't you?"

Turning to look at him properly, I considered this monster. "You have no desire to Return."

Satan's condescending laugh rang around the room. "Fuck no. Up there? Boooring!"

"What are you trying to do? Why are you being so open with me?" What was the catch, what was I missing?

Satan's demeanour changed in an instant as he sat up and caught the back of my neck as I hastily jerked back. "Don't run," he whispered as his eyes changed to the vertical slits. "I will not hurt you…much."

"Satan…" I stopped when he squeezed the back of my neck with hands that had been black with Mammon's blood.

"You have the heart of a Watcher. *The* Watcher. I want it."

Fuck no. "Sam?"

Satan smiled, and I felt my stomach roil again when I saw his teeth were still dark with the blood from Mammon's heart. "Yes." His voice was like a hiss.

"No."

His grip tightened, and he pulled me in closer. His heavy breath on my lips filled me with disgust. "*Yes*. You are nothing but a puppet. A puppet to play with, and I don't like to play with toys." His eyes fixated on my lips. "I like to break my toys."

He crushed his lips to mine, and in fury, I bit his lip hard, blood spilling into my mouth. I bit so hard that as he wrenched himself away with a cry of pain, I jumped to my feet away from him. My powers were very much in my grasp as he turned and faced me. Hate filled his eyes as he readied to fight me.

Well, I wasn't going down without taking the bastard with me.

"You stupid bitch," he snarled as he checked his face and looked at the blood on his hand that was now his.

"No, I'm not stupid, but I *am* a bitch." I called for Hound. "And I'm a bitch with friends."

Hound morphed into his humanoid form smoothly as soon as he entered the room. In two moves, he had Satan pinned to the wall, his feet dangling above the floor as Hound lifted him one-armed into the air.

"You touch what is mine?" Hound asked him as his head cocked to the side in curiosity.

"Morax? I *knew* it was you." For a male being suspended in the air by the strength of one demon, I was astounded to see Satan laugh.

Hound looked at the dead body of Mammon, and Satan preened. "Star?" Hound asked.

"I'm okay," I told him as I walked around the fallen body so Hound could see me. "He wants to use me to get to Sam. He's trying to take over hell."

Hound looked back at Satan. "The General?" And then Hound stunned me when he started to laugh. He dropped Satan like he was yesterday's news. "You were always a fool."

Hound turned to me and held his hand out. "Come, there is no threat to you here."

Looking between the two of them, I was lost. Hound stood tall and confident, while Satan was on his knees, his hands at his throat, which had an angry red welt across it, his hate-filled gaze on us both.

"What am I missing?" I asked Hound hesitantly as I reached out to take his hand.

"I'll explain." His hand closed around mine.

We winked.

CHAPTER 10

"You need to stop calling it winked, it's travelled," Hound admonished me.

"We wink in and out of places. Travelled sounds like a journey; we *wink* in a blink of an eye." As I looked at my hands, I took the offered cloth from Hound wordlessly as I scrubbed my hands clean. I was in the Void. *My* Void. "He ripped Mammon's head off his shoulders like it was paper."

Hound shrugged. "Satan is very powerful compared to some of the princes."

"But not to you?" Hound smiled, and his easy relaxed smile made me smile in return. "You're scary sometimes," I admitted to him.

"Why?" Hound sat on the floor of the Void, completely comfortable in his nakedness. And it was weird, because Hound naked wasn't even strange. My mind just accepted it.

"Because you're a hellhound, which I always thought was a mindless beast, but the more I get to know you, you're more powerful than just a servant of Death." Sitting down across from him, I asked the question that had been waiting for a long time. "What happened to you?"

Hound looked at me and then sat forward. "I fell with the others. Not with the twenty that fell with Samyaza, I was never with the General." He looked thoughtful. "The seven fell next, after the Watchers had paved the way, the princes" —he snorted—"fell looking for worship." Hound's sneer told me exactly what he thought of that. "They sampled the offerings of the world, and then they wanted more." Red eyes held mine. "Meanwhile, the Watchers stopped watching."

"The princes were free to do what they wanted?"

"They were. They wanted to rule." Hound shook his head in disgust. "They had little to do with the fighting of the rebellion, they had little to do with the *living* on earth, all they wanted was a place to rule. The Watchers wanted no power. No authority. Samyaza was steadfast in his desire to live." Hound's gaze fixed on a point over my shoulder. "The Watchers had fallen to enjoy *life*. After the seven followed, more of us fell, seeking the freedom that earth offered. But even angels are creatures of habit. They need law, they need order, and once we fell, we needed an authority to steady us."

"You needed the Watchers?" I guessed.

"We did, but we did not know it. We had the seven, and they found hell." Hound licked his lips. "Humans believe the fallen created hell. It's not true. Hell was waiting for us long before we fell. Many think the Watchers knew, but they told us not." He was quiet.

"You don't think so?"

"The Watchers are not all like the ones you know and care for. Many were like Araqiel, Suriel, Yeqon. Their hearts are not open, their intentions not always for the good of others. Samyaza, Azazel, strong, powerful, but not always good, but still better than their brothers." Hound sighed. "When we left our Father, we allowed temptation into our hearts."

"Lead us not into temptation," I murmured.

"Exactly, and Samyaza paved the way for *all* to fall to temptation."

"Azazel fell first." I felt it necessary to point that out.

"And who do you think told him where to fall?"

Oh. Well, okay, when you put it that way, I guessed Sam looked like the villain of the story after all.

"The fallen enjoyed their newfound freedom, and the seven encouraged all to be tasted. We were a plague on humanity. We were no better than pillagers of land and people that we had no right to, but our arrogance told us that we had a right to them. To their lives, to their livelihoods and to their essence."

"It sounds horrible." My voice was soft in the still quiet of the Void.

"It was a disgrace to the Father we had fled. It was an outrage to who we were, to the beings we had been, and we broke the mould in which we were created so thoroughly it was no wonder that we were lost. The seven relished in our rampage. They watched with glee as we picked sides, and that side was hell. Slowly, in our desperation to belong, we migrated to the depths of hell and the dimensions within it that the seven had carved out for themselves."

"Whose side did you pick?"

"No one's." Hound met my surprised look with a small smile. "I had roamed for years, desolate, lost, empty. What had I become? A monster? A mindless beast that consumed life with no joy. I was despicable."

"What changed?"

"Nothing." Hound snorted. "I got what I wanted. I fell. I tasted freedom. I became a monster."

"But you aren't. You're good!" I protested.

Hound ignored me. "The fallen became too much, the discord they sowed on the earth was too much, and then the Nephilim came." Hound's head bowed. "The devastation of their being...*alive*, it could not go unchecked."

"And it didn't," I murmured sadly.

"The angels came to wage war on them and the ones who would protect them." Hound's look was hard. "There were many who rejoiced in the terror of the Nephilim."

"Not Sam," I countered weakly.

"They were his children. They were his essence. They were *his*, Star."

"He fought for them?" I asked in surprise. I didn't know why, but I had always assumed he had been in agreement with their deaths.

"The General fights from his heart, always."

I recalled what Sam had said to me, and I felt anxiety wash over me. He didn't mean it. Even Naomie said he wouldn't.

"What happened?" I asked as I pushed Sam's words away like the coward I was.

"The demons and the angels fought, and the human casualties became too much, because the Nephilim did not fight and just kept destroying. Sin was winning."

"Sin?" I asked Hound. How was this sin?

"Temptation led to corruption. Corruption led many of us to become twisted, gnarled shadows of our former selves. As we polluted this earth with our depravity, we infected the humans. The floods wiped the earth clean."

"But the demons remained."

Hound nodded as he smirked. "They did. As thousands of souls rose, Death walked among them, collecting them."

"Cross?" I guessed.

But Hound was lost to the past. "I sensed no desire to rule from him, no thirst for power, he just...was. And he was struggling under the weight of the souls he had to carry."

"You helped him," I said with understanding.

"My disgust at what I had become was a heavy burden. As the innocent fell to the wrath of an angry God in order to rid the earth of a blight that we created, I knew what monsters were, and it was not solely the Nephilim."

"You are not a monster," I reminded him.

"Cross saw me. I was on the land, waiting for the water to reach me, waiting to drown." He sat straight as he squared his shoulders, like he was there again. "The water was not simple rainfall. It was the tears of heaven come to cleanse a corrupt and depraved world. I was ready to die. I was ready to be no more. I deserved it." His head dipped down as he spoke. "When I looked up, he was in front of me. He asked me to help him carry his burden. My arms reached out, but I knew it wasn't enough. I asked him how I could serve."

"You became his first reaper?"

"I did. We collected the souls, and we took them over the veil, and we repeated the action for days and days and days." Hound stretched his arms out as he studied his hands. "He was the order that I needed, he was the authority that I had lacked. He was the balance my soul craved."

"Bloody hell, that's huge."

"When the rain stopped, the sun shone through the clouds, and I looked up to the face of my Father. He offered to open the gates for me, knowing that my soul sought to repent for my actions."

"Fucking hell, I take it back, *that's* huge."

"And I looked to Cross, and he simply stood there, waiting. I knew who I had been. I knew I had been part of the reason these souls had passed. I was nothing more than a scurvy dog that had terrorised innocents. I needed to atone for my sins. I needed to pay my dues for the debt that I was in."

"You chose the form of the hellhound?"

"I did. I turned from my Father for the final time, and I followed my new master to do the work that I was meant to do."

"And the others? The other two hellhounds?"

"My brother and sister joined me years later. The demons who survived the flood were more careful. As earth evolved, the sins of the Father did too. My companions grew weary with their own burdens."

I turned as the other two hellhounds walked into the Void. "I don't know their names," I said to Hound.

When I turned back, he was back in his hellhound form.

They do not acknowledge their past. This is who they are.

"Why did you save me?" I asked, scared of the answer.

You are pure. You are not a scapegoat for the Watchers.

"And them?" I flicked my gaze between the two hellhounds who sat on either side of Hound.

Made their own choices.

"Thank you?" I could hear the question in my own voice and was not surprised when Hound chuckled through the link.

The child cannot be.

Screwing my eyes shut, I clenched my teeth. "Hound, after everything you think about me, and everything you know, *how* can I do what you ask?"

The death will be more than you can imagine. Is one life worth so much death?

"Dammit," I grumbled as I stood. "Have you been speaking to Sam? You sound like him."

An honour I have never had said to me before.

"It wasn't a compliment." I thought about what he said.

"Why do you respect him? If it wasn't for him and his Watchers, you would all still be up there." I pointed upwards.

When the water dispersed, the Watchers were changed. They knew the repercussions of their actions, and they repented.

"Did they get an offer to return?"

I do not know. But the Watchers had a fire in their belly. They took the princes in hand, and once again, the fallen had a hierarchy of power to adhere to.

"They restored hell," I realised, "and they what? Watch?"

Every society needs law.

"Why does Satan want Sam?"

Power. Did he bite Mammon's heart?

"Yup." I felt nauseous again at the image in my head. "Snacked on it like it was his favourite treat."

He ingests their power.

"He didn't with Asmodeous." I saw Hound tilt his head. "He didn't eat his heart."

He drank the blood.

The blood from my hand, I remembered. I remembered Sam growling a warning, not at Satan taking liberties with me, but for consuming the blood and therefore the power from his fallen enemy. What had I done?

"Why do you let me live?" I asked him wearily. "I keep fucking up."

You are human. Still.

"Well, that's not comforting." I looked around the Void. "Apparently, this is my own manifestation."

Of course.

Squinting, I looked at my Hound. "Does anything freak you out?"

The promise of destruction that you carry within you.

"Wow."

He shrugged.

"He said he will burn the world if I die," I confessed to the three of them. "He thinks it's a choice I can make. My child or…"

Everything else.

"Yes."

It is as simple as that.

"No, it can't be. I'm not wholly human, we all know this. Hell, being with Cross, it changed me. Look at me!" I demanded as I pulled my hair to show them. "This isn't *my* blonde, this is almost white; my hair was yellower. Have you seen my skin?" I carried on, panic coursing through me. "I haven't got one wrinkle, nothing."

You're twenty-five, Hound deadpanned.

"Look, I had laughter lines, okay? Now, I'm smoother than a polished rock."

You're fixating on the wrong things.

"I can't think of what he said!" I yelled into the Void. "He's going to *burn* the world down, he told *God* this. He said to him, if I die, he tears it all down."

Then you need to find the strength to make sure that doesn't become a reality. You must stop being a pawn in the prince's plan.

"I didn't ask Satan to be a giant psychopath."

But you asked for his aid. The princes will use you only for their gain. Be smarter.

"I'm trying."

You are failing.

Hound was not put off by my angry glare. He merely watched me freak out in the Void of my own creation.

I stilled. "Hound?"

No.

"You don't even know what I was going to say!"

You want to ask me if you are safe here. You are not. You want to ask me if the child is safe here. It is not.

"How do you know?" I challenged him, my eyes narrowing on the hellhound with all the answers.

Because I can find you here without your pulling me in. If I can, anyone can.

"Then I make it stronger," I told him stubbornly.

Or you die and the world burns.

"He wouldn't."

You do not know the General as we do. He knows what needs to be sacrificed to win a war.

"A child?" I asked scathingly.

A monster.

Shaking my head in denial, I turned away from the three hellhounds. I had said all I needed to say.

The plan for the Return continues.

That took me by surprise. "But the angels are here."

You think they are only here for you?

Okay, when he put it like that, I was shocked at my own arrogance. "Sam and the others?"

Will not interfere with the golden on the ground.

"The golden? Sounds pretentious." Rubbing my hand over my stomach, I looked to Hound. "I have to return to Satan."

You are being a fool.

"I am being a survivor."

He will not help you.

"He has three levels of hell, four including his own. He has the majority vote; he can keep us hidden."

Do not do this.

"Before, when the Nephilim were causing the world to end, did the Watchers have the ether?" I asked desperately.

Yes.

Relief swept over me. "Then that's the answer, we can keep my child in the ether."

It won't hold them. They broke free of it before. You think your love for your child will be enough, and it is not. They do not *love. They cared nothing for their human mothers.*

"I'm more than human."

But you are still *human, even if you are a necromancer.*

He had an answer for everything, and I was exhausted. "I'm tired," I snapped. "I have too many things—" I stopped when Cross appeared in front of me. "How did you get here?" I asked him.

"Hellhounds." Cross checked me over and then, placing his hands on my shoulders, he stooped down to eye level. "You must not overreact."

"Okay…"

"Michael and Gabriel have made their first move." Cross squeezed my shoulders lightly. "They are with your parents."

CHAPTER 11

I felt my legs give way, but Cross quickly caught me by my elbows and kept me steady. Everything was spinning, and I was going to be sick.

"Cross…"

"Breathe, Star, I've got you," he assured me. I felt something strong and steady behind me, and I knew it was Hound. Offering me support in case I fell. In case Cross didn't have me. He was letting me know that he did.

"Are they…" I swallowed hard. "Are they alive?"

"Yes, they are. They are merely holding them in the hopes to draw you out."

I was clutching onto Cross's arms as if he were my lifeline, which was hysterically funny considering he was Death. I started to laugh.

"Why is she laughing?" Cross asked Hound, and I felt the hellhound shapeshift.

"Hysteria," he answered gruffly. "Where do they hold them?"

"Their home," Cross said as he watched me.

"Reckless." Hound tentatively pulled my arm. "Star, you need to calm down. This is important."

I did. I really did need to calm down. But if I calmed down, then I needed to face the reality that the angels had my parents. *The angels had my parents.*

Those fuckers.

They had no right to involve them.

No fucking right.

"Here she comes."

I heard Hound speak, and I registered that he morphed back into his hellhound form, but it was as if I were in a dream. My powers curled around me, warm, comforting, and as my head tipped back to look up into the Void, I knew my hair was floating.

Something slid over me, and I looked down to see that I was wearing the black leather trousers that Sam had given me before and a rather flattering black shirt. My eyes met Cross's, and he nodded as he smiled.

"Your eyes are white," he told me.

"Good."

I winked.

My parents' house in Inverness was on a fairly populated street. Although it was a semi-detached house, the neighbours on either side were rarely home. My arrival in my parents' kitchen shook their foundations, and I knew I would have rattled a few of the neighbouring properties also.

The angels were waiting. But I took note of the fact that they were not waiting for what had arrived. Me in full power was not what they were expecting. Me with three hellhounds in tow surprised them. The plain-faced Michael looked us over in consternation, but he did not concern me. The prick who scarred Zel was the one who held my attention.

"Gabriel."

My mum and dad were at the kitchen table, sitting closely together. Mum had my dad's hand in her grip, and I knew she was holding him down, not offering him comfort. I also saw my mother's rage at being held by the angels, and I wondered which Watcher had told her what I had gone and gotten involved in this time. Penemue no doubt, they had a weird connection.

"So…you are her?" Gabriel looked bored. He sniffed. "The other female he sinned with was prettier."

Arsehole.

"She was also human," I countered as I took in my surroundings. "You brought so many of your platoon. Were you scared my parents were going to be too much for you dickless wonders to handle?"

"Your mother is a witch."

"My father is not." I felt my power surging as I raged at his apathy. "We will leave here, you and I and all your flightless birds. We will talk on neutral ground, and I will do my very best not to rip your fucking head off your shoulders for what you have done here."

"Star," my mum's warning was low but heard.

"It's okay, Mum, I have this." My gaze never left the angel. "You have sixty seconds to comply, Gabriel, or I'll start taking heads."

"Your eyes are completely white," he said as he basically ignored everything I had just said.

"You sound surprised." My stare flicked to Michael. "Fifty seconds. He goes first."

"We only wanted to talk."

"Send a fucking text," I snapped.

Gabriel smiled, but there was no humour. If I hadn't known he was an angel, I would have assumed he was a demon. He oozed the aroma of prince-of-hell dickishness like it was an aftershave. A really bad one.

"We will go, but I will leave four behind, for insurance."

"You think I will trick you?" I could have laughed.

"No, I think you forget who watches."

My breath caught. He wasn't referring to my parents, he said *watches*. The Watchers were here. Was Sam?

"I never forget who is with me," I told him. "I think we're down to ten seconds, move."

Before Gabriel could react, I reached out and snatched him, and then we were in the Void. The actual Void, not my version.

Check my parents, I sent to Hound. He didn't move, but I noticed one of the others did. I should have known that Hound would never leave me. I also knew Cross was in my Void, watching. I only hoped that Zel or Sam was with him.

"Your power is impressive." Gabriel looked me over. "But I am an archangel, and parlour tricks impress me not."

As my lightning caught him in the chest, I savoured his cry of surprise. "Impressed now?" I drawled.

Finally, the bored, impassive façade dropped. Amber eyes met mine, and he was angry. "You need to take more care, witch."

"Or what? Going to threaten my family? Me? My friends?" I cast my eyes over the angels who stood behind him, ready to fight. "You're bullies."

Gabriel opened his mouth, but then he closed it again with a snap. I wondered what he had been going to say, when I felt it. Power stalking towards me. Immense power.

Satan stood at my side, his scales on display, his snake eyes fixated on Gabriel, and his power throbbing beside mine.

"Gaby? You look exactly the same. How completely boring...and predictable."

"You run with *him*, witch?" Gabriel actually looked

disgusted, and I knew now was not the time for semantics, but I did want to clarify the confusion.

When I felt another presence, I looked to my right, and I was clueless. The newcomer made all the others pale into insignificance. Long dark hair sat on his shoulders in messy waves. A slim lithe body wearing dark trousers and a black long-sleeved shirt that hugged his physique, which although slim, it was obvious he had muscle. He gave me a wink before he looked at the angels.

"Lucifer," Michael hissed.

Were they fucking kidding me? I had Satan and Lucifer beside me? Where in hell were my Watchers?

"You come to this world, and you don't look me up?" Lucifer spoke, and it was like melted chocolate, thick, glossy, rich and utterly bad for your cholesterol.

"Did we hurt your ego?" Gabriel sneered.

Glancing at sex personified, I realised he was the Prince of Pride. I could totally see it. Why was he here?

"Twenty of your soldiers entered my level of hell and tried to assassinate me," Lucifer sounded amused.

"And?" Michael tried for arrogant. He achieved petulant.

"I killed them."

"Twenty angels?" I asked him in surprise.

Dark blue eyes looked me over, and he smiled lazily. "Without breaking a sweat."

Wow. Love yourself much?

"They told me you were innocent." Gabriel spoke to me, and I had almost forgotten he was there.

"Me? I am." I thought about it. "Mostly."

"You have two princes of hell beside you," he snorted in disbelief.

"I did not ask them here." Which was true, Satan scared me, and Lucifer...well, up to about three minutes ago, I thought he and Satan were the same person. My inner self-preservation knew not to ever voice that observation to them though.

"You have the hellhounds."

"Them I did ask for." I grinned.

"Where is Death?" Gabriel asked me as he looked around.

"I would say all around us." I watched as the souls filled the Void slowly, methodically, carefully. They were here for me, for my use should I need it. I didn't know why Cross wasn't here, but the souls were, and them? *Them* I could use.

"You should go," Satan told them casually, and he jerked his thumb over his shoulder, which made me turn. My blood ran cold as I saw his nightmares released and coming to join us.

Lucifer must have noted my abhorrence as his hand made a come-hither gesture, and I saw the other half of the Void fill with demons.

"You want war," Michael spoke, stating the obvious.

"We want more than war," Satan told him with a grin.

"Is this what *you* want?" Gabriel asked me.

"No," I told them all. "I just want to be left alone."

"You carry something that can destroy it all," Gabriel spoke quietly, as if we were the only two here.

"*Can* and *will* are two different things," I argued, and I saw a brief flicker of sympathy as he looked at me.

"Not in this," he countered gently. "There is still time to put a stop to this."

"It's too late," Satan interrupted. "The die is cast."

"You play a game that is not yours to play," Gabriel told him waspishly.

I actually agreed with Gabriel, neither Satan nor Lucifer had any right to be here. I didn't know them, and I didn't want to. They did not come here today to fight for me or my child. They came to provoke the angels and were using me as an excuse. Reaching for my powers, I gathered them tightly as if I held them in my fist. Releasing them, as if the power of my hand had punched the air around me, I cast the two princes back to their hell.

Gabriel watched me closely as I caught my breath. "Impressive."

"I'm not here to impress you," I snapped. "Why would you take my family? I thought you were supposed to be the good guys?" I heard rather than saw the ones who chuckled at my naivety. "I've seen more integrity in the Watchers."

Gabriel's top lip curled in a sneer at the mention of the Watchers. "Scum."

"Careful now, *they're* my friends." The wind picked up again, and I knew it was me. So did the angels.

"The child needs to die," Gabriel snapped. "You carry death and destruction within you, and it needs to be stopped now."

"I carry an innocent."

"You're a fool." Michael spat on the ground beside him. "If you could see what your precious *innocent* wrecked on this world before, you would be begging for its destruction."

"How can you even say that?" I cried out as I looked at them all. "My child *is* innocent. It has done *nothing*. You cast judgement on a memory, not on what is to come."

"That you think that there will be any difference merely highlights your stupidity," Gabriel said with sadness. "Star, I think you actually believe your own lies. I understand you are scared, that you are alone. But what you are holding onto, this hope that you have that you will be different." He shook his head, and I was beginning to think he was genuine. "You won't be."

"Because you won't give my child a chance."

"Because there is no chance to give."

We stared at each other before I looked away from the ancient wisdom I saw in his amber eyes.

"We will give you a few more days, but time is running out. You can have some time to come to terms with this, and then you need to come to us, and we can stop it together." Michael looked at Gabriel in surprise as he spoke, but Gabriel kept his focus on me.

"And the Return?"

Whatever softness had been in Gabriel's eyes vanished. "They will be dealt with. You aid them?"

"Fuck no." My hand rested on Hound's shoulder. "They fell, they don't get a do over."

"On that, we can agree," Michael muttered.

"The princes?" Gabriel asked.

"They play another game I am not sure of." I decided honesty was the best policy. "The Watchers can help you."

Both angels looked at me as if I were the creepy snake-headed woman that I killed in the ether.

"Don't stare at me like fish out of water. They do not want the Return either. You need to remember who fell and for what reason," I growled at them both.

"Your trust is commendable but sadly misplaced." Gabriel made some weird hand gesture, and his angels snapped to attention. "Four days."

"I—" They were gone.

Hound sat down and looked at me.

"So?" I hedged. "Went well?"

No.

"Yeah, I thought it could have been worse." I spoke as if I hadn't heard him. "They'll leave my parents alone?"

No.

"They didn't even apologise," I carried on. "And four days? Nothing will change in four days. Will it?"

No.

"I agree." I started to walk backwards and forward in front of him. "What was up with Satan, and holy gumdrops, did you see Lucifer? He almost made me forget I was in front of all those angels!"

Ridiculous.

"How many more are there? I can't cope with them just popping in like long-lost friends. Who am I missing?"

The Watchers.

"Ha. Yeah, you're funny." I was freaking out. I recognised it for what it was. I was overwhelmed, and my brain was latching onto anything that wasn't me confronting archangels and princes of hell. Or carrying a child of death and destruction. "Where *are* the Watchers?" I asked Hound, and I knew that invisible eyebrow was raised at me.

You need to stop.

"I do. I do need to stop." I was nodding, but I wasn't sure it mattered. Bending over, I placed my hands on my knees as I concentrated on breathing. "I think I'm hyperventilating."

Really.

It's amazing how much sarcasm Hound could inject into his telepathic voice. "Have they left Mum and Dad's?"

They left two behind.

"To make sure they have leverage?" I understood the reasoning, I just didn't like it.

The hellhounds are watching.

I was still nodding. "Good, that's good." I straightened. "And where is my friend Cross?"

Watching.

"Ha." I resumed my pacing. "And my *actual* Watchers? Are they also just watching?"

No.

My hands were shaking. "Hound?"

It's adrenaline.

"Can you make it stop?"

No.

"I swear if you say *no* one more time!"

You need to call for him.

Tears built behind my closed lids as I shook my head frantically. "No."

He can help you.

"He wants the same thing as the angels."

Star...

"No!" I yelled. "I can do this! I can make the decision on my own."

You are failing. It's not just you. Think of your parents.

"Wow, that was low." I glared at my friend. "Really, really low."

True though.

"He's going to overreact," I warned Hound. "When he finds out I had Satan and Lucifer here, he's going to lose his shit."

As he should.

"I thought you were on my side?" I snarked at Hound as I

pulled my hair up off my shoulders and gathered it into my hands as I set them on my head.

I am.

We shared a look, and then dropping my hands to my sides, I closed my eyes as I called for him.

Sam.

CHAPTER 12

HE WAS IN FRONT OF ME. REALLY IN FRONT OF ME, NOT A projection or a dream, actually here. Had I said Lucifer was sexy? Was I stupid? Sam was everything. Everything I needed and wanted.

"Witch."

The smile at hearing his familiar greeting made me lose some of my tension. "Demon."

"Why are you in the Void?" Sam asked sharply. "Where is Azazel?"

Which was a fantastic question that I didn't have an answer for. "The angels took Mum and Dad hostage."

Sam's whole body froze as he focused on me, and I realised I had maybe blurted that out without much context. "What did you say?"

"The angels went to my mum and dad's house and waited for me to come to them." Was that better? Probably not.

"And you *went*?" Sam asked me incredulously before he turned his furious glare to Hound. "I thought you were protecting her?"

"Hey, they had my mum and dad; your *Father* wouldn't have stopped me from getting to them."

"You cannot be so rash!" Sam growled as he advanced on me, stopping short when his gaze stopped and stayed on my tummy. "You are showing more now." The sadness with which he spoke was too much for me.

Turning from him so he couldn't see my pain, I tried to hide my tears. "Yeah, I suppose I am."

"Your family is okay?" Sam asked me softly, and I felt fresh tears welling in my eyes. This was the demon who had walked into my home and spelled my mum and dad with no thought to me or them. Now he was asking me if they were okay? These hormones were either going to make me cry like a baby or jump his bones…whilst sobbing.

"Yes, I went and got the angels to come with me, here."

Sam tensed and looked around. I saw his hand tighten on the pommel of his sword.

"I haven't trapped you," I said in exasperation.

"Treachery seems to be a common theme in our relationship," he quipped back.

"Yeah, I guess it is." We stared at each other across a short distance. "I have four days."

Sam squinted as he looked at me. "For what?"

"To hand myself over to the angels."

"Fuck that." Sam laughed derisively. "Like that would happen." He lost his smile as he saw my face. "Witch, I warned you what happens if you're reckless with your life."

"You can't kill everyone!"

"Yes. I can. Want to watch me?" He huffed in frustration. "Oh right, you won't be able to, because you'll be dead."

"You need to listen to me."

"When you have something that is worth listening to, I will."

"Sam!" I cried out in frustration. "For fuck's sake, I need you!"

He was in front of me. The intensity in his eyes made my tummy flip as he reached out and caught me by the back of my neck, pulling me close to him, as his lips brushed against mine. Sam pulled back and looked at me with a question in his eyes before I reached up and caught his lips with mine.

The kiss stoked the fire within me, and as I felt him press harder against my mouth, I opened for him as our kiss increased in passion. It was easy to let our physical attraction override all the other crap between us. Sam's hand slipped to my butt as he squeezed me closer, and with little effort from him, I was up and wrapped around him in one smooth effort.

"You taste so good," Sam murmured against my skin as he kissed along my jaw. "I want you," he moaned as my hands tugged his hair to direct him back to my mouth.

I needed him too. I was panting with need. "I'm so ready for you," I whispered as our kiss got hotter. "Have we got time?"

"No," Sam groaned as he pulled back. "But fuck it."

We were somewhere else. As he kissed me again, I opened my eyes to see the room from before in the ether. My shirt was gone, my bra ripped in two, and as Sam kissed his way down my body, I felt his lips still as he reached the swell of my stomach. His whole body stiffened, and slowly he pulled away.

As Sam stood, he turned his back to me as he straightened his clothes.

"Sam?"

"I can't," he said as he looked at me, and the look in his eyes had me pulling my shirt over myself. "You ask too much."

Pissed off, I was on my feet. "Yeah, you seemed to be on board with what I was *asking*."

"We can't stay here, they will come." Sam avoided looking at me.

"I have four days," I snapped as I turned so I couldn't see him avoiding me, while I tried and failed to fix my top.

"Four days for what?" Sam asked me quietly, and I was so peeved at him rejecting me that I missed his tone.

"To hand myself over to the angels."

"What?"

I heard it that time. Fuck. Turning, I looked at him. "Gabriel said I had four days. They want to deal with the same thing you have an issue with."

He was still as stone as he watched me. "What else?" He waited but not patiently. Because he was Sam after all. "What *else* happened?"

"Satan and Lucifer turned up."

"Tell me this is the start of a bad joke."

"No." I felt the panic building again. "I'm out of my depth. And Hound advised that I call for you."

"Lucifer?" Sam asked me with a look that made me want to curl up and cry.

"I didn't ask for him!" I defended myself. "Until today, I thought he was the same guy as Satan!"

Sam stilled in his movements as he looked over at me with confusion. "Why would they be the same?"

"You wouldn't understand."

"Try me."

"Horror movies, media, books, Satan is another name for Lucifer, and vice versa," I explained. "I think."

"No wonder humans these days are idiots." Sam grunted as he walked to the door. "There's a reason I prefer the ether to the earth now."

"You mean when you're not policing hell?" I snarked at him.

Cool green eyes met mine in question. "Should I be flattered you're asking questions about me?"

"No."

He said nothing as he walked out of the room, and I had no choice but to follow him. In the main hall, I didn't know where to look. There were so many Watchers. Who the hell were all these guys? I was still wondering when I saw Watchers I recognised.

Chaz hugged me close as did Ros. The others I knew gave me nods of acknowledgement, but they kept their distance.

"Damn, guys, I'm pregnant not contagious."

"She's been cavorting with the princes of hell again." Sam's stare was flat as he spoke about me to them.

"Star?" Chaz asked as he caught my hand while I sat down. "Talk to us."

Hound appeared and walked through the Watchers like he belonged there. With ease, he morphed into his humanoid form and took a seat beside me. His transitions between forms were easier now, but I knew he preferred his form as a hellhound.

"Gabriel and Michael turned up at her parents' home, and Cross came to get Star to warn her. He didn't know what they were going to do. However, it was to draw Star out only."

"And she went." Sam filled in the shocked silence.

"They're my family."

"How are you still so gullible?" Sam snapped. "They set a trap, and you fell for it."

"It was my mum and dad." Maybe he wasn't hearing me.

"It was a trap, not even a clever one."

I turned to Chaz. "Help me get through to him?"

"What happened when you turned up?" Chaz asked me instead.

"I took Gabriel to the Void, and his angels followed. We were going to talk, and I…well…um…" I didn't know how to say it.

"Lucifer and Satan came too." Hound's tone was dry, and I shot him a glare as he failed to back me up.

Before the Watchers could all tell me that I was a terrible person, I quickly held my hands up for silence. "I sent them back to hell," I told them. "I spoke to Gabriel. He wants me to go to him and allow him to"—I rolled my head uncomfortably on my shoulders—"to take care of…" I gestured down.

"Gabriel knows how to remove it from you with no harm to you?" Chaz asked me excitedly.

"Um." Did he? I never asked.

"You didn't ask, did you?" Sam said as he looked at me with such scorn I shifted in my seat. "And even if you had, you know what he would have told you, witch?" Sam sat in his chair practically vibrating with fury. "He would have told you that there *is* no way, the only way is if you die."

"What—"

"You die," Sam snarled. "That's it. No cure, no alternative."

"Sam," Ros started, but the look from the General silenced him.

"What's happening?" I asked, quickly changing the subject as I looked around.

"War."

My heart was racing as his clipped answer jarred at my senses. "Who are you fighting?" I asked. "Angels?"

"Enemies."

I stood. There was no point being here. There was no help

here for me. "I need to go." I looked at Hound, who remained sitting. "You coming?"

"No."

No? What did he mean no? "Hound?"

"You need to remain here, with your mate. With the Watchers. You need to find a way to remove the thing you carry and stay alive."

"Can we please stop calling my child a thing?"

"Let her go," Sam said, and I turned to look at him as I heard his tiredness.

"Sam?"

"Go find Cross. I'll be there soon." He held my stare, and the small kindling of hope I felt scared me. "Even you can find Cross without any trouble, yes?" His tone was teasing, and I gave a small laugh more from relief than anything.

"Yes, even *I* can do that."

"Okay, go, I'll be right behind you." His eyes held mine, and I nodded when he gave me a slow smile. "I only stab you in the heart, remember? Not the back."

I heard Ros groan at Sam's terrible joke, and shaking my head at his nerve, I winked my way to Cross. I noticed Hound stayed behind, but that was okay. He obviously had something to say to Sam, and I was tired of hearing how much I was disappointing everyone.

I stood in the room above the pit and wondered why I would think Cross was here. They had told me this was not his home. As my attention stayed fixed on the pit, I winked to the edge where I had struck down Araqiel.

"Fond memories?"

I jumped when Satan spoke, and I cursed myself for being predictable. Sam was going to kick my ass.

"No, not really," I answered, pleased that my voice wasn't betraying how nervous I was.

"How's the nugget?" Satan gestured to my stomach, and I remembered I was not really in a presentable state. "Seems like you're having clothing issues."

Before my very eyes, my top was white and billowy. "I really need to learn that trick," I said lightly. "Thanks."

"It's because most clothing has organic matter in it," Satan said as he leaned against a wall, very close to oozing lava. "If it's alive, or been alive, it can be manipulated."

"Makes sense."

"So, you're running out of options."

"Am I?" I asked him as I watched his eyes flick from human to snake. If he was trying to scare me, it was working.

"Girl, you know you are," Satan said as he smiled at me. "I can help you."

I exhaled loudly. "And what can you do for me, Satan, that no one else can?"

"I can keep you alive while the being tries to kill you during childbirth."

"How?"

"Trust me." He grinned wider.

"Despite what many think, I'm not actually suicidal. So I'll pass."

"You'll regret it."

"Will I?" I asked him as I shook my head. "Just say I trust you, what do you get?"

"A feeling of contentment for helping you."

"Quit the bullshit," I snapped. "I already refused to help you kill Sam, I'm not going to say it again."

Satan laughed. "Was that the first time you met Lucifer?"

"You know that it was."

"He's pretty, isn't he? Too pretty. His level of hell is vast."

"I'm not helping you kill Lucifer." My hands were on my hips as I stared at him in outrage.

"I like Lucifer. I hate Beelzebub."

"What?" *What the hell was a Beelzebub?*

"He's a prince of hell. Prince of Envy to be exact. Hateful demon."

"You want to kill the Prince of Envy?" Did he see the irony? "You're envious of envy. Really? You're such a cliché."

"With more levels of hell under my control, the better life here can be for you, witch."

"They'll never allow it."

"Who? The angels? I enjoy slaying the brothers we left behind." Satan spoke about death and killing like I spoke about getting the weekly shopping. Bored. Blasé. Cool.

"I meant the Watchers." I took some satisfaction in the fact Satan lost a little bit of confidence.

"The Watchers have more important things to worry about." He glanced at my belly. "And let's not forget the Return."

"What are you doing?" I asked him as I watched him. "What game are you playing?"

Satan started to walk towards me, and unless I wanted to end up in the hellfire, I had nowhere to back up to. I could wink, but I wanted to hear what he was saying.

"I'm not playing." He looked me over. "You really are a tasty witch, and I can make you very, *very* happy." When my eyes widened, he grinned. "No, sweetheart, not like that. I can give you your healthy little bundle of joy and keep you alive."

My lips felt cracked, they were so dry. "What do you get?" I asked. "In return."

"Why, little witch, I get what no one else has. A necromancer."

"You want the souls."

"I want the souls," he confirmed.

"Cross will—"

"Be my problem, not yours." Satan was watching me intently.

"No."

"You sure?" His head tilted to the side playfully.

"The souls are not bargaining tools."

"Oh child, you have no idea." With another grin, he disappeared.

"Fucking hell." I breathed out, feeling like it was the first time since I left Sam.

"He's well suited as a snake, yes?"

I yelped as Lucifer stood behind me. Far too close to me. "How long have you been here?"

"Long enough."

"What do *you* want?" I demanded. Only I would get tag teamed in the pit of hell by wicked demons.

"I have a vast area of hell," Lucifer told me conversationally. "Satan, through his duplicity and deceit, now has a larger area of hell than I do."

"So?" He was the Prince of Pride, not envy; would it make a difference to him?

"Do you think size matters?"

Oh my Lord, this was even more bizarre than talking to Satan. I was losing my mind. "I don't care."

"Oh, you're one of them. It's how you *use* it that matters." Lucifer snorted. "Bullshit. It's all about the size."

"I *do* believe it's quality over quantity."

"No. It's quantity. He has more than me," Lucifer said as he leaned into my face. "And I don't like it."

"I suggest you raise it with the management; I'm just a witch."

Lucifer looked upward for a second and then back at me. "So much more than a witch."

He vanished as Sam appeared, and I could have flung myself at him in relief.

"I thought I said go straight to Cross?" He frowned at me. "What are you doing?"

"Trying to stay alive," I snapped.

"Is it working?" he mocked me.

"No. Too many demon princes are offering me the impossible."

"Demon princes?" Sam stepped forward, his gaze severe. "Explain."

"I don't think it's safe here," I replied. "You have no idea how easy it is for princes to just appear."

"Where did you get the shirt?" Sam asked as he reached out to touch the white top.

"Satan." I cried out in surprise when Sam ripped it in two and, without any preamble, threw the ripped shirt to the pit behind us. "What the hell?"

"You think I'm going to let *that* male dress you?" Sam scoffed as he pulled his own shirt off and gestured for me to raise my arms as he draped it over me.

"You can't manifest clothing?" I asked in surprise as I straightened the shirt.

"Of course I can," Sam snorted as a shirt appeared on him. "I just like you wearing my clothes." His look was heated as I tried to figure out if he was going to ruin it by saying something horrible, but when he didn't, I fought my smile.

"Possessive," I murmured as I tugged his shirt into place.

"You know it," Sam whispered before he placed a kiss on my lips. "Come, we need to talk."

I was in the Land of the Souls, and I immediately looked for Gran or Naomie. I didn't expect Zel.

"Why is she alone?" Sam demanded of him. "Where in hell have you been?"

"She isn't alone, she's with you." Zel walked towards us, and I saw his fresh wounds as he ignored the other question.

"You've been fighting?" I asked him as I took note of the damage.

"Angels are bloodthirsty," Zel answered me gruffly.

"Angels are bloodthirsty? Really?" My look was scathing. "You should have been with me when Satan ripped Mammon's head off his shoulders with his *bare hands*! I'll show you bloodthirsty."

Sam caught my arm. "Mammon?" His eyes were wide as he looked at me before he turned to Zel. "Why the fuck was she with Mammon?"

"Because Cross told her she would be hidden there." Zel looked me over. "I left you for *one* day."

"Why did you leave her?" Sam asked sharply. "For fuck's sake, Zel, aren't you supposed to be protecting her?"

"Aren't *you* supposed to be hunting her?" Zel bit back. "She's your mess, not mine."

"Mess?" I objected. "I think that's harsh, no?"

"No, I think it suits you perfectly," Zel scoffed as he strode up beside me. "You call for him, or did he find you?"

"Does it matter?" Sam growled. "In your absence, she's been cavorting with more princes of hell." He looked at me with his eyes narrowed, and I braced myself. "What are you doing, witch?"

"Um." I looked between the two of them. *Rock and a hard place* sprang to mind. "Well, you see…"

"Oh fuck me, it's going to be ridiculous," Zel muttered as he stood watching me impatiently.

"Mammon was horrible, Satan turned up to try to convince me he can protect me and talked to me about his plans for the future, Mammon interrupted him—which to be honest was welcome—but then they fought, Satan took his head, and then Hound turned up and took me away." I was breathless as they both watched me. The look of disbelief on their faces at any other time would have been comical.

"And Satan and Lucifer?" Sam asked coolly, and I saw Zel's eyes widen.

"Well, after I took the angels from my parents' into the Void," I started to answer, but I saw Zel's look of confusion. "Michael and Gabriel took my mum and dad kind of hostage to draw me out," I explained, but when I saw him away to launch into a lecture, I hurried on. "So, in the Void, Satan and then Lucifer turned up, and I got rid of them, and the angels gave me four days to hand myself over." I avoided looking at either of them. I could almost *feel* their frustration building. "And then Sam and I had a conversation, and then I went to the ether with Sam." I rushed on when I saw Sam's countenance darken. "Sam said to find Cross, and I tried, but I ended up at the pit, and Satan—honestly, he must have a tracker on me or something—he turned up, spoke about expansion again, and then Lucifer came when Satan was gone, and he's... well, he's possibly more insane than Satan."

"Explain *expansion*," Zel demanded.

"Satan is trying to take over hell. He fancies himself king. That's why he's killing his fellow *royals*." I hoped, in their anger, they appreciated my sarcasm, but they both looked so pissed off that I think they missed it. I watched them exchange a look, and Sam shook his head slightly at Zel when he went to speak. Zel's jaw tightened, but he said nothing as he looked away. "What was that?" I asked them both as I looked between them. "I have to tell you all my things. Share."

"What did he offer you?" Sam asked me instead. "I assume he offered you something. Satan is only revealing about his plans when he wants something."

"He offered to shelter us." My hand dropped to my belly, and as I did, I felt Sam's wince like a physical blow.

"He said he can take both of you?" Zel asked me quietly. When I nodded, he looked away from us as he stared out over the Void. "There is dark magic at play here, and we both know, if anyone could keep her and the child safe, at least until the birthing time, it could be him."

"At least until the birthing time," Sam said, his voice low and full of bitterness. He glared at Zel, and I saw Zel take a deep breath. "That's your plan? Ship her off to Satan, the Prince of *Wrath*, until she dies in childbirth anyway?"

"Ensuring she lives until it's time to give birth is more important than letting her die now. You heard her. I left her one fucking day and she's been with three princes of hell and a platoon of fucking angels. She is a walking disaster. How the hell she has lived this long astonishes me!"

"Hey!" I protested weakly. "I am not *that* bad, and how many times do I need to tell you both, I can hear you when you speak about me like I'm not here!"

They both ignored me, which was usual but still pissed me off. I felt my powers move through me, and they had been in and out so much since I became pregnant that I was almost shocked I felt them again. I understood their appearance when I learned the angels had my parents: fury did seem to be my strongest motivator. But at the moment, I was tired, thirsty, hungry and really wanted to lie down and nap.

Or have wild sex with Sam.

Whilst sleeping.

And snacking.

And possibly crying.

Holy shit, Zel was right, I *was* a mess. Holy cow, I just

thought Zel was right. Was this pregnancy brain? Was any of this normal? Were my wild emotions a result of the pregnancy? Women did this more than once? Voluntarily? Maybe *they* were crazy?

Sam and Zel were both still arguing over my life, it seemed, and as I looked around the Land of the Souls, I'd had enough. I called for my little cyclone. Wind arrived, and I stepped right into it while those two idiots continued to talk about me like I was a possession. Wind took me to the Waterfall of Solitude, and after thanking him, I went and sat on the wall and watched the waterfall.

It was my first time being here with no one looking for me. Or with me freaking out that I was a witch, necromancer, destroyer of all. *Drama Queen*, I mocked myself.

Watching the waterfall, I felt a sense of peace as some of the tension in my body eased. Everything was white, and I knew that me seeing it that way was odd, but the reality was, I liked it white. It was pure, untouched, unmarked. The water ran clear, and the pool did too. Looking up, I saw that the sky was actually a pale blue. Had it always been? What was the colour before? Had I ever looked up? I felt the itch at my elbow, and I smiled that some things never changed even when I had changed so much.

"Are you okay?" Gran asked from beside me.

"Got knocked up by a Watcher," I told her bluntly. "Most likely going to die before it's born, or during childbirth." I looked at her and saw the sadness in her eyes. "If it's half angel, can it actually be called childbirth? Angelbirth?" I tested the word. No not that, somehow I'd managed to merge angel, birth, and placenta together in my head and now had a craving for Angel Delight.

"If you die before the child is born, your soul will pass," Gran told me as she looked out over the water. "If you see this through, the child consumes your soul to be born."

I felt like I had been frozen as I sat there unmoving. "If I die before my child is born, my child dies."

"Your soul or your child, it's the choice you have to make." Gran kicked her legs gently off the side of the wall as we both sat there, staring at the same thing and seeing nothing. "Of course, the thousands who die when the being grows and comes into its power is no little matter."

I barked out a laugh at her usual candidness. "It could be different. He's different now, more prepared. And the baby is half me, and I'm not a monster."

"The fact you carry it still is monstrous in itself."

"Seriously, Gran." I pushed off the wall. "He's innocent."

"It may be born innocent, but it will not stay that way. Death and destruction are all they know. You are a necromancer, lass, the thirst for death will be on the babe's tongue the second it's free of you." Gran remained on the wall, her stare flat. "Its father, Samyaza? A General of war. You may as well go hit the button topside now, lass, put the world out of its misery before it has a chance to know what true horror is."

I felt the tears spill, but I was too numb to wipe them away. "No."

"No?" She scoffed as she looked away and then back at me with such unhappiness in her eyes. "*Yes*, Star. I am your grandmother. I know these Watchers. I know their curse. Your child is this world's undoing."

"So what? You want to just get rid of it?"

"Yes."

"Gran!"

"It's not a child, Star. My Lord, lass, you can have as many babies as you want, but not *this*. This is not a babe. This is death."

Her words cut deep, but one did not cut. One caught my attention and caused me to look up at her. "Death."

Looking around at the Land of the Souls, I took it all in. "Oh fuck, why didn't I see it before?" Whirling in a circle, I ran my gaze over the souls that had migrated towards me as I sat and wallowed. "Cross!" I yelled into the air. "Cross, you sneaky fucker, get here right now!"

Hound appeared, and I reached out for him, taking the silent support he offered. I saw Sam and Zel in my peripheral vision, but I was only interested in one dark-haired demon, and he wasn't coming.

"Cross!" I yelled again. "I swear, you do not want me to come get you!"

"You seem agitated," he said from behind me, and I spun so quickly I almost lost my balance.

"You!"

He smiled slowly as he watched me. "I must say, it took you long enough."

"Why would you not tell me?" I demanded as he leaned back in his white suit, looking every bit the picture of innocence. Like an angel.

But he was never an angel.

"I can only teach you so much in the short time that you have graced me with." His tone was scathing. "I have done what I can. If you wish to continue to be so completely ignorant, I cannot force you."

"You could have told me." I wasn't falling for this guilt trip.

"You are never shy in telling me anything else. This. *This* I needed to know!"

"What are you talking about?" Zel demanded as Sam stayed silent with his gaze on Cross.

"I am pregnant with one of the Nephilim," I answered. "A child of an angel, even if he has fallen. He was an angel first."

Sam now held my stare, and his expression was emotionless.

"I know this," Zel snapped. "Why are you reacting *now*?"

"Because my child is half angel and half *me*." I walked towards Sam and looked up at him, and as he looked down at me, I understood. "You knew?" He said nothing, and I turned away, so very tired of it all. "Of course you knew."

"Knew what?" Zel demanded again. I wondered how he liked being the last to know, and I hoped he realised how much it sucked.

"I am a necromancer. My child will be of my blood and his, or her, father's. But it will be a necromancer." I looked over to Cross, who was watching intently. "And as a necromancer, it commands the dead." With my hands on my stomach, I felt my powers slosh inside of me as the pool within me churned with emotions. I looked up at the light blue sky as if for an answer, but the answer was already inside me.

"Will one of you explain it to me?" Zel was nearly apoplectic in his fury.

"I carry death," I whispered on the quiet of the wind. "My child won't be born to *cause* death and destruction. It *is* death already. Every soul, living and dead, will be its to command." I saw Zel pale, and I felt my throat tighten with words I wasn't sure I was strong enough to say.

"That's impossible, that's…that's…" His eyes were wild.

"The apocalypse?" Zel asked as he looked around, desperate for someone to correct him.

I had finally stunned the great Azazel, and somehow the very thought made me laugh. "I carry the end of the world within me, more than you even thought. My stubbornness to have his child will be the end of everything. Imagine that? To give birth to my baby, I kill it all. What power that must take." I shook my head as I fought the rising hysteria, as my rage wanted to lash out at the two males who knew and withheld it from me. "All that *power* within me, and yet, no one thought I was strong enough to know the truth."

Cross was silent and calm, unmoved by my scorn. But Sam, he was torn, his anguish plain on his face. "I'm sorry."

"Yeah? Me too, fucker, me too." *He was sorry?* I genuinely believed that he was.

It didn't matter.

Nothing mattered.

CHAPTER 14

"What now?" Zel asked as he walked over to stand by Sam. Looked like the bromance was back on.

Joy.

"You come with me," Cross said as he stood fluidly. His smile was warm, but it didn't reach his eyes. "It is time, Star."

"No." Sam was rigid with fury. "She is going nowhere with you. She stays with me."

"You can no longer aid her. She is mine. Your hold over her is done."

"My hold?" Sam scoffed. "I have no *hold* over her, Cross. She is and always will be mine." Forest green eyes met mine, and I saw the hardness soften. "Witch."

"Demon," I answered softly. "You fight to keep me, but what about our child?"

"You would still go through with everything when you know what it is that is inside you?" Sam asked me carefully. As if I were fragile.

"I don't know," I admitted as I looked at them all and my gran, who still sat on the wall, watching us all.

Sam's jaw clenched, but I saw him nod before he made the few steps to reach me. His hand cupped my jaw softly as he tilted my head up to look at him. "I know you're scared, and I know this is something you never expected, but let me help you."

"And if it's too late?" I asked him as I tried to see past his walls to the depth of his soul like when he looked at me and it felt like he saw every secret I had ever kept.

"I will find a way, but you need to be here, with me, to let me do that. I need time, and I lose that if you go with Cross."

As we stood so close and he finally dropped that wall, I almost staggered at the revelation. "You were never going to hurt me," I realised.

Sam stepped back as if I had struck him, and I guess in a way I had. "Hurt you?" He looked over at Zel. "What did you say to her, brother?"

"No, he didn't," I cut in quickly. "Zel has only tried to protect me and the baby." When I saw Sam's wall go back up, I nodded in resignation. "You wouldn't hurt me, but you are still against the choice I have made."

"Star," Sam said as he reached for me. "Woman, please, listen to me. Listen to us all."

I had to stop crying at everything. I could feel the lump in my throat, and I knew I was seconds from bawling my eyes out. Again. "Sam," I pleaded as he pulled me into his arms and held me tight. "Please."

"I'm sorry. I'm so sorry I did this to you, and I would take it all back if I could." His lips moved over my hair as he spoke. "I thought it was over. I thought it could never happen again. When the rains passed the last time, and they were gone, we asked..." His breath caught, and I heard movement behind me.

"We asked for it to be that this would never happen again," Zel spoke, finishing Sam's sentence. "Since we fell, we asked for nothing, only to be left alone, to live as we wanted, to cause no harm."

"But the Nephilim cause harm. They cause more than harm," Cross said in the quiet that followed. "And you were granted that request. Or so you thought."

Sam's arms were wrapped around me as he held me close to him as if he was scared that I would leave. Now that I knew he hadn't intended on killing me, this time, I felt more settled. But I was a woman. And I was carrying a child. And there were beings here who wanted harm to come to my unborn child.

Call me stupid.

Call me selfish.

Call me a fool.

But I was a mother.

And nothing and no one was causing my child harm.

"I know what you're thinking," Gran spoke for the first time since the Watchers had come. "I know you, Starlight, don't."

Pushing away from Sam, I looked at Cross. "Tell me more about where you want me to go."

"The rooms you were in before are not my domain. I hold a fondness for the pit, I won't lie. The chaos is soothing." Cross cared little for the opinion or the looks of the Watchers. "My domain is safe. Nothing can follow unless I allow it, and even then, well, it can be a struggle."

"No angels?" I asked with wild hope.

"No angels," Cross confirmed before his gaze flicked to Sam and Zel. "Heavenly or otherwise."

"What?" I felt the panic rising.

"I cannot follow," Sam told me bluntly. "If you go with Cross, you're lost to me."

"But I can come back?" I asked Cross as I looked at him and Sam. "I can pop in and out like you can?"

"You lose your life." My gran got off the wall as she fixed me with a look I knew well. Hard and blunt. My gran didn't speak in riddles, and sometimes she didn't need to speak at all.

"Why am I *always* dying?" I demanded in frustration. "Why don't I get to be a hybrid like everyone else?"

"A hybrid?" Cross asked in confusion.

"You know, like you and the Watchers are. Alive with souls and not dead."

"You are not like us," Cross told me gravely. "You were human first."

"My humanity holds me back?" I asked sceptically. "I thought that's what you were all concerned with?"

"Had you been like us, it would not matter. But you were born as a human. Albeit you have the blood of your ancestors and witchcraft is rich in your blood, human you are."

Cross just went full Yoda on me. The unfortunate thing was that none of them would know what that was. "But I'm a necromancer."

"You are." Cross gave me that familiar smile of his, and I felt like my feet were on firmer footing. "Which is why I am quite eager to train you, but I cannot do that and develop you to be all that you can be, if you keep up this insanity."

"Cross, I…"

"I don't care what you say to her or what you promise her." Sam stepped between us. "You're not taking her." His hand curled around my bicep and tugged me back into his chest. "I know what she is to you, but she is more to me. She's mine."

Oh, not this again. Shaking his hand off my arm, I turned to my gran and went and stood by her. "Gran, you've known me all my life. You've always been honest with me. Tell me what you think."

"Your grandmother is a soul," Zel spoke suddenly. "That

you think she is not influenced by Death confirms my belief that you are an inexperienced child."

"Fine, insult Cross, insult my gran. C'mon, big guy, tell me what I should do."

"Angels!" Cross warned suddenly.

The Watchers turned and drew their weapons as Cross vanished and left only Sam and Zel to protect me.

Gabriel walked over the land like he owned it, and I completely understood Zel's low growl of discontent as we watched their approach.

"Scum," Gabriel announced as he slowed to a stop in front of them. I noticed that they were both angled in front of me, offering me some protection. Sam may not want the child to be born for apocalyptic reasons, but he still wasn't letting them come for me.

This was how you knew you're hopelessly in love with someone. When they will quite literally burn the world down to save you, instead of being horrified that they would be so villainous, your heart skips a beat with happiness that they could love you so much.

And he *did* love me. Fuck, I needed to stop having epiphanies at the worst times.

"You said four days," I spoke to Gabriel before they could start laying into each other. "It has not been four days."

Gabriel looked me over and dismissed me as he turned his attention back to Sam. "Michael told me you had agreed to cooperate."

Moving slightly, I positioned myself better to see Sam as he spoke to Gabriel and hadn't realised I was anxious of his reply until I saw the obvious contempt on Sam's face.

"I have no issue with you stepping in and eradicating the

problem of those who wish to Return," Sam said with a confidence and casualness that I envied. He was always so cool. "But to harm my witch?" That smirk that would drive me insane one day curled his upper lip. "No. No one touches my witch."

"Your witch?" Gabriel laughed. "Your woman carries an abomination within her."

"And it's not your problem," Sam said smoothly. "Now, should you wish to discuss the matter of the Return, I am more than happy to have that discussion with you. Just not here. Not now."

Gabriel's eyes were wide with disbelief, and I felt for the guy, I really did. I'd been on the receiving end of Sam the Wanker, and he was bringing it in spades right now.

"I am sure you and your Watchers have the rebellion covered, unless you are telling me, *General*, you're no longer up to the task?"

Hmm, taunting him. Bad move.

"My Watchers have policed the fallen since the day they fell. It was in the terms of severance. I'm sure you'll recall them; you did after all, bleed for them." Sam's grin was wicked.

However, my attention had snagged on a phrase I had never expected to hear in a conversation between angels, fallen or otherwise. "Terms of severance?" I asked, bewildered.

Zel turned to me and for once actually looked amused. "What, you think contracts are a human invention?"

"I didn't expect angels to be haggling over redundancy pay!" I exclaimed as I saw Sam's lips twitch.

"We are not animals," Gabriel spoke stiffly as he addressed

me. "Where do you think your customs come from if not the realm of heaven?"

"I had been pretty sure lawyers were spawned in hell," I quipped back.

"Lawyers and accountants," Sam said as he looked over his shoulder at me quickly, and I saw the twinkle in his eye as he joked about my own job before he turned back to face his old adversaries.

"This is irrelevant," Michael protested suddenly. "The whore cannot live."

As the shout of protest left my lips, I choked on it with the speed Sam was in front of Michael, a blade at his throat and murder in his eyes. "You will not speak of her like that," he warned quietly, his eyes meeting every angel standing there. "She is innocent. She did not know, and I can tell you all now, any of you, *any* of you, touch her...I will slay you all." His grip on Michael tightened as he looked at the angel in his hold. "*All.*"

I couldn't take my eyes off him. I saw his shadows curl and swirl as he let his power seep out, and somehow whilst I watched him, I saw Zel grow larger. He didn't do anything, he was just more *present*. How was that possible? I really needed to know more about these Watchers. Them and the fact that Gabriel looked apprehensive.

"Samyaza," Gabriel cautioned as he moved towards Sam, who was still holding the furious Michael. "He is rash, you know he is, he speaks without thought."

They were placating him? What the hell was happening? They were angels, and Sam was fallen, and they looked like they were deferring to him? I was missing something, and I had a feeling it was huge.

Sam let go of Michael as he pushed him away, and the angel stumbled. "The Return, focus on it. Fix it. You need do nothing else here."

Gabriel looked at all three of us before he shook his head. "I cannot leave this alone, you know that. If you were in my shoes, you would have killed her already."

"I'm still here," I snapped. Seriously? Was it an angel-like thing? "I can hear you."

Gabriel looked at me as if I were an insect. "You don't feel evil."

I waited. He didn't say anything else. "Um…okay?"

"It means they know you are an innocent," Zel explained.

Hope bloomed inside me. "That's a good thing?" I asked carefully.

"Yes." Gabriel nodded as he assessed me. "We will kill you quickly."

Hope died within me as quickly as it had arrived. "Well, me and my innocence thank you." Did angels get sarcasm? From the look on Michael's face, I would say that was a yes.

Sam was back in front of me. "Go," he told the angels.

Gabriel's hackles rose. I could tell, and so could the two Watchers beside me. "You order me no more, General."

Sam's hand rested casually at his hip. Sometimes he carried his swords openly, and other times, like now, they were hidden. Knowing my Watcher, I took a step back.

"Pity," Sam scoffed. "Your lack of discipline within the platoon is embarrassing."

Gabriel caught himself from looking, but he had already given himself away when he started to look at the angels behind him. "I will not be lured into action with your taunts. I am here for the witch and nothing else."

Had he not already reacted to Sam, I may have been more impressed. As it was, he was completely underwhelming in his attempt to wield authority.

"Go now, and no one dies." Zel had his sword in his hand already.

"There are only two of you." Gabriel sniffed as if he had been insulted. "We will not enter combat against two."

Sam and Zel exchanged a grin, and I decided subtlety was overrated as I put distance between them and me. As the first weapons clashed, causing my sanctuary to ring with the sound of metal against metal, I wondered what my best course of action was. Stay and be captured? Run and risk the wrath of a Watcher? Where was Cross when I needed him?

Wind came hurtling towards me, and I gladly jumped into his cyclone, carrying myself far from the skirmish at the waterfall.

On the Plains of the Dead, I waited, anxious an angel followed me, more anxious a Watcher had not.

Zel appeared in front of me, panting but exhilarated. "Do you want the child to live?" he asked me hurriedly.

"Yes," I answered with no hesitation.

"We haven't got much time. If you want it to live, come with me."

And I went.

CHAPTER 15

"Does Sam know?" I asked as we walked through woods with lots of trees and weird noises that I wasn't sure were natural. "Also, where are we?"

"Where we are is unimportant, we are not staying." Zel looked over his shoulder as he yanked me along with him. "Where we're going isn't important either."

"Okay, but I think asking if Sam knows is important."

Zel stopped and looked at me, his face set like the stone I had no doubt he was. "Did you hear what they said?"

"You know I did," I answered him as I stared at the trees, flinching when I heard a sound like no animal I knew could make.

"He may love you, witch. But he has not changed his course."

Tugging my hand free of Zel's hold, I wrapped my arms around myself as I fought off the sadness. "And you? Now that you know, does it change *your* path?"

"No." Zel didn't even blink as he answered me honestly. "I won't lie to you, it will be hard for him when you're gone, but I do believe, really believe, this child will be different."

There was brutal, and then there was Zel. He didn't mince his words, and tact was not in his vocabulary. "How can you be so sure?" It was insanely important to me that Zel had a good reason for his belief.

Zel grinned, and it was wicked and it startled me. "Because this child is *your* child; how can it be bad?"

Squeezing my eyes shut, I had to force the tears back.

Firstly, Zel being nice. No. I wasn't ready. Secondly, we were doomed if he thought half of this little guy inside me being *me* was a good thing. I was a disastrous child, completely hopeless teenager, and well…my twenties weren't covering me in glory either.

"Come, we need to go. Samyaza will be hunting."

"You're not worried the angels took him?" I asked as we hurried through the trees, and I looked over my shoulder, convinced I would see a platoon of angry angels chasing us.

Zel barked out a laugh and gave a rueful shake of his head, but he didn't slow down, and he didn't answer. Guess that was my answer. Zel had confidence in himself to outsmart angels *and* Sam; who was I to argue?

"If we keep moving, we can avoid their gaze," Zel said as he ducked under a low hanging branch. "Samyaza will be angry right now, but he has no intention of handing you over to Gabriel or his soldiers and will slow their pursuit down."

"But they want the same thing," I protested as a branch slapped me in the face. "Neither wants the child to be born."

Zel gave me one of his famous looks that made me feel incredibly stupid. "The angels want you and what you carry dead," he told me bluntly.

"And Sam wants that too."

"No, Samyaza is trying everything he can to save *you*."

I pulled on Zel's tunic to halt him. "He really doesn't want me to die."

Zel shook his head as he looked around us. "Of course not, did you hear me when I told you that he loved you? You're his *soulmate*, for fuck's sake. Why the fuck would he want you dead?"

"And how will he save me, then?" I demanded as Zel

hauled me forward again.

"Can you ask the hundred questions when I have us in shelter for tonight?" Zel looked up at the canopy of trees and then at me.

"No." I looked up. "And no, I'm not a freaking squirrel. I am *not* climbing a tree."

"You're climbing a tree," he told me as he grabbed my hips and lifted me skywards. "And keep it down, there are more in the trees than squirrels."

Looking down at him in horror, he winked at me as he thrust me higher. "Climb, little nutcracker, shit just got real."

Grabbing onto a branch, I very inelegantly and with no finesse, hoisted myself onto a branch. With the aid of some very rough manhandling of my lower body, I ended up prone over a branch. Clumsily I tried to fix my position, and as I did, I scowled as Zel climbed the branches like a natural.

"Well, it wasn't pretty and it wasn't easy, but you're up," he commented drily as he continued past me. "For all your training with Cross and Ros, you have zero upper body strength." Looking back at me, he looked as always, disappointed. "Did I not tell you that I was the best teacher?"

"Yes," I admitted as I followed the way he was leading and refused to look down. "But you're also a psychopath who would rather eat my heart than teach me anything." His look was comical, and he pointedly looked at me and our surroundings. "Okay, well, if I weren't pregnant with Pol, then you would rather eat my heart."

"Pol?"

"The baby," I answered, testing a branch before I lifted myself up. "By the way, why on earth are we in a tree?"

"Pol!" Zel was open-mouthed and genuinely looked like he

was in shock.

"Apocalypse baby." I pointed at my tummy. "I can't say that more than once. My brain will explode, and I may just swan dive out of this tree, but Pol...Pol I can cope with and compartmentalise until the full breakdown hits me or the angels kill me." Zel still looked unsure about what he was going to say, or maybe he doubted what he was hearing? "You can't be speechless, Zel. You know this is how I deal with things."

"But Pol?" he protested weakly. "There's inappropriate and then there's just batshit crazy; you can't *nickname* the apocalypse," he said as we both resumed climbing. I could have answered, but honestly, scaling a tree in an unknown dimension and having a normal conversation with Zel was kind of... nice. We would never be friends, but this demon, he inherently believed that my child would be good because it was *my* child. We never needed to be friends, we never needed to sit and have coffee together or go for a beer together. He was running through dimensions with me to keep me safe, because he believed *in* me.

How many people in your life could you count on for that?

Look at Ruairidh. I'd known him most of my life, and what did I get from him? Half-hearted gestures of affection when he felt like it. Would he be here with me now, knowing what I carried inside me and what my fate was? No. He would be running so far from me I wouldn't see him for dust.

"You make me nervous when you're thoughtful," Zel said as he tested the next branch above us.

I grinned as he gave me a wary look. "What kind of tree is this?"

"It's native to this dimension. Think of a good old oak tree and a California redwood, and throw in some Douglas fir."

"A strong evergreen that's really tall?" I asked as I stared up at the branches we still had to climb.

"Exactly." Zel stepped back slightly. The branches were wider than I would have thought possible, but then, I hadn't been climbing trees as a child, I had been talking to the dead and having tea parties with souls. Maybe trees in my dimension had these thick branches.

My dimension?

Dammit, how easily I fell into the world of other worlds.

"Are there aliens?"

Zel had been doing something to the tree trunk and paused as he looked at me. "You have souls, princes of hell, demons, and angels. Why would you need more?"

Pursing my lips, I thought about it. "It can't just be us though, can it?" I gestured to the trees. "I mean, I'm in another dimension. How do we know that somewhere in the universe there isn't an alien race doing exactly the same thing as me?"

"Having a fallen angel's child, committing the ultimate sin against the creator? You think somewhere else, someone or something else is doing the same thing?" Zel looked me over. "Arrogant much? Catch."

I laughed at his mocking tone as I sat down on my branch and caught the end of a rope as it was thrown at me. "Where'd this come from?"

"The trees. They are almost like vines, but they hang loose, mostly around the trunk. Wrap it around yourself. If you sleep, then you won't fall out."

"If I sleep," I repeated. "I've never slept in a tree before."

"There are many things you have never done," Zel spoke with a soft sadness. "Or will ever do."

"Don't," I pleaded quietly. "I can do everything you ask of me, Azazel, if you don't remind me what I'm facing."

He went to speak, but instead he nodded. We sat in silence for a while, Zel doing whatever it was Zel did and me staring out and across at the trees. There were few spaces between them, limiting my visual range. I couldn't see the sky, and I refused to look down, so out and across was my option as it grew darker. I wasn't going to lie to myself—I was still looking to see the other "squirrels" Zel had mentioned. I had an active imagination, so for me, squirrels had morphed into flesh-eating monsters with companions like killer monkeys. Or snakes. Lots of snakes.

Snakes made me think of Satan. Was his offer genuine? Had he somehow the power to shield us both? Had Satan the means to *save* us both?

"He only wants the child," Zel said as balanced beside me and checked my tree rope.

"How did you know what I was thinking?" I asked him. "I thought I could shield now."

"You can, but it's the first time we've stopped, and you have nothing to distract you from your thoughts."

"Ah." I nodded my thanks as he moved back and up, taking the branch above me. "So not mind reading, I'm just that predictable."

"Anyone would think the same," Zel huffed as he sat down, and I appreciated that the tree was strong and the branches unnaturally wide, but I did doubt their ability to hold Zel with any comfort for the warrior above me.

"What do we do?" I asked him as I rested my head against the trunk and closed my eyes.

"Try to sleep. I've shielded us for now, but it won't last

long before one of my brothers recognises the ward."

"Ros," I murmured.

"Yeah."

I heard his smile, and I marvelled at this Zel. I liked who he was with me just now. I welcomed it. "And then?"

"We keep moving." I heard his own tiredness.

"For how long?"

"Sam is wise." He hesitated. "Not when it comes to you, as we have all seen, but in general, he is."

"The General is *generally* wise." I smiled, not looking at him but hearing his sharp intake. I knew I had annoyed him, but now I wasn't worried about the repercussions and felt more at ease with this Zel.

In true Zel style, he ignored my wit. "He will provoke either Gabriel or those that wish to Return to action."

My eyes snapped open as I looked at Zel in disbelief. "Why?"

"To cause a distraction. If they fight amongst themselves, you are free of their attention."

"Satan doesn't wish to return to heaven," I told him as I thought it over. "No distraction is going to shift Satan's attention from taking over hell."

Zel was already nodding. "And Sam will have a plan in place for that." His hard stare at his boots made me feel for the leather.

"You should be with him." I knew it to be true, but selfishly, I wanted him to stay with me. Zel believed in my child as much as I did.

"My place is here, serving him as I have always served."

"Served?" I asked, curious at the terminology.

Zel gave a half shrug. "There are those who are created to

lead and those who are created to serve. I serve."

Was he serious? "Zel? Are you telling me you're merely a follower?"

"A subordinate, yes."

Oh, he was serious. "Azazel, the angel who fell first from heaven to ensure the way was safe for his friends, his brothers?"

"My General, yes."

"Azazel, the warrior who is protecting the one woman in any dimension who has the power to start the apocalypse, off his own back?"

"What's your point?" Zel asked me as he closed his eyes.

"You're no more a follower than I am a leader," I scoffed as I looked up at him. "You're delusional, demon."

One eye opened as he looked at me, and when it closed again, I saw the small smile playing around his lips.

The minutes passed, and I knew I should sleep, and I knew I needed it, but my brain was awake. You know that way when you're absolutely knackered all day, and then as soon as you lie down to sleep, your brain asks you things like how do dragons blow out candles? Or was there really room on that door for two and not just Rose? Or where do a fallen angel's wings go?

"Zel..."

"No."

I frowned at his instant shut down, but I wasn't to be put off. "Zel?"

"What?" he asked me tiredly.

"Why can't I see Gabriel's wings or any of their wings?"

"Because you are an imbecile and think you are looking at them in their true form," Zel answered. "Your very eyes would burn in their sockets if you were to look upon an angel in its true form."

Huh. "But in the Bible, it says—"

"Really? The Bible is what you're referencing right now?" Zel mocked.

"Whatever," I muttered as I shifted on my branch.

More minutes passed, and I opened my eyes again. "Zel?"

"Fuck me," he groaned. "What?"

"Are you in your true form?"

Two light blue eyes pulsed with power as they focused on me in the dark. "No."

"The shadows around Sam, they're his true form?" I probed.

"Yes."

"What's yours?"

"It's different for us," Zel said eventually. "When we fell, we lost our Angelic Essence, obviously."

"Essence?" I asked as I sat up straighter. "I know that term."

Zel shook his head to stop me. "No, not like that. When you are with Sam, or any of us, or anyone is with any of us, they have a scent of our essence, but not an Angelic Essence."

"So without that, that's what makes you demons?"

Zel snorted in the dark. "Very basically, yes. Our very natures were corrupted the day our Angelic Essence was removed. We had free will, choice, options."

"You were like humans," I said in wonder. "Like when Adam and Eve ate the forbidden fruit, they were cast out for having the ability to have additional knowledge and stuff."

Zel fixed me with a long hard look. "And stuff?"

I hid my grin behind my hand. "Or something."

"Sleep, witch, we have a long day tomorrow."

"But I want to know about the loss of the essence!" I protested, and when he said nothing, I rushed on. "So, losing your Angelic Essence made you demons but not humans?"

"We can never be human, we are not born."

Why did that surprise me? I never even thought about it, but when I did, really, why was it a shock? I mean, who would their mother even *be*? "Oh."

"Anything else?"

"But you have power. You have something supernatural left."

"Of course. We have the residual power left over. We have our own abilities that we had before, they are merely… watered down. As when we were above, there are levels of power and ability, and that allowed us to be ranked. That ranking still exists even with the Angelic Essence removed."

"Do you wish for it back?" I asked as I tried to process everything.

"No. Why?"

"You're so just. And righteous. And strict."

"I have a moral compass because of *who* I am, not *what* I am. Life is on earth, not in the lofty heights above."

"Or below," I whispered.

"Hell is full of the broken and the damned."

"Not for you," I teased.

"We are happier in the ether."

"Thank you. For sharing." I heard his grunt in reply. My eyes drifted closed again, and I was almost asleep when I had my final thought. "Do your wings go when your Angelic Essence is lost?"

"Sleep, witch, now."

Seems we were over our bonding session.

CHAPTER 16

When I woke in the morning, I was still in a tree, but I had Amaros the Watcher in front of me, grinning like a cat, and when I yelped in fright—because who needs a grinning Viking in front of them when they wake up?—he laughed.

"Little witch, look at you, sleeping in a tree like a bird."

"How are you here?" I asked as I tried to see past him. Which was impossible because Ros was huge. They were all huge.

"Azazel has really shitty wards," he told me with a low whisper. "Wanna come down?" I shook my head in denial, which made Ros laugh more. "C'mon, Tweety, let's go." Ros leaned forward and merely snapped my tree rope in two as he stood with a grace and balance I envied. When I went to push his hand away, he grabbed my hand and held tight until I looked up at him and felt fear as he looked at me with a seriousness I didn't expect from him. "For the sake of my brother, my General, please, Star, don't react badly."

"Wha— Why?" I stammered.

Ros leaned forward and pressed a quick kiss to the top of my head. "Be strong, Starlight."

I hesitated. That was what my gran called me. Ros held his hand out to me, and bracing myself, I took it.

On the ground, there were Watchers. Lots of Watchers. They were all here? I looked for Zel and saw him listening intently to Der. He didn't look harmed, but Zel would have the same facial expression if he had his arm chopped off, I was sure of it.

"Where is he?" I asked Ros quietly as he led me towards my two threes that I knew. I almost stumbled when I saw Hound sitting on his haunches, watching the clearing with what I knew to be contempt. He had given me that look many a time during my training.

"Shh, not yet," Ros warned.

I saw others pitching tents, and I realised I was in the middle of a camp. They were making camp. Here? The feeling of dread rose as I realised this was a war camp.

"Amaros," I whispered urgently as he marched me through the throngs of Watchers, who watched me either openly or with curious glances. Either way, I was their sole object of notice.

"Eyes on your tasks!" Sam barked as he strode amongst them, and I stopped walking as he advanced towards me.

Holy shit.

Sam in full Watcher gear, ready for war? If I weren't already carrying his kid, my ovaries would have exploded. Wow, I really had the most inappropriate thoughts.

"Damn, is it wrong to mount him and ride him like a pony?" I asked Ros without any thought at all.

His burst of surprised laughter echoed around us as he walked away from me and joined the others, leaving me alone in front of the General…alone and drooling, forgetting something serious had happened.

"Witch," Sam said as he checked me over, I assumed for damage, but what did I know?

"Demon." I waited. He said nothing, and I rolled my eyes at his stubbornness. "What is it this time?"

"We need to talk."

"If it's about killing innocents, I'm not listening."

Sam's expression was blank, but I saw his jaw tighten. His hand curled around my bicep, and without a word, he was leading me to a tent. I met the looks of Chaz and Pen as I passed, and both looked away.

"Sam?" I asked as the panic returned. "Sam, what's happened?"

"In the tent."

When I saw Zel looking at me with what could only be described as sorrow, I stopped. My power kicked in, and my feet dug into the soft earth beneath me. "Sam!"

"I told her not to react badly," Ros hissed to Der.

"Shut up," Der hissed back.

"Ros?" I demanded as I turned to him and saw my hair floating around me. My Viking demon bowed his head as if he was preparing himself for something bad.

And I knew.

"No." The cold shiver ran over me. "You called me Starlight." I backed away. "*No!*"

"Star," Sam's voice was beside me as I stayed staring at Ros. "Please, in the tent."

"She's gone?" I asked him, feeling something inside me break.

"Star," he tried again.

"*Answer me!*" I screamed in fury, and the thunder and lightning crashed through the sky, racing towards me to be the outlet for the anger and devastation battling within me.

"Her soul has been destroyed." Sam was stoic in front of me.

"How?" I was being torn open. I could feel parts of me unravelling as I stood still in front of a camp full of Watchers.

"Can we talk about this inside?"

"No." I stepped back, and he stepped forward. "Stay back."

"It was not us," Sam told me.

"I know that," I bit back. "But I have zero control right now, and I only want to hurt the one who did this, and that is not you."

"Star."

My hands were in my hair as I tried so hard not to pull it out and scream. I had to contain it. Ros had asked me not to react badly, Ros knew. And I was going to lose it, I knew I was, but Ros's words were the only thing I was holding onto.

"Amaros!" I called as I kept my eyes on Sam. "Tell me."

"They took her in the Land of the Souls." Ros was to the side of me, but all I could see was my fury reflected in Sam's eyes.

"They?"

"Michael." Sam's lips twisted in a sneer when he spoke.

"Where is he?"

"You can't." It was Chaz who spoke, but still I was looking at Sam.

"Why?"

"Star, please, we need to talk." I flinched when someone, probably Chaz, touched my arm.

"Tell me why I can't kill him." I felt the pull of Sam's anger as I spoke, and it spiked my own.

"We need to plan a coordinated attack." Pen walked into my line of vision. "He wants you to react, and by being rash and unchecked, you're playing into his hands."

Thunder boomed above us, and I closed my eyes against the pain I felt coming from within me.

Cool hands cupped my face, soft warm lips caressed mine as I felt him press close to me. Reaching my hands up, I curled them around his wrists, not to pull him away but to hold on to the support that he was.

Sam pressed his forehead to mine, and I was back in my garden under the blood moon. Clinging onto the demon who owned my heart, sure he would never hurt me, and now I was clinging onto the demon who stabbed me through my heart, wishing my life was as simple as a witch being stabbed by her lover under a blood moon in a midnight sky.

"I'm not holding on," I whispered against his lips.

"I know." His arms slipped around my waist, and I was curled around him.

"I need them to die."

"They will."

Green power pulsed around us, and I welcomed the rage radiating from him. "She was my gran."

"I know."

"They took her to the pit?" I asked before I lost the ability to speak.

"I'm so sorry."

"I can't," I whispered as I clutched his tunic, twisting the cloth in my fingers, desperate to hold on before my fury ripped through the dimension. "I can't hold it back."

"You can let it go," Sam whispered into my hair. "I'm here with you."

I heard the collective gasp and groans, and I knew this was what Ros had tried to warn me against.

Opening my eyes, I met Hound's gaze, and he stared back at me. My eyes flicked to Zel's, who shook his head once. Squeezing my eyes shut, I burrowed into Sam's chest. I was so close. If I could have gotten closer, I would have.

"What do you want?" Sam asked me softly.

Unbidden, my eyes opened, and I saw them. Zel, Ros, Chaz, Pen, Der, waiting. Waiting with their breaths held, it seemed, waiting for me to give Sam the power to go to war.

They weren't ready.

He wasn't ready.

Holding Ros's stare, I uncurled my fingers from Sam's tunic, and I pushed myself back slightly. Not yet ready to let go, but not needing to hold on, because if I did, I would break.

"Let's go inside, talk about how best to fight back."

Sam's eyes widened in surprise, but when he asked me if I was sure, I nodded and raised myself on my toes to kiss him briefly. "He wants to push us to react in anger, but we need to be smarter."

Sam watched me carefully for a moment, and when he nodded once and turned to lead the way, I looked to the Watchers, and I saw their gratitude. Not because they wouldn't stand with him, not because they didn't want to fight, but because he was being reckless.

He would burn it all down. This male would, and could, destroy it all. I was all that was holding him back, and I wasn't sure I should be the one with that power.

Because I wanted to *let* him. I *wanted* him to rip their heaven from the sky and watch the fuckers who erased my gran's soul out of spite. Out of malice.

Malice? Before I was done with this world, I would watch them burn in the pit for this.

HOURS later and with more tea consumed than was good for a person, I felt my head droop as I listened to the Watchers and their war council.

The storm still brewed outside because I was grieving, and no matter how many times I told myself I was being a mature, sensible person, my grief wanted to smash it all down.

Arms lifted me, and I curled into Sam, my head nuzzling his neck as he carried me somewhere. I didn't bother opening my eyes, and when he laid me down on a bed, I simply curled up into a ball. When the bed dipped and his arms pulled me back into his body, I went easily, and within moments, I was asleep.

Heat licked at my skin, waking me from a slumber filled with sadness and desolation.

I was naked, and my fingers were in Sam's hair as his lips moved over my body. Teeth grazed my nipple as he sucked, and my body burst into awareness as his other hand dipped between my legs.

Green eyes looked up at me as Sam drew his head back. "You were crying in your sleep. I couldn't listen anymore."

Wiping at my eyes with one hand, I felt the wetness on my cheeks. "Sex was your solution?" I teased softly as I pushed his mouth back to my breast.

"Sex with you is always the solution," Sam murmured against my skin as he kissed lower. This time he didn't hesitate at the swollen belly but kissed over it as he made his way down. "You're so wet," he said in approval.

"You know how to please me," I whispered back as his fingers parted my folds and his tongue dipped inside, tasting delicately before sweeping over me in one long delicious lick.

"Oh shit" left me breathlessly, and I felt his smile as he sucked softly.

"You taste like heaven." His words were muffled as he spoke, but I didn't care; I heard him clearly, and as he licked and nibbled and sucked me to a glorious orgasm, the fire within me stirred at his words.

Heaven.

Moving up my body, he pushed my legs wider. "Open," he growled as his tip pushed at my entrance.

Widening my legs, I arched my back as he slid inside, my body stretching and protesting at the sudden fullness, but the sharp sting of pain was soon replaced with pleasure as his hips started to roll, and I met his thrusts with my own.

"Put your legs around me."

Complying, I cried out when he tilted his hips at an angle that hit me deeper. His movements became more forceful, his hands no longer as gentle.

"I lose myself when I'm with you."

My legs tightened in answer as Sam pushed harder.

"I only want to be inside you, like this, fucking you like this."

His hand was between us, rubbing me in time with the rhythm of his hips.

"You're so fucking beautiful, so fucking stubborn, so fucking perfect."

My head was tilted back, my eyes closed as he set a relentless pace above me, and my body hurtled along towards the edge, beneath him.

"Look at me."

I opened my eyes and looked into dark green pools of desire.

Of lust.

Of love.

"Keep your eyes open, witch," he ordered with a smirk as he picked up his pace.

"Demon," I sassed back as I felt it building.

His thumb circled my nub relentlessly as he drew his hips back and slammed back into me. My cry of need was loud in the quiet of the tent.

"More," I urged as Sam did it again.

My fingers curled into his shoulders, and my legs tightened around his waist as I crested, and my cry was almost soundless as I crashed over into oblivion. My body felt Sam follow me, but I was still drifting in bliss.

As we caught our breath and clung to each other, Sam kissed me long and deep. Finally detangling from each other, Sam lay beside me, picking me up to drape me over him, my head resting on his chest.

"I love you."

Had I stopped breathing?

I felt his rumble of laughter. "Breathe, witch," Sam teased as he kissed my head.

"Say it again."

"I love you." Sam's hands trailed over my arm. "I've said it before."

"Say it a million more times?" I asked quietly as we lay there, wrapped in each other.

"Until the end of time."

The first tear slipped free, and I knew the dam was going to break. "I'm going to lose it," I warned him. "Make me angry."

"I don't want you angry," he pulled me closer. "You need to grieve."

"She was everything to me," I whispered. "Who will be next?"

Sam's fingers stilled, and I felt him tense beside me. "I have Watchers at your parents'."

Fresh fear flooded over me. "Thank you." I tried not to let my terror overcome me. "Where was Cross?"

"I don't know. He was only at the pit so long for you."

Another tear slid down my cheek. "No one will be safe."

"We can send them back."

"By fighting."

"It's war." I felt him shrug.

"We've lost so much already." My hand touched my stomach, and I froze when Sam's hand covered mine, the gentleness with which he held me bringing the tears back.

"Go to sleep, Star."

Tilting to look up at him, I traced my hand over his jaw. "I think I prefer it when you call me witch."

His laughter lightened the mood and lifted the seriousness from his face. "Sleep, little witch."

"What happens tomorrow?"

"We start afresh."

"More people I love and care for are in danger." I drew a shaky breath. "Will…eradicating my gran be enough for them?"

"No."

Swallowing past my fear, I struggled not to let it show. "What do we do?"

"Fight," Sam sighed.

"All for me."

"They want to kill you, and that's not an option."

The knot in my chest echoed the fear I heard in his voice. "Sam?"

"Mm-hmm?" His eyes were closed, the low light casting his beautiful face in shadows, making him seem even more ethereal.

"I'm not sleepy," I whispered against his chest as I pressed my lips to his skin.

Looking up, I saw his slow smile as he opened his eyes to look at me. "I can take care of that."

I knew what I needed to happen in the morning, I knew what needed to be done. As Sam turned me in his arms and his lips caressed over my jawline, I felt the knot within me tighten.

I knew what I had to do, I just needed one more night before I had to face it.

THEY WERE EASY TO FIND. APPALLINGLY EASY. BUT THEN WHEN you were the soldiers of heaven, I guessed you had little to fear. They'd already stunned me with their arrogance and then wounded me with their cruelty. *Of course* they would be easy to find. They thought they were untouchable.

Standing at the edge of their camp, I felt the knot in my chest tighten further. It had been there since I learned of what they did to my gran. Grief so sharp and sudden almost made me stagger under the force of it.

Taking a moment to control myself, I rolled my neck on my shoulders as I prepared myself. My body ached in a low delicious throb. A night with Sam would do that to you, and my smile was brief as I recalled how well he put me to sleep, utterly sated and exhausted from his lovemaking.

And he *had* made love to me.

He may talk like a sailor in bed, but the actions, touches and caresses had been made with love. I'd had two previous boyfriends, and neither had been close to making me feel what Sam did. My elbow itched, and the pain of loss gripped my throat so hard it took a moment before I could turn my head, knowing Gran would never be beside me again.

Naomie stood staring at the piece of land the angels had occupied. "I am sorry for your loss," she spoke softly, her eyes trained on the camp the same as mine had been.

"Were you there?" I asked her as I turned back to look at the scattered tents and fire pits.

"No, I would have come for you." She sounded pissed that I

asked, and I knew I was wrong and she was right to be annoyed at the question.

"Sorry."

I heard her make a sound of acknowledgement, and we both stood in silence for a while. Watching.

"I think you are being reckless."

"It's a thing I do," I tried to joke, but she didn't laugh.

"You cannot control the outcome of this. There are too many variables."

"I know."

"Star." She hesitated. "She would not want this."

"I know." The knot in my chest was making it hard to breathe.

"Then why?"

"He loves me." I blinked back the tears. I was so sick and tired of crying. "He really does." Naomie said nothing, and I continued. "This will hurt him, but he knows me, and he knows how I think. And he'll understand."

"He won't." Her voice was strong with her conviction. "He loves you. I know it as you do. But this? This he will not understand."

"He understood what happened with Araqiel."

"Maybe, but up until the moment of your first cut, he didn't. He adapts to the situation in front of him." She smoothed her hands over the front of her skirt. "He will not adapt to this."

Turning, I looked at her, this woman, this soul who was my ancestor. This woman who cast a spell hundreds of years ago, and everything thereafter that had happened to me had been a result of her refusal to bow to a prince of hell. Naomie knew strength. Naomie *was* strength.

And I was her granddaughter. Many, *many* times removed.

She saw the resolution in my eyes and gave a curt nod. "I'll be watching."

"Thank you." Squeezing her hand, I started to walk towards the camp of the angels.

Halfway there, Gabriel came out to meet me, the bastard by his side wearing a smirk that fuelled the fire within me.

"Gabriel," I greeted.

"Star." He searched behind me and quickly to the side, looking for the trap. "You're early."

"I'm alone." I saw Michael's smirk turn to an incredulous grin, and I felt the knot tighten further.

Gabriel looked at me, and I saw understanding in his eyes. He held his hand out to me. "Come," he invited.

I ignored the offered hand, but I did walk with him into the camp and to the tent that was in the middle of it all. In his tent, I sat at a table of polished mahogany with velvet-covered chairs.

The Watchers' table in their camp had been made of a large piece of broken wood and two stumps of trees they hadn't made firewood from. There had been no chairs; they had stood or sat on the ground.

How similar these angels were to the world of men. I wondered if they knew that. Their actions were like men of old, the aristocrats and the commoners. Those who had and thus felt superior and those who had not and got on with it. Looking around and seeing the opulence, I longed for my rough and ready Watchers.

Was this what heaven was like? If it was, I knew why my Watchers had left. When I refused the offer of tea, Gabriel sat across from me, Michael beside him.

Him, I couldn't look at.

"How long do we have before they come?"

"I always thought you would be taller." Blond hair, amber eyes, handsome. Boring. "In the stories, you're always depicted as larger than life." Cocking my head to the side, I studied him. "But you're not, you're just…you."

He bowed in his seat graciously and grinned. "I don't know whether that was an insult or a compliment. But I am, thankfully, just me." His smile was warm, his eyes…kind.

"You have no idea that he took my grandmother's soul to the pit and burned her in the hellfire, do you?"

Gabriel whitened as he sat up straighter. "Samyaza?" he asked in shock.

"Michael."

The blond angel turned to look at Michael, who looked absolutely fine with what he had done.

"Michael?" Gabriel questioned, and Michael kept his eyes trained on me.

"You asked for a result, I got you a result." He pointed at me as he spoke. "She's here, isn't she?"

"I think he knows who I am, and we both know I'm here." I watched Gabriel struggle to control his temper, and I watched Michael not give one single fuck that his comrade was pissed off at him.

"Star, I…" Gabriel floundered.

"How long has it been since you've been here?" I asked Gabriel curiously. "It's been a long time, hasn't it?"

"What makes you think that?" Gabriel asked as he tried to force his shoulders to relax. But he was struggling, and I actually appreciated the effort he was making to keep this business-like.

"Your furnishings are dated. We moved out of the nineteenth century some time ago. You offered me your hand to walk beside you. You treat me like I'm a porcelain doll." I looked at Michael, and I smiled. "I'm not a doll. When you knock me down, I won't break."

The knot in my chest pulsed, and my power hit Michael in the gut, wrenching him from his chair and thrusting him up to the canopy of the tent. I was on my feet, and I heard my storm arrive outside.

Hound and the other two hellhounds walked into the tent, and I heard cries and shouts from outside, but in here, I had control. Hound morphed and looked at Gabriel, and I heard the angel's sharp inhale. I heard it all, but all I saw...was Michael.

"You don't look smug anymore," I told him conversationally as I moved around the table. "You look...panicked." My hair swirled around me. "Did you laugh? Did you watch with glee, you sick fucker, as her soul was wiped from this world? From *all* dimensions? Did you wear that fucking smirk as you destroyed her?"

He didn't answer, but then he couldn't, as my power was gagging him.

"You want my child," I spoke to Gabriel. "You want to remove the threat to humanity that I carry."

"You carry the end of days." Gabriel was trying so hard to remain calm. I had to give him credit.

"I know." Turning around as I turned Michael with me, so I had him in my sights as well as Gabriel, I faced the golden-haired angel head-on. "I know now, but I didn't. Before." I ignored the muffled shout above me but noticed the scowl Gabriel sent upwards. "I only found out. I mean, I knew it was

Nephilim, but the characteristics of my child will be different." I still couldn't believe it, but I had been given no time to sit and think about it, and maybe that was for the best. "This is so very hard for me. The fear and anger I feel that this is happening to me is outweighed by the complete love I feel for my baby." I held my hand up as Gabriel went to speak. "I know what you're going to say, it's a monster, blah blah blah. To me, it isn't."

"Star." Gabriel was fully focused on me, Michael seemingly forgotten by him.

"I'm not very good at being a witch," I confessed to Gabriel. "I'm a bit shit as a necromancer to be honest. But a mother?" Tears flooded my eyes, and I had to blink them away. "I would have rocked at that. Like a goddamn fucking rockstar."

He stayed silent, and I sniffed loudly.

"I can't." I gulped. "I can't allow my child to be the earth's destruction." Pain raced through me as I said the words out loud, and I shook my head as if I could shake it off. "Fuck, this is killing me to say this." I rubbed my nose as I fought back the emotion. "You can remove him?"

Gabriel nodded once.

"Will he, she, ugh, fuck." I swallowed again. "Will there be any pain, for it?"

Gabriel hesitated and then shook his head.

"I have a condition." I told him in the silence of the tent.

"Yes?"

"He dies." My stare was on Michael. "An eye for an eye. You know that law, don't you?"

"I am sorry for his actions," Gabriel told me, "but your grandmother was already dead."

Wow. He wanted to deal in semantics? Fine. "You've never been born. You had no mother. You have never been human. Do you even have a soul?"

"Of course." Gabriel actually looked affronted I had questioned it.

"And to have your soul lost forever, never to have existed, no redemption, no afterlife. What would that mean to you?" I asked, and I saw his eyes flash with…something. Fury, I hoped. "That's what he took from me. From her. I am a *necromancer*, and he *took* her from me. My grandmother's soul was dragged into the hellfire in the pit of hell, and he watched while she burned."

"I'm so—"

"Yeah, I know, you said," I snarled. "I'm going to take this piece of shit to the pit, I'm going to remove his head, and then when Morax collects his soul, he's going to hand it to me, and I'm going to walk into the hellfire, and I'm dragging that motherfucker's soul with me, and I will watch him burn." I leaned forward into Gabriel's face. "Do you hear me?"

He nodded.

"Do you understand?"

He nodded again.

"When I am done, I will come back here. You will have your wish, and we will end this before it becomes more death, more pain, more horror. More loss."

"I cannot let you have Michael," Gabriel spoke clearly. "I understand your pain, and I will make him pay for his indiscretions, but his soul, you cannot take."

Indiscretions? "It wasn't a dirty stop out with his best mate's girlfriend, it was an act of violence so abhorrent that even you feel sick."

Gabriel swallowed. "Even so, you cannot take him."

"Watch me." We winked.

I was in the pit, on the edge where I had been when I rose against my Watchers. Michael was at my feet, my power keeping him there. I knew he was fighting. I knew he was trying, but he had no idea how strong my hate and my rage against him were. He would tire long before I would.

"You fucked with the wrong family," I told him as my power dragged him up to his knees. In my hand was a knife, but as I looked at the plain-faced murdering bastard, I remembered something. "You were there when they blinded Azazel, weren't you? Yeah, you're the kind of sick and twisted shit that would get his kicks out of that."

The contemptuous bastard had the cheek to look smug.

With a level of force I didn't know I possessed, I buried the knife into his eye socket. His shock and pain broke my gag on him, and his screams filled the pit. "Hurts, doesn't it?" I whispered in his ear. Twisting my wrist to cause the most damage, like Ros had taught me, I withdrew the dagger.

"Star!"

Looking up, I met Sam's furious gaze. Wetting my lips, I straightened. "Sam."

"What the *fuck* are you doing?" he demanded as he stood across from me, hands on his hips.

"Blinding this piece of scum before I remove his head and burn his soul in the hellfire." I looked over at him. "Problem?"

Ros's mouth was hanging open. Zel looked delighted, Chaz and Pen were on either side of Sam, and Sam...he looked...torn. "No problem with that, but what happens next?"

"I go back to Gabriel."

"For?"

"He's going to…" I shook my head and looked back down at Michael, who was clawing at his face as he moaned in pain. If I were a better person, I may have felt remorse.

"He's going to kill you." Sam interrupted my thoughts and was obviously pissed.

"Not me," I said quietly, but I knew he heard me.

"Did he say that?"

I frowned. Yes? No? I thought about it, I wasn't sure. "Why?"

"Because there's nothing to say that when we remove this child from you, you won't create another again." Sam spoke calmly, pleasantly even, and he knew exactly what he was doing, because I was listening. "They will kill *you* first, the human body will die, the child will be removed and killed. Your soul they will take to this very pit, and they will burn you both in the hellfire. Because they will not allow you to live. We created Nephilim once, and we can do it again. Heaven will not leave the threat unanswered."

Michael's cries had quieted, and I looked into his one remaining eye. "Seriously?" He didn't need to speak for me to see the truth, and I screamed in frustration. "And you all scorn Satan. At least he wears his true colours on his skin!"

"You should have spoken to me first, witch," Sam admonished from across the pit.

"You would have tried to reason with me," I protested as I dug my hand into Michael's hair and yanked his head back. "And I would have listened, and I wouldn't get to do *this*."

"Star?" Zel spoke as he stepped forward. "Star, listen to me."

"What?" I was feeling more pissed off than before, and my patience was thin.

"Don't."

It was my turn to have my mouth hanging open. "*What?*"

"Let me across, let me come to you," Zel spoke in a smooth even tone, and somewhere my brain registered that it's how police and other emergency responders speak to suicide jumpers or mad men.

"Why?"

"You took a Watcher's life, and it tarnished your soul. You're good, Star, remember?" Zel nodded encouragingly, and I felt my head nodding along with him.

"Remember the split, Star?" Pen stepped forward. "*Your* split, Star, is almost all good, remember?"

"Yes," my voice was hoarse.

"Let me across," Zel spoke again. "Let me wield the blade."

"He burned her in the pit," I wailed, and I felt the knot tighten once more. So did Michael, because he screamed out in pain.

"Her grief is tuned to him," Chaz whispered urgently to Sam. "We need to move, now."

"Witch!" Sam barked.

My head snapped up. "Demon?"

"Let us across, part your barricade of souls, and hand this burden over."

My barricade was protection; I wasn't as stupid as I looked. I knew the angels wouldn't find me here, because the souls cloaked us. It was my luck the Watchers knew me so well that they came here. "You'll let him go." I felt the tears start to flow.

"Star," Zel spoke as he stepped too close to the edge, the

hellfire bubbling in anticipation beneath him. "Look at me." He pointed to his scars. "Thank you for repaying my pain, but let me take it from here." Zel watched me. "Please. Don't do this, he isn't worth it."

No, he wasn't.

But Gran was.

"*She* was." I plunged the knife into Michael's neck, and I felt nothing. His hands caught the side of my face, knocking me off balance as he scrambled to break free of me and my power.

Dark hands steadied me, and I looked up into Hound's red eyes. "Let go." He felt my pain, I knew he did, and his forehead leaned against mine. "Let go, it's okay, let go."

Hands pulled me back, and with a giant sob, I let go of the knife as Zel appeared beside Michael, and with a mighty blow, he severed his head.

Turning, I looked up at Sam, and I tried to stay on my feet, but the knot was crippling. He took me down to the ground and gathered me in his arms. "Let it go."

"Sam." I was breaking. I knew I was.

"I have you, I will always have you." He kissed my temple. "Grieve, Star. Let it go."

In the bottom of hell, beside the pit of hellfire, while the Watchers exacted my revenge on the Angel of War who burned my gran's soul, I let go of the grief. As I sobbed, the knot loosened, and I knew I could breathe again.

CHAPTER 18

THERE WAS A STRANGE STAGNANT FEEL TO THE WATCHER CAMP. Gabriel hadn't come screaming for my blood, and the Watchers hadn't rushed off to take his head.

Days passed, well, it felt like days, but in this dimension, it could have been hours, or it could have been weeks.

I cried, I mourned, I slept.

On repeat.

I'd never been that fragile girl. The one you needed kid gloves to handle. The gentle, sensitive soul. I was the kind of girl that got kicked in the teeth and then got back up swinging. Yes, life knocked me down. Life knocked everyone down. It's how you got back up that defined you.

My gran's soul burning…that was taking its toll.

The fact I had to die, in all ways, so my child could never be born? That was knocking me down on repeat.

How many times did you get that kick in the teeth before you stopped swinging? How many times did life fuck you over before you decided it wasn't worthwhile getting back up only to be knocked down again?

One more time?

Ten more times?

How much was *too* much?

"Witch," Sam greeted me as he ducked into the tent. "Did you sleep?"

"Yes," I answered immediately. He got very vocal when I didn't. I knew he loved me, and I knew he was worried, and I knew he was biding his time, but I also knew he was losing patience.

Because *time* was something we didn't have much of.

"Any movement?" I asked.

"No, they're sticking to their camp."

"Does someone new get promoted?" I'd been thinking about this. "Does the Angel of War have an understudy?"

Sam sat on the edge of the bed as he stroked a hand over my hair. I liked this softness he showed me now, and had my days not been numbered, I would have been scared he would think me weak as I lay broken on his bed.

"Yes, actually, he did. That would have been Satan."

That got a reaction from me. "No!"

Sam smiled, the corners of his eyes crinkling with amusement. "Yes," he confirmed. "You think the Prince of Wrath was a nobody?"

"I didn't think of it," I admitted. "Shit, I don't think that's a good job for him."

Sam's laughter made me feel warm inside. "Which is why he was an *understudy* only."

My fingers traced his jawline. "Why not you? You're the General after all."

He smiled as he grabbed my hand, kissing my knuckles as he stood. "You want something to eat?" When I went to refuse, I saw his face and instead nodded. "Okay, be right back."

Alone in the tent, I looked at the roof. "Are you going to speak?"

"You're taking too long," Cross spoke from across the room.

"Did you move them?"

"Your parents are safe, as I said they would be." I heard his huff of displeasure. "Your lack of confidence in me is displeasing."

"Bite me," I muttered as I rolled out of bed. I was in leggings, a loose jumper, my hair in a messy braid. Quite frankly, I looked like a mess.

"I thought I brought you clothes." Cross looked me over with a frown. "Why are you so…dishevelled?"

"I gave up on caring," I answered honestly as I walked over to him. "Hound will be okay?"

"Any more questions on my competence, and I will be my namesake."

That earned a smile, and I raised on my tippy toes to kiss his cheek. "Don't be, I was just checking."

"You're ready?"

What a loaded question. Was I? "Yeah." I checked the tent and looked to Cross. "They can't follow?"

"Again with the doubt?" Cross held his hand out to me. "You need to learn discipline and faith."

I snorted as I reached for him. "Faith? After the shitshow I've lived through the last year, my faith is shot to dust."

"You think the letter is wise?" Cross asked me with a hooded look.

"Well, I thought I hid it better," I snarked at him. "But yes, he needs to know why."

We stared at each other for a few moments before Death nodded. "Very well, we waste time."

I was no longer in the tent.

I knew for certain I was no longer anywhere I had been before. The air tasted…sweet.

"Do you breathe here?" I asked as we walked through

white marble halls with no doors, leading me to who knew where.

"I do not need to breathe."

"But can you breathe?" I asked as I reached out and trailed my hand along the cool marble. "You have a huge hard-on for white. Aren't you supposed to be all gothicky and love black?"

"Do I need to know what *gothicky* means?" Cross replied as we approached massive wooden doors. "I'm quite partial to Gothic style architecture, if that's what you mean."

"No, it isn't." I followed as he pushed the doors open, and we were in…paradise? "Holy shit."

I walked forward and looked at what I was amongst. The door was gone. We were on a beach. Crystal clear turquoise waters lapped at white sand. Palm trees swayed in the breeze, but that was only one part. I saw mountains with snow on them. To my left, there was an almost urban area, with… movement? Was it people? Higher up, there were clouds, just loads and loads of fluffy clouds, but even though they were high, I knew I could touch them. Walk amongst them if I wanted.

"Cross?"

"Hmm?"

He was already sitting at a table, on a chair that looked both inviting and comfy, as it sat amongst the sand. I was still gawking as I approached and sat down across from him. "This is why you always look like you're fresh off a beach, because you're literally fresh off a beach."

Cross grinned as he leaned back and looked out over the water. "I like long walks on the beach at sunset."

I giggled.

"I'm serious."

I laughed harder.

"You are a terrible disciple."

I was doubled over and couldn't stop laughing. Tears streamed down my face as he sat affronted across from me. Eventually, I wiped my eyes and willed myself to calm down. "Sorry."

"You're not though."

"I'm not." I grinned again.

"You don't approve of my home?" I could see his tension, and I felt guilty.

Looking around, I felt the happy smile. "Your home rocks," I told him happily. "And I can stay here?"

"Obviously." Cross settled back and looked out over the water.

"Is it modelled on anything? Here?"

"Things from here and there, places lost, places found, places created."

"Who knew you would be even more evasive in your home?" I looked up at the mountains. "How do I get up there?"

"Travel."

I tried to wink, but I stayed where I was. "I'm broken?"

"You are the very definition of a flight risk," Cross told me easily. "I have prevented you from *winking* at will."

"I'm grounded?" I asked him incredulously.

"Yes, for want of a better term."

"I came here with you. I left them all. I didn't even say goodbye to my parents!"

"Your guilt at the death of your grandmother makes you emotional. You've proven this for the last *many* days. If I had allowed you visitation to your parents, you would never have come here."

"That doesn't make it right," I snapped.

"We spoke about this, Star. You are merely protesting because you don't want to do any exercise and actually *walk* to the peak."

My eyes narrowed on his. "It's not fair you know me so well and you're still all dark and mysterious…with a longing for sunsets."

"Take a moment, breathe," he spoke to me as he fixed his eyes on the horizon once more. "Just *be*, Star."

"No one can come for me?" I asked again hesitantly.

"No angel, demon or their creator can enter my realm. I told you."

Hope rose within me. "And time is…"

"Malleable."

After a few minutes, I leaned back in my own chair and closed my eyes. Time had no meaning here. I was moving forward at such a slow pace it was like I was frozen in time. Cross had explained it to me. We weren't frozen, but the sand in *this* hourglass trickled slowly.

For those who I left behind, they would continue, but when I came back out of here, I would enter their timeline exactly where I left it, or near to it at least. If I chose. I wasn't time travelling. I couldn't go back and change the past, and I couldn't jump forward too much or change the future, but I had a window of time that allowed me to manipulate when my return was. Depending on how long I spent here, it meant I was either a few days or months away from my loved ones. Or if I never left, well, that was a thought for another day.

I didn't really understand it, if I were completely honest with myself. I never understood time travel, and the whole concept of it baffled me. Time hopping was not something I wanted to do. I just needed a place to come to terms with what had happened, was still happening, and learn to be who I was.

However, I knew better than anyone, death was not the end. Well, not for most souls. Only the ones related to or associated with me met a final end. Pushing my anger and pain away again, I opened my eyes to see a darkening sky.

"Are you okay?"

"Yes." My hand smoothed over my swollen belly. "How angry do you think he'll be?"

"He is what you term as apoplectic."

"I thought the note would help?" I winced at Cross's amused look.

"I think it's safe to say it did not achieve the result you hoped for."

We sat in silence for a while longer. "And the Return?"

"The angels have sensed your departure, and Gabriel has turned his attention to yet another rebellion against his beloved heaven."

"As he should," I mumbled as I thought of the angel.

The sun set, and I was under a million stars, on a beach with Cross. How my life had changed. "I have to remember not to stay too long," I warned Cross as I closed my eyes again and let peace settle over me.

I would not hide here for long, but for now, I let myself breathe.

LANDING flat on my arse wasn't made any easier because I was landing on sand. "Motherfucker!" I cried out as I glared up at Cross.

He was bouncing from one foot to the other, bare chested, black training trousers, and bare feet. In my time that I had been here, I now knew why his feet were always bare. The romantic in him liked to walk along the beach.

The beach that was currently my place of torture.

I got back up to my feet, the intent to maim Death very much the centre of my attention. It didn't help that he was grinning like an idiot at me.

My soul was fast though, so when I crashed my fist into his face, I yelled with glee.

"Ha!"

Cross shook his head to clear it before he laughed. "That all you got?"

We resumed our sparring match, and as we did, I felt myself get stronger. Every day, I got stronger here. My training was coming along well, and I knew soon I would need to visit the Land of the Souls to put method into practice.

But not yet.

I wasn't ready to go back. I wasn't ready to face them. I wasn't ready to go to the Land of the Souls knowing Gran wasn't there.

"Stop," Cross commanded as he looked up at the sky. "Time to feed you."

Rolling my eyes, I took the small bottle of clear liquid he handed me and dutifully walked to the hut where my body lay. The Watchers had, unknowingly, taught me the spell to separate myself from my body and my soul. So, while I trained and learned my craft in my soul form, my body lay in stasis with my unborn child cocooned within it.

Easily, I merged into my body, and when I was in, I opened my eyes and drank my vial. As agreed with *Death the Dictator*, I walked around the hut for a while, making sure I was active and allowing my body exercise. Walking out onto the sand, I made my way to the water's edge. Cool water washed over my feet, and I spent a few moments curling my toes into the wet sand beneath my feet.

"Hmm." Cross looked me over. "I think you grew."

Rolling my eyes, I looked down at my bump. "I think your vial boosts everything," I told him. "I'll waddle soon."

"Like a duck," Cross agreed as he splashed water over his torso.

"You look like a sexy playboy," I mocked him. "Only you're no boy."

"But sexy?" he said with a playful wink.

I snorted in answer as I turned to go back to the hut. I stopped dead when I saw Hound on the beach.

"Um, Cross?"

He came to stand beside me as Hound morphed into his humanoid shape. "I found you."

"How did he find me when you told me no one could find me?" I asked Cross angrily.

"Hound is a reaper, and he is attuned to you." Cross walked out of the sea like it was perfectly okay for us to be followed to the place where I was promised there was no possible way to follow me. "Plus, he was becoming so annoying, it was either this or pin him to the pit."

Hound didn't look Cross's way, but I wished he would. His disappointment was heavy, and I didn't want the burden of it.

Slowly I made my way to the hut where, lying on my bed, I said the spell, and when my soul was free, I reluctantly went back outside.

You had to admire the patience of a hellhound. They're not rabid, mindless monsters, they're methodical calm machines that do not give up.

Or appreciate people who do.

"You're pissed?"

"Yes."

I nodded, as I expected that. "I'm getting better."

"I will try to contain my excitement."

Damn. "So, on a scale of one to ten, how pissed?"

"Which number is beyond furious?" Hound asked calmly.

"Mmm, ten?"

"Then I'm probably about fifteen."

Ha.

"Samyaza is more akin to one hundred," Hound continued.

"You didn't bring him?" I asked desperately.

"I, unlike you, am not an idiot."

Ooh, name calling. Goody. "I thought you'd understand."

"I do."

"Then why are you angry?" I demanded with my hands on my hips.

"You left."

I waited, and then I got it. "I left you behind."

"Chicken winner."

I snorted out a laugh as Hound deadpanned the saying wrong, but I knew I couldn't correct him. He may be calm and methodical, but he was still a hellhound and, from the looks of him, really pissed off with me.

"How's my Watcher?" I asked casually.

"He is one of the reasons I am here."

Cross joined us and folded his arms as he looked at Hound. "They are being rash."

"Who is?" I asked, alarmed.

"It is who they are," Hound answered as he looked around. "Where did the fire pit go?"

"You've been here before?" Why would that surprise me?

"I thought it best that Star not be reminded of fire or pits," Cross answered Hound.

"Are you both ignoring me?" I asked suspiciously.

"A good idea," Hound said to Cross and resumed his hellhound form.

"The cold shoulder?" I turned to Cross. "Why isn't he mad at you?"

"Why would he be?" Cross went back to the training mat. "Come."

Stalking over to the mat, now I was pissed off. "You brought me here, you hid me here, so how come *you're* innocent?"

"Pft." Cross flexed his arms. "I am Death, I am accountable to no one. You, on the other hand, you were his friend."

"Am. I *am* his friend."

"And you left that friend without a note or a goodbye."

My mouth was opening and closing as I stared at him in disbelief. "You!"

"What about me?" Cross bent over and stretched.

"You told me we couldn't tell anyone!"

"I know."

Looking between the hellhound, who was sitting on the sand watching us, and the male that was Cross, I felt lost. "Then why is my friend not angry at you?"

Cross shrugged. "You should ask him."

My jaw was so tight I could only talk through clenched teeth. "He isn't talking to me."

"I know." Cross fell into his sparring position. "Be ready."

I missed the jab to the jaw by centimetres. "What the hell!" I cried as he got me on the second punch.

"Focus and fight."

When he clipped the back of my leg and I fell to the sand, I was beyond agitated. Jumping back to my feet, I hit back. When Cross brought me down again, Hound was at the edge of the mat.

Too slow. Be faster.

"I'm trying," I panted as I broke Death's hold.

Try harder. I thought you said you were better?

So it was going to be like that? Fine. Furiously I wrestled and boxed with Cross, and all the while, a hellhound ran a derisory commentary in my head.

When I was on my back again, I called time. "You win."

"I always win," Cross said above me.

"Which is why I'm the disciple and you're the main man."

"Man?"

"Shut up." I got to my feet and turned to look at Hound. "Your hints and tips were welcome."

Liar.

"You want to morph and we can go a round on the mat?" I offered flippantly.

I would annihilate you.

With hands on hips, I tossed my ponytail off my shoulder. "Bring it."

He hesitated, and then fluidly Hound was walking towards

me and the mat. With no words, a pair of black shorts were on his hips, and I looked to Cross, who smirked.

"I wasn't going to go for his nuts," I protested.

"Course you weren't," Cross scoffed as he settled on the sand, cross-legged, to watch us.

"I'm going to get my arse kicked, aren't I?" I suddenly realised.

"Oh yes."

CHAPTER 19

T HREE DAYS LATER, AND H OUND WAS SATISFIED THAT I WAS better. He didn't say I was ready, but he grudgingly allowed that I was better than I had been.

Just.

He was grumpy still. After kicking my arse on the sand and bruising my soul until I thought even my body felt it, he acted like nothing had happened. Still, I thought he went easy on me. *Note to self, don't piss off the hellhound.*

"It has not been that long," Cross murmured as I sat at our table set on the beach and watched the dawn.

"I know, but it needs to happen. I have family to return to, to talk to."

"And is the Watcher your family?" Cross asked casually.

"The Watchers are part of my family. Sam is…" *Everything?* Seemed anticlimactic. He was more than that.

"Hmm." Cross looked skywards. "It's been busy." He changed the subject.

"Why can't I be two things?"

"One of you is enough," Cross answered smoothly.

"Comedy gold," I deadpanned.

While Cross was here with me, he was also collecting souls everywhere else. It was a trick he had yet to show his only disciple. Because Cross could do all things and was apparently omnipresent, or whatever the word was for something that can be here, there, and everywhere all at the same time. But as a result of him being who he was, he had seen the few skirmishes that there had been between the angels and those who would fight them.

The Watchers were not fighting. Not yet. But they were keeping vigilance, waiting. Which is why I was getting today to go see Mum and Dad and explain my life. I was excited to see them but also terrified.

"I can come with you," Cross offered again.

"No, I turn up with Death beside me, and we may as well cart Dad's soul over the veil there and then."

Cross's lips pressed together to stop his laugh at my inappropriate humour, but his attempt to repress his humour made me giggle.

"Oh thank Christ I can still laugh." I stood and looked over at Hound. "You sure?"

Of course I will come with you.

He may still be salty with me, but he wasn't letting me out of his sight again. Me traipsing back into the world alone? Not happening. Not on Hound's watch.

"Alrighty, how do I look?"

"With your eyes," Cross sassed back.

"You been quaffing the wine when I wasn't looking?" I asked him suspiciously.

"Just go," he said with a shake of his head as he settled back in his beach chair.

"And Hound will be allowed to come back?" It wasn't that I didn't trust Cross, I just didn't trust him with his realm. He was possessive.

"You wound me," he drawled with his eyes closed.

"Well, that would be a first," I muttered as I felt a whoosh, and then Hound and I were outside my mum and dad's house in Inverness. "It freaks me out that he can do that," I told Hound as I walked up the path.

Should they be here?

I hesitated. That was a very good point. Cross told me he moved them to safety. "He did send us here?"

Unless he lied the first time.

My reply was stolen from me as my dad yanked the door open and stared at me. "Star?"

"Hey, Dad."

Stepping out onto the path, he went to grab me, but I danced out of reach and saw his hurt. "I can explain inside."

"Quick, it isn't safe."

I followed him to the living room where my mum was on the floor with every crystal known to man on a cloth in front of her.

"Mum?"

She gaped at me for a few seconds before her eyes narrowed. "A soul? You come with just your soul?"

"Not safe for me otherwise." I wasn't showing up heavily pregnant. Things were hard enough. "It's why I didn't want you to touch me," I explained to Dad.

"Where's your body?" Dad asked as he sat down in his armchair. He took a drink of tea and winced.

"Oh, you're on the potion tea?" I felt for him. I bet she had given him the bad one.

"Every hour." His look spoke volumes, while his voice remained neutral. Mum was moving crystals around on the floor, and I shared a grin with my dad before I took a seat.

"You can sit?" Dad asked me in surprise.

"Yes." I patted the couch. "Inanimate object. They've

explained it to me, but to be honest, it was a lot of physics and mumbo jumbo."

Mum snorted from her prone position. Mum was like Hound: fucking furious and trying not to show it.

"I'm sorry," I told her.

I received a grunt as an answer.

"Have you seen any of them?" I asked them both.

"The Viking comes every other day, the hippy with the long hair every two or three days," Dad spoke gruffly. "The bearded big fella stops by now and again. He and your mum… have difficulties."

"Der?" I asked in surprise. "Why?"

"He may have made some witty comment about Jean's tea." Dad sipped his hastily when my mum scowled at him. "It wasn't funny."

"Pen?"

My dad was stiff this time. "The handsy one with his sly smile is not welcome."

My dad was jealous of Pen. It was kind of cute. I noticed my mum was now more pissed off.

"Your boyfriend doesn't feel inclined to grace us with his presence," my mum spoke tightly. "Why is that?" Frigid blue eyes met mine.

"He is possibly busy." Lame. So lame.

"*Busy?*"

If she squeezed that crystal any more, she was going to bleed. "Mum." I reached out to her, but she flinched back.

"My mother's soul burned in the hellfire."

Nodding, I swallowed my tears. "Who told you?"

"Penemue."

"I'm really sorry."

"You're pregnant. With one of the Nephilim?"

I was glad it was my soul that was here. My mother's glare and fury would have stopped my heart with fear, and I would most definitely have swallowed my tongue by now.

"Yes."

"Reckless," she snapped as she returned to her stones.

"It wasn't planned." Great defence. Made me sound very responsible.

"Where are you? And the child?" Dad asked gruffly.

"Safe."

"Are you safe here? In this form," Mum demanded as she tossed a crystal into the mortar and started to crush it with the pestle.

"I can defend myself."

"Whoop-de-doo." The crystal was being ground to dust with my mother's sheer force of will, I was sure of it. "I *asked* if you were safe."

"I'm okay."

We sat in uncomfortable silence as Mum took her anger out on a selection of crystals. It was clear my dad wanted to ask me many things, but we both knew to let my mum get it out of her system first.

When she was finished, she pulled a small pouch from her pocket and added a pungent smelling herb. Leaning forward to look, I reared back when the black smoke rose from it. Hound was alert and watching, and I saw him turn his head to me right before he vanished.

His disappearance made me stand, and my mum gave a low mocking laugh. "Be still, you silly girl. The hellhound knows we will see him if he stays."

"Hellhound?" Dad asked as he looked around the room. "Why is that monster back here?"

"Hound is my friend," I explained. Again. "What's in the spell, Mum?"

"It's a warding to reveal those who would be hidden." She stood and looked around. "He knows we would see him."

To see a hellhound meant death. Hound was gone for their protection. "A warning would have been nice," I muttered as I sat back down.

"Like you warned us that you had run off with Death while pregnant with a Watcher's child?" Mum asked scathingly.

And here it comes.

"What the hell were you thinking? *Pregnant*? And keeping it? Are you insane? You have no idea the damage you cause. We've already lost Mum, you're hiding your body God knows where, your body harbours *evil*, and you sit here and want to tell me, *me*, about fair warning?"

"I can explain," I started. *Evil* was unjust, I thought.

"I don't want your explanation!" she yelled. "Jesus Christ, Star! It's the end of the fucking world!"

"I'm taking care of everything!" I screeched back. "I have a plan. I needed to be somewhere to be better, stronger. I need to stay as this just now because the angels want to put my body *and* my soul into the hellfire." I shook my head as I looked away. "I cannot give them my body."

"The Watcher has already been today. He enhanced his wards, so they won't be back today."

Running my hands over my face, I sighed. "I'm not here for them."

"The solution to your problems is not in this room."

"Mum," I protested weakly. "I just wanted to see you both."

"To say goodbye." Her voice was flat. Angry. I heard Dad's sharp intake of breath, and I wanted to throttle my mum for being so blunt.

"It's not goodbye, it's however long I have, to see how you are, make sure you are safe, make sure you *know*, even if you don't understand."

"It's very hard to understand," Dad admitted. "I mean, all the extra things that go with it, but I do feel, like your mother is failing to communicate well, that this is a goodbye," he said sadly.

"No." I looked between the two of them. "I am safe, for now. If…" I paused. "And it's a huge if, like *massive* if. *If* I am in real mortal or, you know, immortal danger, I promise I am running right here to be with you."

"Well, I feel all better, then," Mum snarked.

"Okay, it's not the best, Mum, I know that," I said waspishly. "But I'm in shit, and I'm trying my best to win."

"Why would you fall in love with a Watcher?" my mum said with exasperation. "Of all the hare-brained, nonsensical, reckless things! A Watcher!"

"He's…" What? Charming? No. Kind? Definitely not. Understanding? Fuck no. Sexy? Absolutely, but that was a really poor reason to give my parents. "He's my soulmate."

Well, if Mum hadn't been pale and angry before, now she was ghostly white and quite possibly as near to explosive as I had ever seen her. "No."

"Why does soulmate sound bad?" Dad asked perplexedly.

"She's a necromancer." My mum glared at me like it was all my fault that my powers manifested this way. "It means she's absolutely Friar Tucked with no way out."

I sat on the couch as she fumed silently in her chair.

"It could be worse," I ventured eventually. "I turned down Satan."

My dad choked on his tea, and my mum may have passed out. Maybe I needed to let them beat the shit out of me too?

"Satan?" Dad spluttered.

"Mm-hmm. Prince of hell. Prince of Wrath to be exact. He's trying to take over hell and offered to shelter me."

Dad gaped at me as he leaned forward. "You said no?"

"Yes, Dad, I said no."

"Well, thank heaven for small mercies." He sat back in his chair. "Why can you not be with the angels? Why are they the bad guys?"

"Because I'm pregnant. I can be pregnant again; therefore, even were I to hand my child over for them to kill, my body can still conceive again."

"They need to kill the shell as well as the soul," Mum added on bitterly. "Such a mess."

I had to agree with her.

"You will always be separate?" Dad asked as he waved his hand up and down slowly over my form.

"For now, it is easier."

"Your body's incubating it?" Mum asked me, and I nodded. "Risky."

"No more than falling in love with a Watcher."

She levelled me with such a flat stare I dropped my gaze.

"You need blood magic," she declared suddenly as she got to her feet.

"I do?"

"Up! Follow me. Roy! I need you too."

Like obedient children, Dad and I followed her through to the kitchen, where she led us outside to the back garden.

Hound was there in seconds, and I saw that neither Mum nor Dad noticed. So her spell was only for inside? That wasn't good enough. I would need to talk to Ros about that. He did enchantments. He would help her whether she wanted it or not. Stubborn woman. From her trouser pocket, she produced a flip knife, and my dad made a gargled sound of protest as I stared at the blade and my mum.

"Isn't that illegal?" I asked her incredulously.

"My house is overrun with demons," she told me curtly. "Plus, my husband used to be a policeman; we can say he confiscated it off a youth, and I'm blameless."

"Mum!"

"Jean!"

She shrugged us both off. "Bigger shit to deal with," she reminded us both. "Arms."

"Why?" I asked as I immediately thrust my hands behind my back.

"Because your soul is untethered," she explained as she hissed in pain when she drew the blade over her forearm. "Books and movies, they always show the blade across the palm. Do you know how many nerve endings you're cutting that way? Too many. Painful. This little nick? Hardly a scratch." She made a come-hither gesture to my dad, her finger movements sharp with impatience. "Now, Roy."

Dad was sliced like a chicken breast ready for stuffing next. "You."

I looked at Hound. He nodded.

"This ties my soul to you?" I asked hesitantly.

"No, idiot." She practically rolled her eyes at me. "I thought you had been trained. Your body still lives, and in your body is the blood of your father and me. This? This strengthens the tie to your body."

"But—"

Mum had no patience. She grabbed my arm and slashed across it, which freaked me out when the skin split from the slice of the blade but no blood spilled.

"What?"

"You're a soul." Her tone was gentler. "You can't bleed."

With low words of a spell I didn't know but my soul recognised, she held her arm and Dad's arm over my cut, and I was too fascinated with the spell to freak out over the fact they were dripping their blood into my open wound.

I felt it. The pull. The tie was tighter.

"It's working."

"I may be a *weak witch*," she muttered as she finished up, "but I know my craft."

"A fact she never shared before we married," Dad added dryly.

"Hush now, you've benefitted over the years."

"How?" I blurted.

"Best stew in the Highlands," Dad answered promptly. "Never makes a soggy dumpling."

My eyes were wide as saucers. "*Cooking*, Dad? Really?"

"We don't all get soulmates that fell from heaven, Starlight. Some of us know the right one when they can cook up a storm and look pretty damn hot doing it." His look to my mum was particularly salacious, causing her to giggle.

She giggled.

As my parents made googly eyes at each other over my open wound that their blood was dripping into, I wondered if I was officially in hell again.

CHAPTER 20

I LEFT MY MUM AND DAD'S AFTER HOUND SAT AND STARED pointedly at me until I could no longer avoid his judgement for wasting time. I wasn't able to hug them for as long as I wanted, which hurt so much, but they knew I was okay, and although they tried to hide their worry, they knew I was equipped to handle it. Plus, my mum had complete faith in the Watchers to protect me, and even though she hated it, she convinced Dad it was a good thing.

However, what stayed with me most from my brief time with them was that my mum also thought my child needed to be "dealt with." No one had any faith that what they all thought might not happen.

What if we were wrong? What if my child was none of these things? What if they were all wrong? How did I live with myself?

You're overthinking.

Glancing down at Hound, I resisted the urge to shrug. "Am I?"

We were walking along the banks of Loch Ness, and I kept stopping and staring at the water.

What are you stopping for? I told you that monster is fictional.

I smiled at his exasperation. "I'm enjoying the view," I replied as I looked at the rich greenery and the hills. "I could look at this all day, every day, and never be bored."

Hound turned to the water and the view and gave a very derisive sniff.

"Seriously?" I nudged him with my shoulder as we resumed walking. "You're so silly," I joked lightly.

When you are ready, you can return to the Land of the Souls, and I will bring the souls to the Waterfall.

"When I am ready, I would like that." I stopped again and just looked at the view. Hound was huge in hellhound form, and my head rested against his shoulder easily. We stayed like that for a while, me with my head against a hellhound as we watched the sun lower in the sky.

His head snapped up, and we both turned, Hound in front of me, ready. Naomie hovered a few yards from us.

"Star, come!"

As she reached for me, I went to grab her hand when Hound snapped his jaw at her, and she sprung back.

"Hound!" I chastised him as he fixed me with a dead stare.

Caution!

Biting my lip, I knew he was right. "Why?"

Her eyes widened in surprise, but I could see she understood. "They fight."

Hound couldn't have stopped me had he even tried this time; I was already grabbing Naomie's hand.

In the land where she had told me to come to find her, she led me through trees to the edge of the treeline, where she stopped, and I looked out over the clearing.

"What the hell?"

They were lined up against each other. Golden armoured angels and demons. Ranging from ones that looked like men to the misshapen nightmares that Satan had in his army. There were no princes that I could see, and as I scanned through the gathered demons, I saw no Watcher that I knew.

"Where are they?" I asked Naomie desperately.

"Not here, yet." She eyed me, and I nodded. "I didn't know if you knew."

"No, I've been…"

Careful, Hound warned.

"Away," I finished with a wide-eyed look to Hound. I wasn't entirely clueless; I didn't need his caution.

"They have been merciless," she spoke quietly as she shielded us in the trees.

"The angels?" I guessed.

"Michael is missing," she whispered. "They think that the demons of hell have taken him."

I searched the angels for Gabriel and saw him striding, hanging back as he assessed his…platoon. Which was what Sam had called it, but now it was bigger. Was it still a platoon? Whatever the fuck it was called, Gabriel knew exactly who had taken Michael. It wasn't any of the demons gathered in front of him.

What was his angle?

"Something isn't right," I whispered to Naomie. "The Watchers will not come. This is a battle not against them, but for those who wish to Return."

"And Michael?"

I looked between both sides. "Is their problem, not ours."

Taking her hand, I backed us slowly into the trees so we could once again be hidden. As Naomie turned away, I stopped, scanning the treeline on the other side of the clearing.

Movement.

Focusing, I called my power to enhance my sight, a handy trick Cross had taught me recently. He completely missed all my comic book references for it, but it had amused me for hours.

Movement again. There.

Eyes met mine, and my absent heart would have been pounding. Soft glowing green camouflaged in the greenery of the trees. I swallowed as he moved forward slightly, and I felt my soul reaching for him.

"Come, Star, he cannot cross," Naomie said as she tugged me backwards.

"How?" I asked as I fought the urge to claw her hand off of me so I could stay.

"This is our domain, the witches. He does not belong here."

Did I?

"If you think that will stop him, you're a fool." With an anguished cry, I turned away and followed her through the trees. "How come we can be in both?"

"We are witches," Naomie answered easily as the treeline once again thinned, and we were back on the rolling grasslands from before. "It's a mirroring effect," she explained. "The dimension they are in can be replicated. Centuries ago, I don't know when"—she looked at me with a smile—"but even *I* wasn't born, our ancestors were able to mirror it."

"How?"

"I don't know," she answered truthfully. "The spell is lost to us now, but the dimension is not."

"Can living witches come here?" I asked as Naomie sat on the grass.

"You're here, aren't you?"

I grimaced as I thought about it. "Am I?" I pointed down at myself. "Only our souls are here," I reminded her.

"When you were here before, you were human."

"It was my soul," I reminded her. "My awareness splits when I sleep, sometimes."

"How do you get around that?" Naomie asked me curiously.

"Don't sleep."

"He pulls you," she said thoughtfully, and I had to stop my laughter at the phrase. Naomie had no idea that "to pull" in Scotland had different connotations than what she was thinking. I'd gone out "on the pull" many a night in Inverness and St Andrews when I was a student, hoping to find a guy who I could connect with. I'd gone home many a night empty-handed. Now, I knew I would never have found him, no matter how many nights I spent in clubs and pubs searching.

My guy was a demon. A fallen angel. He owned my heart, and his soul matched mine.

"When a spell is cast, how long does it last?" I asked Naomie as we both sat in the long grass, listening to the fighting behind us through the bank of trees.

"Depends on the strength of the spell, the strength of the caster," she said as she held her left hand out. "Here, I'll demonstrate."

With her left hand facing up, she spread her fingers, and from her other hand, she poured water. Not from anywhere, just from her hand, and I stared at that longer than I should have. "How are you doing that?"

"This?" She gave a light laugh. "A simple spell. My affinity was water," she explained, as if that was supposed to make sense to me. "So look at my palm." I did. "This is the strength of the witch and the water is the spell."

Her hand poured more water over her hand, and I

watched as the palm collected some, but most of it ran through her open fingers.

"The palm is strong but look how much of the spell we are losing. Now, look." She closed her fingers, and she caught more water in the palm. "Stronger, right?"

I nodded.

Naomie turned her hand over so the back of her hand was facing upwards. "Now here, a more solid, stable strength, the water flows over and around, and the water is always running off back into the earth where it came from."

"Shouldn't you be catching the water?" I asked in confusion.

"Why?" Naomie shook her hand out, flicking water away from her. "Our power comes from nature. It is always moving. It is not a fixed thing." Her hand formed a fist, and she held it upright, her fingers clenched facing me, and once again her other hand poured water. "Look, strong you would think? But look at the top, no matter how hard I clench my fist, water is getting in. The spell is not working for what I need it to do." The fist was turned at a forty-five-degree angle and now her knuckles were facing me. The water ran over it and off, dripping onto the ground but not before covering the whole area.

"Strong surface, spell constantly moving, adapting." I reached out and touched her fist, and the water covered my finger.

"Strong witch, strong spell."

"You're strong," I mused. "You held off Asmodeous for centuries."

Naomie rubbed her hands dry on her skirt. "Time moves differently in hell."

"I hope for your sake it was quick."

Naomie looked away, and I knew without her confirming it, she had felt every moment of the torture she had endured at the hands of Asmodeous.

"I wish we knew this spell," I said, abruptly changing the subject.

"It merely gives us a safe place to practice and learn. I don't think we need more than one dimension."

With a smile, I stood and looked to the trees behind us, my smile fading. "They're still fighting."

"Until the end of time," she scoffed as she rose too. "Do you want to learn?"

"To fight?" I asked in surprise.

"No, I think you have enough teachers for that skill. I thought you may want to start working on controlling your powers, maybe your storm?"

I wanted to hug her, but the sounds of battle kept distracting me. "Should we check?"

"No." She saw my surprise and defended her words. "That you can still hear them fighting means that no one is winning."

"I never thought about it that way."

"When you are angry, you call the elements." Naomie wasn't asking a question, she was telling me. "Wind, rain, thunder, electricity." She reached out and tugged on my hair. "You lose your colour, yes?"

"Yes, I was more golden than white."

"Not white, *white blonde*. In my day, this colour was so rare we would have chained the child in the darkest dungeons, sure they were possessed."

"You were rovers?" I asked.

"Yes." Naomie pointed to her own black hair. "You would have caused quite the stir."

"I don't think much has changed," I joked as I jerked my thumb over my shoulder, causing her to laugh.

"The elements are essential for a witch. Nature is everywhere, all around us, and balance must always be maintained." Naomie spread her arms wide. "We are in the world, and what we take, we must give back."

"Give back?"

"When you call the elements, you are taking them from somewhere else. You upset the balance. That is why you cannot control it. You hold too much, you feed your anger out into the wild, but the wild has nowhere to put it. So it churns, and then when you are finished with it, where does it go?"

"I'm causing weather problems?"

"Yes, floods, hurricanes, earthquakes, forest fires."

"Holy crap."

"It's okay, we're going to stop it."

"How?" I asked her. Who needed the Nephilim? I was akin to the end of days in my ignorance.

"You only call what you need, and then you send it back, peacefully." My look must have been sceptical, because Naomie grinned. "Trust me?"

I nodded. "Yes, but I'm warning you, I'm difficult. Apparently." I did not look at Hound, but I felt his challenge.

"You've been taught by males," Naomie said with ease. "It's a woman's touch you need."

While the demons battled angels behind me, through the woods, I learned to call the wind at my command. Coaxing the wind and trying to persuade it not to get excited or start gusting was bloody hard. Wind was flighty. It wanted to be everywhere at once; it was like trying to teach a puppy to sit. It just wanted to bound up to you and lick your face.

If I had been in my body, I would have been drenched in sweat. After what felt like days, I had a mini tornado in my palm.

"He's kind of cute," I said as it bowed and twirled in my hand.

"You did very well, but did we not agree that *this* time, you were going to release it?"

"But what if he doesn't come back?" I looked up at Naomie and then back to my mini wind. "I have Wind in the Land of the Souls. He carries me around."

"Why don't you travel?" Naomie asked in confusion.

"When I first went there, I didn't know I could. Now, I think Wind would be upset."

"You can command the wind in the Soul dimension?"

I really should have picked up on her tone. "Yeah, he's fab."

I was drenched head to foot in water.

"Why?" I asked in shock.

"Four days I've spent on this, and you can do it in the Land of the Souls without conscious thought?"

Huh? *Ohhhh.* "Oops." I bit my lip. "I think I just had an epiphany."

Naomie threw her hands in the air before she turned and stormed away from me, leaving me dripping wet. I giggled when my little tornado started to whirl around me in an effort to keep me dry.

"Star."

Looking up, I saw Ros in front of me. "Ros?"

"Hey," he said solemnly.

"How did you get in here?"

"Enchantments, remember?" With a murmur, my clothes were dry.

"Thanks." I got to my feet and faced him. "You're alone?"

"Yes."

The tightness eased in my chest. "What do you want?"

"Hear me out."

"Why?"

"I think you need to go to the Tree."

CHAPTER 21

"THE TREE?" I ASKED HIM, COMPLETELY CONFUSED AS TO WHY. "I'm not in danger from a Watcher, am I?"

Ros blinked once as if he were confused. "What?"

"My gr—" I hesitated. "I was told that the Tree was what could save me from him. Him was a Watcher."

Ros still looked stumped. "Which Watcher?"

"Araqiel."

"Where the fuck do you come up with these notions?" Ros shook his head at me in wonder. "If only a Watcher can take you to the Tree," he said, "why would the *Tree* then be what *saves* you from a Watcher?"

He waited to let that sink in. "Well, I thought you or Sam would take me to the Tree, and then I'd be safe from Araqiel."

It did sound kind of flimsy now that I thought about it.

"You chopped his head off just fine with no help from the Tree of Life."

"But you knew I needed the Tree!" I protested wildly. "You said you could understand why I needed the Tree."

"Because you're a witch and a necromancer," Ros explained slowly. "The Tree of Life is what they may use to return to heaven and fuck it all up. I didn't think you wanted the millions of dead to deal with."

"Oh." I was so confused. "Then who am I being saved from?"

"You need to ask?" Ros's eyes were wide again.

"Gabriel?" I guessed.

"He's going to come for you, he's gunning for your head,

just like you were for Michael." Ros took a step closer to me. "You need to get to the Tree. You need to get there, and if the Tree chooses, you'll be safe from Gabriel."

"If the Tree *chooses*?"

"I don't think you have anything to worry about," Ros said. "Not really."

"You're not selling me on the whole *let's go to the Tree* idea," I snapped at him.

"I can explain on the way." He looked at me hopefully. "Yeah?"

I wanted to say no, a sensible person would say no. "How do I get there?"

"You crazy? I'm taking you."

"Just you?" I asked warily.

"I may need help." Ros didn't even blink. Ros held his hand out to me. "Do you trust me?"

I looked back over my shoulder to where Naomie had gone before turning back to Ros. "You fuck me over, Viking, and they'll need more than a longboat to burn your corpse." I took his hand as he chuckled.

We were no longer in the mirrored dimension. We were at the start of the white marble hall I had walked along with Cross.

"Ros?"

"I need all of you for the Tree," Ros explained. "Body too."

My heart was racing. This didn't feel right. Cross protected me. Me and my child. Chewing my bottom lip, I hesitated.

"Cross doesn't care about your body or what you carry," Ros spoke quietly beside me, and I turned to face him. "He's all about collecting souls, processing souls, the next step, the next stage, the afterlife. My Father watches from his perch on high, watches his creations *live*. Love. Laugh. Create new life." Ros gave me a sad smile. "I think it's why he let us fall; he knew what it was like to watch and understood we wanted more."

"But you fought." I pointed to the scar on the side of his face. It didn't detract from his good looks. It enhanced them. The beard he wore when we first met was gone. Now he merely had a light scruff across his face. I took in his features, and reaching out, I traced the curve of the scar down the side of his face. "You didn't get this because Daddy was happy to let you go."

Ros smiled as he took my hand away, kissing the palm as he dropped it back to my side. "Gabriel fought us—whether it was on my Father's orders or not, I'll never know. Haven't kept in touch."

"Gabriel," I hissed. "He blinded Zel."

"He was always a dick." Ros didn't sound that put out about Gabriel, and I assumed it was because he had been with him a lot longer than I ever would.

"Cross is my friend," I reminded Ros. "He won't appreciate you sneaking into his domain to steal my body." My brow furrowed. "He definitely won't appreciate me being with you."

"You won't be with me." Ros grinned wickedly. "You would trigger his return. Don't worry. I've been sneaking into Cross's domain for years."

I knew my eyes were wide, and Ros chuckled. "Do you know how boring some centuries are?" He shook his head as he started to walk up the hallway. "Seriously, you have no idea. Stay here, I won't be long."

Watching Ros disappear along the marble-walled corridor,

I contemplated my situation. I was a soul. I was a human. I was a witch. I was a necromancer.

I was a mess.

Cross understood my situation, but Ros was right, he wasn't too fussed about my human body. All Cross was interested in was my soul. Even when we trained, from the moment I had woken in his rooms above the pit, he had been content to let the Watchers keep my body as he trained my soul. My body could die, and Cross would be fine with it because he *only* needed my soul.

My *soul* was his disciple. The things I needed to learn, to train to be able to do, for Cross, my body held me back. When he taught me to fight, he hadn't resisted Sam showing me how much more I could be, because Sam was improving my skills in my soul.

Naomie was the same. She instructed me to come to learn from her in my soul form. Of course, she had a weird kind of vibe going on with Cross that I was refusing to explore. She was in Asmodeous's hold for so long because of a curse and her love for Zel, I didn't want to know how close she was with Death.

Was this why Ros was taking me to the Tree? With my body? Was this how it ended for me?

Ros was walking back towards me, my body cradled in his arms and with a huge grin. "That place gets weirder, I swear," he told me conversationally as he jerked his head back to indicate where he had been. "The cloud platform is new," he continued. "It's all very Salvador Dali, don't you think? The beach, the sand, the forest, the snow-capped mountains, the clouds, it's like a romantic fantasy threw up in there."

Cross was a romantic? Of course he was. "He likes long

walks on the beach at sunset," I told him as I looked at my body in his arms. "If I die, do I lose my humanity?"

Ros—who had been about to say something entirely different, I thought—closed his mouth with a snap. "What the fuck are you talking about?"

"I'm human." I pointed to my body. "Yes?"

"How long was I gone for?" Ros asked suspiciously.

"If or when I die, and I'm separated like this, and I'm all cremated or whatever my parents choose to do with me, and I'm just a soul, do I lose my humanity?"

"Star?" Ros looked me over. "I don't have time for this," he said seriously. "Your brain, I can't cope with it without lots of beer and at least two of my brothers beside me. Okay?" He started to walk. "So let's park the deep questions until we sort one crisis at a time, okay? Can we do that?"

"I thought it was a simple question," I muttered as I followed behind him.

"Course you did, because you're you."

"Meanie."

We left Cross's…tunnel? Ros caught my hand once, and I was in the ether. I knew it from the smell in the air and also the fact there was a huge freaking castle in front of me.

The pull to my body was strong, and I was resisting it. "You put me back in there after I've been out for so long, I'm going to be horny," I warned him.

There are lots of fun things in the world to see. Amazing things. Seeing Ros try not to drop my body while he stumbled with his face beet red was definitely one of them.

"Ugh, you're a freaking nightmare," he growled as he steadied himself and me. "Tell me, does Sam gag you when you're doing it?"

"I'm only gagged when he puts something in my mouth," I whispered in his ear as I smacked the Viking's arse before I cackled at how uncomfortable he was.

"Stop it," Ros warned me as he walked over to a grassy little hill thing. It looked like a harmless bump, but I could feel the low power coming off it.

"Seriously? You're putting my body on top of a mound of graves?" I snapped.

As he placed me gently on the knoll, I guessed you would call it, he straightened and met my eye. "I'm not unaware of the effect of the soul split, and you have a mighty fine set of tits, my girl, but I respect you too much to bring you down to my level of dirty."

Now *I* was red faced.

"And my brother would cut my balls off and feed me them. So to temper your lust"—he grinned—"by placing you on a grave, it negates the effect."

Was this fucked up? Was he serious? How was that a thing? "Huh?"

"Balance." Ros pointed at me and then the knoll. "You wake up, you're hungry for some sexual healing. Apart from the joys of sex, the main point of any creature's sexual organs is to procreate. So when you give a huge bolt of electricity to a body by placing a soul back in, you waken everything up. Which is why the…" He looked to be searching for the word. "Craving is so high. But you can counter that by putting that screaming need for life on hold, and you do that by placing it on a whole heap of death."

"Why am I just learning this now?" I asked Ros suspiciously.

"Because Sam's a male. His woman waking up horny and begging? Jackpot."

I narrowed my eyes on Ros, and he looked completely relaxed. How…barbarian. "You're just all complete wankers."

He shrugged. "It is what it is, little Star. Come on, hop in, we're running out of time. Cross will know you're gone soon. And I don't want to deal with Hound."

"You shouldn't piss off Death." I gave Ros the evil eye. "Or Hound." I merged with my body.

The pain wasn't as sharp as it had been when I did this at first. I was more or less used to the dull aching everywhere, the sharp niggling of pain that ran through me. It annoyed me that Ros was right. I could feel my need, but I could also feel the lingering death in the ground underneath me. As I checked to make sure I was okay, my hand strayed over my abdomen. The bump was fine. I felt fingers touch the back of my hand, and I opened my eyes.

I was no longer on grass, I was on sand, golden sand. Dunes rose and fell in front of me. "And this is?" I asked as I sat up.

"The desert." Zel spoke beside me.

"Earth?"

"Well, it's not the moon," Zel snapped.

I looked at Ros with a frown. "I thought you said help?"

The Viking demon merely grinned at me as he helped me to my feet.

In my soul form, I would have been able to stand on the sand and be completely unaffected by the sun in the desert of whichever continent I was on. In my pregnant body, I was struck by immense suffocating heat, and my body was screaming for hydration. My black jeans and black top were stifling me.

"Holy hell, it's hot." I was already unbuttoning my jeans. "Ros, I need a sundress or something." Wordlessly a printed fabric was held out to me as I peeled off my clothes. "And sunscreen. I'm blonde and Scottish; I'm going to burn quicker than a marshmallow in a fire."

Pulling the dress on, which was actually more like robes and covered most of my skin, I yelped when Zel slapped lotion on my face and rubbed with no gentleness or care. "I'm not wood that needs sanding," I grumbled. "Spell me?"

"Won't work, enchantments aren't as effective as we get closer to the Tree. There's no telling how long they'll last. Better to stick to what we know. Plus, if we use power, we're traceable."

I looked around the vast expanse of desert. "I have to walk? In this heat?"

"We're with you," Zel said quietly beside me. "We can do as much as we can until we can't."

With a sigh, I started walking.

"You're going the wrong way," Ros said with a laugh.

With a glare, I turned on my heel and started walking in the other direction. "You want to tell her?" I heard him ask Zel.

"No, she'll eventually notice we're walking away from her. She's slow, but not entirely stupid; she won't go far."

I heard the two comedians moving away. I could be stubborn, I could keep walking the wrong way just to make them come and get me. Or I could swallow my pride and follow them like a good little puppy.

I ground my teeth together.

There was so much more going on in the world. In other dimensions. I was above being childish. They were helping me. They were my friends. I thought of Zel. Okay, we were acquaintances.

I was bigger than this. I just needed to turn around and follow.

I started walking.

The wrong way.

To hell with them. If they wanted me to go with them, they needed to ask me.

Nicely.

CHAPTER 22

Ros had come and picked me up and merely carried me back to where Zel had waited, impatiently, pissed off at my stubbornness.

"I don't know how he hasn't spanked the shit out of her," he muttered to Zel as he put me on my feet, and the three of us started walking.

"Spanked her?" Zel snorted. "I don't know how he hasn't strangled her."

"*Her* can hear you," I reminded them. "Is this like a demon thing? Are you so used to people not sensing you that you just speak and think, because you're invisible, they're deaf?"

"Why are we invisible?" Ros asked curiously as we walked over the sand. Which was hell itself. The sand was deep and fluid; it was like walking through water. You felt that you were getting somewhere only to find you'd put in all that effort to move three feet.

"You let people see you?" I asked in surprise. "Normal people?"

"Define normal," Zel muttered, giving me a look that left me in no doubt that he thought I was definitely not normal.

"Humans, not witches or wizards or...what else is there?" I asked Ros curiously.

"Wizards?" Ros was beaming.

"No wizards or warlocks?" I realised.

"Just witches," he confirmed. "But you can be either male or female. The blood, once corrupted, isn't fussy on gender."

"I thought *witch* was a feminine term." I thought about it. Why would I think that? Who decided that?

"Wicca is male," Zel explained. "Wicce is female. Both mean witch."

"Sometimes males prefer druid," Ros carried on. "But again, druid is gender-free. It's all moot at the end of the day. Both have the ability to be more than human due to the corruption of their blood."

"How far removed from the first witch is Naomie?" I asked Zel. Blue eyes flashed at me before he looked ahead again. "She's not the first?"

"No, the first was along the river Nile many, many years ago," Ros spoke up quickly to avoid any uncomfortable silence.

I breathed a sigh of relief. I didn't want it to be Naomie, I didn't know why.

"She burned in oil daily," I told him. "He tortured her daily."

"He did." Zel was resolute. Unmoved.

"You feel nothing?" I asked him incredulously as I panted beside him with exertion.

Zel stopped and glared at me. "Did she tell you what she did?"

"She said she betrayed you."

"And still you think you can push with your questions? Tell me, Star, when did you become part of the brotherhood?"

"I'm not, I'm just a—"

"A pain in the arse," Zel growled and resumed walking. "Keep your questions to yourself. We're not here to bond, we're here to stop fucking Armageddon."

I looked at Ros, who was watching me with amusement.

"Touchy much?" I whispered to him as Zel strode on in front of us.

"If I didn't watch you fight so hard to survive, girl, I'd swear you have a death wish."

"He's such a grump." We both followed after him. "Have you seen her? She's stunning, and she spent centuries, *centuries* holding on, refusing Asmodeous. You'd think even if he was ignorant to her beauty, he would be impressed with her conviction."

"You don't know the whole story, little witch. Best keep your thoughts to yourself."

"How long before we reach the Tree?" I asked, trying to be innocent.

Ros was not to be fooled. "I'm not falling for that." He chuckled. "You can look as angelic as you want, I'm not telling you their story," he added.

"Ugh, you guys know everything about me," I protested. "Why can't I know your sordid pasts?"

"You know the gist of it," Ros said as he handed me a flask of water from a backpack that he didn't have before. "We were made in heaven, we watched life below us, we wanted more than we had." He took a drink when I handed the flask back to him. "End of story."

"But when you settled down, like when you were here before the floods or whatever, maybe after, were you happy?" This had bothered me for some time, and I guess as we trekked over the desert, now was as good a time to ask as any.

"Happy?" Ros looked thoughtful.

"I mean, you risked and lost so much, and you got what you wanted." I gestured to the sun in the sky and the desert sands. "You're no longer just watching, but I don't know if you are living." His brow furrowed, and I hurried on, too caught up in my own stride to notice that Zel had stopped. "You all live in that drafty castle and are together all the time. What did you gain? You could have had that up there." I pointed upwards.

"Sex," Ros answered and then laughed as I wrinkled my nose at his crudeness. "Laughter. Friendships. Families. Life." My usual laughing demon was now serious. "You don't know us, Star. Not yet." He glanced at my bump. "We're meeting under very unusual circumstances. We're soldiers. We were always soldiers, and we are fighting in a war that you are in the middle of, through no fault of your own." He patted my shoulder as he passed me. "Keep an open mind. What you see isn't always what you think it is."

Was that a warning? I hesitated. I was traipsing over the desert, sweating buckets, in a robe that was clinging to me, with two Watchers, just because Ros had asked me to.

"He doesn't mean us, witch!" Zel called over his shoulder, and I laughed at how predictable I was to these males who told me I didn't know them, but they somehow knew me well. *So* well.

"So we won't bond today," I teased as I caught up to them. "You may as well tell me about the Tree."

"It's a tree," Zel responded gruffly.

"Well, it's more than a tree, no?"

"What do you know about the Tree?" Ros reasoned. "Tell me what you've been taught, and I'll tell you what's right, wrong and Starisms."

"Starisms?"

"Logic fucked up beyond all possible reason," Zel said with a smirk as he exchanged a look with Ros, who laughed.

"You're such a dick," I mumbled as I struggled up a dune that was intent on sending me back to the bottom. Zel caught me as I started to slide. Picking me up, he carried me to the top of the dune, where he set me down. "Thanks."

"Mm-hmm."

Ros looked at me and the sand dune. "This is usually the fun part," he said and pointed downwards. "It's like downhill skiing without the skies. You can force yourself to stay upright and, with a little bit of momentum and power, just slide."

My eyes, which had been widening in horror the whole time he spoke, were looking between the seemingly innocent dunes and Ros. "Have you met me?" I exclaimed.

"Unfortunately," Zel grunted as he took a drink of water.

"I will not manage this," I told Ros, ignoring Zel.

"We could sledge it?" Ros asked Zel.

Zel looked at his fellow Watcher with amusement and shook his head even as he smiled. Genuinely smiled. "This is not the time, brother," he told Ros and grinned wider when Ros pouted.

"But it's the best part."

"If we are still standing when this is over, we'll come back," Zel assured him as he clasped Ros's shoulder. "We'll bring Der."

Ros looked delighted, and I would have been happy too if I hadn't been thinking of Zel's words. If. He wasn't confident of the outcome.

"I could roll down?" I suggested.

"You're pregnant." Zel's grin was gone.

"Oh yeah, oh well." I held my arms out to Ros. "Piggyback?"

With a short laugh, he crouched, and I clambered onto his back as Zel looked on with disapproval. When I was secure on the blond demon's back, I leaned forward, the bump making it slightly uncomfortable, and whispered in his ear.

"You can't slide, but you can still run, right?"

Ros turned his head to look at me, and I saw him start to smile. "Quick before Grim-and-Grumpy stops us," I urged.

"Wait!" Zel shouted, but we ignored him.

Ros was off, and we were slipping, sliding, running down a sand dune, and I felt like I was flying. Ros gave a whoop of joy as we careened down the dune, and I laughed along with him. He staggered at the bottom as he struggled to catch his balance, and then I was off his back, being whirled through the air as he spun us both in a circle of joy, our laughter ringing out in the desert.

"Put her down!" Zel commanded, but we both could see he wasn't really upset.

"That was great!" I was buzzing. "I want to go again!" I clung onto Ros's arm and jumped up and down.

Ros threw his head back and laughed. Slinging his arm around me, he pushed me as we both started to follow Zel. "We'll come back when this is over, and you can do it the other way."

"What if I'm dead then?" I looked between the two of them and then back at the sand dune. Neither of them had an answer, and I poked Ros in his side. "Come on, demon, one more time? For luck?"

"Luck has nothing…" Zel started to protest, but Ros had already grabbed my hand, and we were heading back up the dune.

It was just as exhilarating and fun the second time, but we

both knew that Zel would not permit a third time, and reluctantly we resumed our trek.

We'd been walking for what felt like years. My body was dehydrated, my feet were going to drop off, my legs were using muscles I hadn't known were muscles. I was bone weary, and the more I struggled onwards, the more I resented the fact that we couldn't just wink where we needed to be. "They don't know where you are?"

"I'm shielding us," Ros informed me. The two demons looked picture perfect. Not one bead of sweat on their brows. Their clothes were dusty from the sand, because they weren't completely infallible. But they were close. They kept producing water, which I had been suspicious of for a long time. *Someone* was using their power.

It was also dark, and the temperature had dropped so significantly I was in danger of shivering to the next dune.

"We will stop soon," Zel spoke for the first time in a while. "You need to sleep."

"How much longer?" I asked.

"The morning should bring us there," Zel answered, and when he looked at me properly, he stopped. "We stop now."

I settled into the sand as they produced and erected a tent. "Your backpacks are like bottomless carpet bags," I chuckled. "Got a standard lamp in there?"

"Could be sunstroke," Ros offered to Zel, who shook his head.

"Just her brain," he grunted. "Feed her this." He handed a packet to Ros, who took it and walked over to me, opening it.

I was starving, so when he gave me a protein bar, I felt cheated. "Zel? Where's my chicken and potatoes?"

"I can't travel right now," he reminded me, but I saw his smile and knew he wasn't mad.

"I forgot." I took the offered protein bar. "Thank you."

After my protein bar, I ate what I thought was beef jerky. I'd never had beef jerky, and I was sure after tonight, I wouldn't eat it again.

"You walk around with these packs prepared like this for times when you don't want to be detected?"

"Or when we go hiking," Ros said as he leaned back on his elbows and stared up at the stars.

They had to stop reminding me they weren't all-powerful demons all the time. Their love of life was sobering. They had erected a small fire, and it was actually a pleasant night despite the circumstances. Ros had given me a warm blanket, and I was under it, lying close to the fire.

"When I found out what the Return was," I told them as I followed Ros's example and stared up at the sky, "I for sure thought you may all want to go back." There were so many stars in the sky. "But you would never return."

"But too many want to," Zel said gruffly.

"For revenge?" I asked.

"Who knows?" Ros murmured, and Zel grunted his agreement.

"Can they still fall? If they want? To be like you?"

"No. One time only offer," Ros replied.

"But what if new ones want to do it?"

"New what?" Zel asked me as he checked his backpack.

"Angels."

They both laughed. Like really hard. I felt stupid, and I didn't know why.

"There are no new angels." Ros lay flat on his back and stared upwards. "All that there were, is all that there is."

"But he can create."

"Remember the balance, Star," Ros said softly.

There were no new angels. But there were so many demons. How many angels were there?

"Not enough," Zel answered before I asked. His hooded stare told me more than his words.

"Which is why you'll fight," I said with understanding. "Their numbers can't afford to fall?"

Zel nodded once.

"Shit." I heard a huff of laughter from Ros. "So, the Tree that's a tree," I said as I stuck my tongue out at Zel. "Tell me what to do."

"Can't." Ros now had his eyes closed. "Each time is different."

"Well, you could tell me about some of the other times?"

"No," Zel spoke. "May influence you."

"How?" I asked in exasperation.

"Just could."

I bit my tongue from being snarky as all three of us watched the millions of stars above us. "So, what is it?" I heard them both groan, and I sat up. "C'mon, you cannot lead me over the desert and then not tell me something?"

"The Tree of Life is exactly what its name says," Zel began, and I was about to protest when I realised he was going to tell me more. "You've seen the symbol?" I nodded. "Whichever way you turn it, up or down, the roots are branches, the branches roots. The trunk of the Tree is thick and vast. When you approach the Tree, you have to physically fight to stand against it."

"Why?"

"The power is overwhelming," Ros answered. "It's crippling."

"Nothing lives in it, no birds nest, no squirrels hoard for the winter." Zel stared at the firelight. "For a Tree of Life, there is no *life* within it."

"Who created it?"

"No one knows. Maybe it was always here." Ros rolled onto his side as the firelight cast shadows over his face.

"It wasn't you know?" I pointed upwards.

"No." Zel was quick to answer.

"And it connects heaven to hell?"

"No," Zel answered again. "It connects everything to *everything*."

"And how do the demons who want to, shall we say… ascend? How do they use it? I mean, I'm guessing since I don't see a massive tree reaching into the sky when I'm on a plane, they can't climb up it?"

"You're so literal," Zel scolded. "It's not a giant beanstalk."

"You *enter* the Tree," Ros answered. "You enter it, and it takes you where you need to be."

"Then why would it take them back? Why not just spit them back out?"

"The Tree is not heaven. It is not hell. You go to the Tree to be given a choice."

I knew I was frowning. I knew I was going to get wrinkles from the amount of times I was confused with the things these demons said. "Choice? What choice? Does it judge you? Like purgatory?"

"Purgatory is different, obviously."

"Yeah, obviously." I shook my head at Zel's tone. "I don't think I understand," I admitted.

"You will understand better when you are in front of it," Ros said with a confidence I wasn't feeling.

Zel was watching me. "Go to sleep," he said quietly. "You'll need your rest."

Picking up my blanket and looking over at Ros, who was once again staring at the stars, I ducked into the tent and lay down.

I wasn't scared. Either I had become immune to fear or maybe I trusted these Watchers too much. As I prepared for sleep, I knew one thing that had nothing to do with anything other than my heart...I wished Sam were here.

CHAPTER 23

I FELT IT BEFORE I WAS EVEN OVER THE SAND DUNE. THE AIR throbbed with it, pulsed with the power, and I understood what Ros and Zel meant. I felt it beating down on me, and I wasn't even in front of it yet.

"Fucking hell," I muttered to Ros, who nodded grimly as he hauled my arse over the crest, and I stood staring down at a perfect oasis. There was a pool, shrubbery, greenery, and in the centre, a big, huge gnarly oak tree.

Gingerly we walked down the dune, no running or laughter this time. As we got halfway, the surface we walked over became less sand, more grass-like until we were on firmer footing. I hadn't been scared last night. I was scared shitless now. The Tree was huge. Thick leaves hung on twisted, thick branches. The green on the leaves was almost glossy in appearance.

"I don't see a door," I whispered urgently to Ros. "How do I enter?"

Despite the reverence both demons had for the Tree, Ros snorted out a laugh. "I fucking love you, Star," he told me with a huge grin.

I didn't know what he was laughing for; they told me I needed to enter, but there was nothing *to* enter. The wave of ancient power rolled over me continuously as we approached, and all my thoughts dissipated as I struggled to stay upright. When the three of us were about ten feet from the Tree, the power ebbed to a low thrum.

I tried to take in everything around me, but I quickly

realised that Zel was right: this may be the Tree of Life, but we were the only three living things here.

Four.

He stepped out from the shade of the Tree, and my heart leaped to my throat. Sam's dark hair fell in his eyes, eyes blazing with green energy. He was in his leathers and fighting tunic and had so much weaponry on him he looked like an armoury. Still, he was the most welcome sight as my feet carried me forward, and I flung myself into his arms.

He caught me easily, and his lips devoured me as I kissed him back. Why did I leave him again? I made terrible decisions all the time. Zel was right, I was a liability.

When we broke apart, our foreheads pressed together. "Witch," he growled.

"Demon." I felt the tears spill over, and he brushed them away with his thumbs as he brought his lips to my forehead. Bringing me in close to him, he looked past me to his brothers.

"You disobeyed orders."

Ros blanched, but Zel merely shrugged. "This needs to happen. You were just too blind to see it."

Sam's hand tightened around me, but he didn't answer.

"How does the war fare?" Ros asked.

"Skirmishes, nothing more," Sam answered him as he pushed me away from him and started checking me over. "She isn't hurt?"

"I'm fine," I assured him.

"When this is over and we survive, brother," Zel said, "I owe you a drink."

Ros turned his head away so quickly I was instantly suspicious. "Why?" I asked Zel with narrowed eyes.

"Because you drive me to drink. How he isn't a raging alcoholic is beyond my comprehension," Zel replied dryly.

My burst of laughter was loud, but it felt so good. "Zel, we both know you really do like me," I teased as I looked up at Sam and saw his answering grin.

"I tolerate you," Zel muttered as he shed his pack and stretched his arms.

As Sam said something to him in reply, I felt it, pulsing behind me.

Calling me.

It wanted me to turn.

I swallowed and fought the urge to do what it asked.

It was Ros who noticed I had stilled. "Star?" He took a step forward, and then with a cry, he was on his knees, his hands at the sides of his head. Zel was at his side in an instant, weapons ready.

Sam was propelled forward, away from me, but he spun and, with flaming swords in his hands, he was ready to fight.

"Star!" he called in warning.

Turn.

With my eyes on the three of them, I saw Zel yell out, and he too was on his knees in front of me, his head in his hands as he fought the onslaught of power that flowed from behind me and around me to them.

Sam stood straight. "I will not yield," he said through gritted teeth, and I felt the power flicker.

It was laughing?

Turn.

Sam's eyes met mine, and I reached for him. "Don't. Witch!" he yelled at me as I slowly turned to face the Tree.

"Shit," I cursed as I felt it tether to my midsection and pull. "Don't you hurt him."

The power tugged me forward, and I bit my lip to stop from screaming as I squeezed my eyes shut.

Be easy, child.

This voice was different. I hesitated before I opened my eyes.

There was a woman in front of me. Her hair was long, so long it kissed the grass at her feet. A golden circlet held the white hair from her face. Not white hair, I realised. Blonde. White blonde like mine. An oval face, wide pale green eyes, her skin pale but with a dewy glow.

If she'd had pointed ears, I wouldn't have been surprised; she was the very picture of elven. Or maybe I had watched too many movie adaptations of good fantasy books. It didn't help that she wore a floor-length gown with a scoop neck that clung to her curves, while it showed barely any skin.

You seek knowledge?

"Yes."

Then come.

Fuckity, fuck, fuck. I wanted to look over my shoulder. I wanted to look at Sam one more time, as I had a very bad feeling about this.

But I was here because I knew the Tree would help me. I had been told only the Tree would save me, and I was definitely in need of saving. Wasn't I? The angels wanted to kill me, kill us both.

I walked forward, and when she extended her hand, I took it.

Holy shit, I was inside the Tree.

I spun slowly as I took it in. The grass was still under my

feet. The walls, if they were walls, were wooden. I mean, it was kind of a given, but it was still kind of unexpected. Looking up, I saw there was no ceiling, just darkness. When I turned back around again, there were three paths. One directly in front of me, and two on either side.

"Do I have to choose?" I asked her.

"Yes." I heard the smile in her voice, and I glanced at her.

"Can you help?"

"No."

"Shock." I deliberated. Which one did I pick? I felt no pull to either of them.

She leaned forward to speak to me as though she were telling me a secret. "You need to enter them all."

Oh. I hadn't expected that. It wasn't an either-or option. It was a which-one-first option.

"Do they have an order?" I asked her.

A light chuckle reverberated around the hollow of the Tree. "You must choose."

"Right, of course." *Shit shit shit.* Left to right? Right to left? Middle first? "Ah, fuck it." I walked to the path to the left of middle, and as I was about to step onto the path, I looked back at the woman. "Do I need a weapon?"

"You are the weapon." There was a flash of light, and I was halfway down a path with overhanging roots above me.

"I am the weapon? What the hell does that mean?" I muttered as I ducked under a gnarly tree root. "Roots?" I looked up. "I'm under the Tree? Why am I under the Tree?"

I stopped and thought about it. I then realised I could have been hanging from a tree branch for all the good it would do me. Under it, in it, above it, it made no difference. I started to walk again.

Nothing moved. Nothing stirred. The air was stagnant, and every step I took echoed in the dark.

"But it's not dark," I said to nothing. "I can see." Which is when I realised my hand was holding a lantern. "Where did you come from?" I asked it suspiciously.

I wasn't suited to these kinds of things. I liked to read books with adventures and quests, but me? I was so far from quest-like it wasn't funny. Yet here I was, on a quest. To live? To find answers? What was the question again?

I giggled.

Dammit, I was shit at this. Zel was going to tan my hide.

I felt a small breeze, and I faltered. "Oh Jesus, if you're a minotaur or something equally horrifying, please don't come at me."

When nothing beast-like or otherwise appeared, I resumed walking. The path was long, and I got the distinct impression I was heading down, but the tree roots stayed above me and never got further away, which meant either they were really long deep roots or I had a better imagination than I thought.

And suddenly I wasn't on a path. I was in front of the Waterfall of Solitude in the Land of the Souls, and the whole place was bursting with colour.

"What the..." Walking forward, I took it all in. Tree leaves were green, the water was a warm inviting blue, the rock of the waterfall was grey, and the walkway was loose pebbles of multicoloured stones. Gran's wall was a traditional stone dyke.

When I saw myself swimming in the pool beneath the waterfall, I almost fainted. Cross sat on the rock above the pool, and he was reading a book.

I'm swimming and he's reading. Looking around, I looked for Hound. I spotted him lazing under a tree.

"What's wrong with this picture?" I muttered as I took another step forward and felt my elbow itch.

Please, I begged.

When I looked to my right, Gran stood beside me. Tears poured down my face, and as I reached to hug her, she walked right by me and sat down on the rock beside Cross, her feet trailing into the water.

"How long do you two think you'll be cavorting here?" she asked me. Well, she didn't ask me. She asked swimming me.

"We're not cavorting," the other me laughed as she splashed Gran. "My dear master is teaching me," I told her as I turned onto my back and floated.

Master? Was I drugged?

"Uh-huh, and he's teaching you what? Breaststroke?" Gran snarked as she splashed me back with her feet.

Cross looked up from his book and grinned. "I do like to stroke her breasts."

Eeew. No. Gross.

Gran muttered something about us both being hopeless, and then she was gone. I was getting out of the water, stark naked, and as I straddled Cross's lap, we began making out.

"No! No! Make it stop!" I had my hand over my eyes. "Oh shit, I will never unsee that." I felt the atmosphere change, and I peeked through my fingers. I was back in front of the three paths.

Looking at the woman, I didn't know whether to throw up or not. "What the hell was that?" I demanded.

"Choose." She looked at the paths, and realising I was

going to get no answer from her, I marched straight to the one in front of me.

The flash happened as soon as I stepped foot on the path. The path was overgrown with grass, and there were no tree roots this time hanging over me. There was sky. Stars. Trees lined my path, and I breathed in deep. I knew this place.

Hurrying along the path, I longed for the sight I was sure I would see. And sure enough, after I almost fell many times, the castle was in front of me.

"Thank you." I ran off the path towards the Watchers' home. It felt like I zapped forward, and I was in the hall.

Both of me.

I was sitting on Sam's lap, laughing so hard I was holding onto my sides. My hair was loose and hiding half of my face. Sam's head was thrown back as he roared with laughter. I stayed still for a moment as I watched him. Had I ever seen him that carefree with me? Maybe? Tearing my eyes from him, I looked at me. I'd turned to look at him, and my white blonde hair now concealed all of my face, but I could see Sam. His eyes were filled with love, and as his laughter quietened, he leaned forward and whispered in my ear. I heard a familiar groan and looked to the other occupants of the table. They were all there, even Bara, who they had kept away from me since the pit. Zel was pointedly ignoring Sam and the other me, while Ros was talking animatedly to Chaz and Der. They all looked...relaxed. Easy.

Looking back at Sam, I saw that he was speaking to the other me again. She was nodding, and then the other me slipped off of his lap and held her hand out. Sam spoke to the others, all who just waved him off, and then with his arms around my—her—waist, they turned to leave. Jeans and a loose T-shirt that slipped off my shoulder showed healthy tanned skin. As Sam swept the hair out of my eyes, I saw the long angry scar down my face, from forehead to chin, right through my left eye. My scar rivalled Zel's.

I stepped back in shock.

And I was back in the chamber with the three paths.

"What happened?" I demanded of the woman.

She gave me a serene smile. "Choose."

"If it's sharks, I'm going to kill someone," I muttered as I stepped onto the path.

The flash didn't take me to the middle of the path, like the other times. This time, it took me to the middle of a war zone.

Destruction was everywhere, like when the news reported fighting abroad, and you saw places that had been heavily bombed for days. I didn't recognise where it used to be; all I knew was that it wasn't a place where people were anymore. Tentatively I walked forward, booms sounded around me, and even though I obviously wasn't there, I still ducked when an explosion went off not far from me.

Cars that had burned were strewn everywhere like discarded toys. Shops were gutted and burnt out. Smoke rose from buildings that looked like they would topple over at a gust of wind.

Did someone hit the button? What was this?

I saw him walk around a car that was on its side. Light brown hair, pushed back from his forehead, slight in shoulder, slim, he wore jeans and a black T-shirt. He looked like a normal teenage boy. Except his green eyes glowed with power that a normal teenager didn't have.

With a casualness that made my chest hurt, he looked around and smiled.

He was beautiful.

He was devastation.

He was my son.

Drawing in a shaky breath, I took a step forward towards him.

He yawned. I was one of the best at the fake yawn, and he'd just fake yawned. Why? Turning, I saw them, a handful of Watchers approaching stealthily. Did they know he knew they were there? Darting my eyes over the debris, I saw the next group approaching…angels.

I went to cry out a warning to the Watchers, him, either, when I saw one of the angels signal to the Watchers. They were working together?

What the fuck was happening?

I searched the whole scene, looking for a clue, and then in the shadows, I saw them. Lucifer and Satan. Laughing.

It was not the time for laughing.

My son straightened and stretched his arms. "Is this the best you have?" he called out. "Seriously, Dad, I thought you had more skills."

My heart stopped when Sam stood up from behind a mound of rubble. "Not the best I have," Sam spoke with a coldness I'd only heard from him a few times.

No, no, no, no. He was fighting him? Wildly, I looked between the two of them, struck speechless by the similarities of them.

"Just hurry up, attack me," my son said casually. "I'm hungry and I need to eat."

Had he looked around? He was hardly going to walk into a flipping fast-food restaurant.

"You have already destroyed half of the world with your hunger," Sam snarled.

He had? He had done *this*? Horror was making me sway on my feet.

But my attention kept being pulled to the corner where Satan stood with Lucifer, watching the scene in front of them. Why were they here? Were they also working together with Sam and the others? Peering closer, I tried to see behind them, and like a film was lifted from my eyes, I saw, and I felt true fear as I saw what was really happening.

"No."

CHAPTER 24

I WAS BACK IN THE CHAMBER. I LOOKED AT HER, AND SHE WAS waiting. "I need to get out."

"Choose."

I was anxiety personified. "I need to leave."

"Choose."

I was going to scream soon. "Please, let me out." I took a step towards her, but I was suddenly immobile. "What is happening out there?"

"Choose."

Closing my eyes, I willed myself calm.

"There is nothing *to* choose," I snapped at her. "None of it is real."

"Choose."

As I was unable to move, she was also unmoving. I clenched my teeth together and tried to move. Nothing.

My powers were dormant.

I would not be held here.

I was the weapon.

I *was* the weapon.

I was *the* weapon.

I screamed.

I felt the hold break like shackles dropping from my body, and I burst forward. As I reached her, my hand wrapped around her throat, and I squeezed. "You bitch, you know what I saw."

"Choose."

Throwing her away from me, I paced the chamber. "I have my power. I can get out."

My power winked out like a candle in a storm.

"Damn you to hell!" I yelled at her. "You know what I saw! Let me out!"

"You must choose."

"I choose to leave."

She smiled.

My hands ran into my hair in frustration as my fingers twisted and clutched at the roots, tugging at my scalp. Tears ran freely down my face as I crumbled to the floor.

Soft hands touched mine, gently extracting my hands from my hair. Looking up at her, I noticed our hair was so similar in colour I couldn't tell which was mine and which was hers.

She smiled at me as she helped me to my feet, fingers gently wiping away my tears. Catching and clasping our hands together, she brought them to our chests, between us. We were the same height. Forehead pressed to forehead, she looked at me, and she saw past my pain, past my anger, past all my barriers.

"Choose, Star."

"How?" I asked brokenly. "How can I choose?"

"I saw what you saw," she said softly. "I know what you know."

"It's not real."

"Little Star," she whispered in the stillness between us. "*Everything* is real."

I hiccupped as my tears fell.

"No." I stepped back. "Everything may be real, but that in there"—I gestured to the three paths—"that wasn't true."

She said nothing as she watched and waited. I bit my lip.

"That's not right." I squeezed my eyes shut as I thought about it. "Something in there *was* true," I told her as I opened my eyes.

She smiled, her hands still holding onto me. I stared at her as I thought about it. I tried to see it from every angle. "My gran." I glared at her because that hurt, to show me her, happy in her soul. "Not true."

Her head tilted in consideration.

"Cross." I paused. "Real...but not true."

A small smile.

"Sam. True." I had no hesitation there.

She waited.

My eyes closed as I recalled the devastation. "My son..." I choked on more tears. "Not true."

Open your eyes.

I was back in the war zone. I wasn't looking at my son. Or my soulmate. I was looking in the shadows. As Lucifer and Satan stood together and pulled strings like puppeteers.

Who is the puppet?

"Me."

Choose.

"Samyaza," I answered without looking over at either of them, as father and son faced off in a war zone that would never happen. "Sam is real. Sam is true."

The scene faded, and I was outside of the Tree, but my danger had not ended. I was facing an army of angels, and they held three Watchers captive.

"Let them go," I ordered as I walked forward, noting that I had on the jeans and T-shirt from the path with Sam. I held Gabriel's stare as I approached. Holding my arms out, I didn't break my gaze from his. "As you can see, I am no longer a threat."

Gabriel's eyes flicked down to my stomach, and his eyes widened as I lifted my T-shirt and showed him my flat stomach.

"Star?" Sam's voice was tortured, and I almost wished I was back in the Tree.

"Explain," Gabriel demanded.

"Let them go, and I will."

"You are a witch and a necromancer. A powerful one, I know." Gabriel looked behind me to the Tree, and his brow furrowed. "But you have come out of the Tree and—" He looked at me and then the Tree again. "We will talk."

"Let them go," I repeated softly. "No harm will come to you, just let my family go."

"Your family?" Gabriel looked taken aback for a moment, but when I didn't move and neither of the males in front of him rebuked my claim, his look went from disbelief to… acceptance? "Release them."

His angels didn't hesitate. They stepped back from Sam, Zel and Ros as one, and then I was wrapped around Sam as he held me close, and I felt the other two beside us. Reaching out, I grabbed for Ros, and with a look at Zel, I gave a slight nod.

We winked.

Not far. Just far enough from the Tree and the angels. I knew that they could still see us, and within moments, Zel had erected a tent and we were inside. The whole time, Sam clung to me like he was afraid to let go, and I was okay with that. A table and some chairs appeared, and I knew one day I would have to ask how they could just conjure things without winking to go get them. I had done it in the Void, but the Void was different; this was earth.

"She needs to breathe," Zel told Sam dryly. "She's still human."

I felt the rumble of laughter as Sam squeezed me tight to him once more, and then he stepped back. His hands cupped my face before he kissed me gently, so softly. His kiss told me more than his words ever had.

"You know?" I asked as I felt the tears well.

"As soon as you crossed the barrier, the enchantment fell away," Ros explained. "We saw. We just didn't know if we should believe."

"Did Gabriel see?" I asked them, but I kept my eyes locked on Sam as he stared down at me.

"No, they came later." Zel's lip was curled with disgust.

"You got caught?" I finally looked away from Sam and turned to the other two. "Seriously? I'm in there risking my sanity, and you can't even evade the angels?" I teased.

"You were gone for some days, and some of us refused to move from our position." Zel's look to Sam was pointed.

A large hand slipped over my abdomen, and Sam noticed my flinch as his hand trailed smoothly over my stomach, pulling me tight into his body. My back to his chest, I felt a little bit more secure and so incredibly safe with him.

"Tell us," Ros asked me as he sat on the ground, ignoring the chairs. "It will help."

"I've been used." I took a deep breath. It still hurt so much as I took a seat at the table. "I don't know how they fooled everyone."

"They?" Zel and Ros exchanged a look, and I turned to look up at Sam, who was also frowning.

"Lucifer and Satan," I explained. "Who did you think it was?" I asked them when I saw their surprise.

"Me." Cross was sitting in one of the chairs, and he looked pissed.

"Why would it be you?" I looked at the other three in confusion. "Cross is my friend." I had a very vivid flashback to straddling him naked, and I turned my head away quickly as heat flamed my cheeks.

"I don't enjoy accusations, especially ones not spoken. I don't appreciate bumbling demons breaking into my home and stealing, and I most certainly do not appreciate that rotten piece of wood conjuring me into visions that involve naked disciples straddling me and shoving their tongue down my throat." He looked at me and then smiled that sly smile of his. "Well, I may have appreciated a little part of it."

"What?" Sam stared right at me, face like thunder.

"Okay, he makes it sound so much worse than it was," I protested. "It wasn't even me, it was like a mirror of me."

"Definitely felt like you," Cross said primly. "Tasted like you."

"Tasted like..." Sam looked murderous as he glared at Cross, and I was half off my seat to stop doomsday, or whatever it would be if Death died, when Zel cleared his throat.

"Can we please stay on topic?"

Watching the two dark-haired males across from me, I cautiously sat back down. "I was shown three paths. Each one had a different scenario. In one was me, Gran"—my voice hitched—"and Cross at the Land of the Souls. We were at the Waterfall of Solitude."

"You got hot and heavy with him in front of your grandmother?" Ros looked appalled. "That is totally fucked up, even for you."

"No! Gran left us alone, so then I got out of the water, and we..." I saw Sam's knuckles whiten, and I widened my eyes at Ros to get him to shut up. "It wasn't real. I was watching it happen. I was totally grossed out, and when I reacted that way, I was back at the chamber to pick the next path."

"Grossed out?" Sam looked at Cross with a shit-eating grin.

"Can you both just put your dicks away?" I snapped. The fact that both of them looked down to see if they were exposed made me want to hit them. "It's a saying, okay?"

"Would it be entirely possible for you to *say* what happened within the Tree?" Zel's voice was drier than the desert outside.

"The next path I went down, we were in the ether, all of us. Well, not Cross, but anyway, we were all at dinner, and we were laughing, and it was nice." I recalled the laughter, the easiness. "It was good."

"What made you react to leave?" Zel asked me.

"What?" I shifted in my chair, remembering the horrific scar on my face.

"You were grossed out with Death, so you were taken off that path. You say you were happy with us, so what made you leave?"

"I knew I had to come back to you," I lied. Four pairs of eyes stared at me, and not one of them believed me, I could tell.

"And in the third?" Sam asked me, breaking the silence.

"War." I looked around and then back at Ros. "Got a drink for your favourite necromancer?"

Cross handed me a glass of wine, and I smiled at him as I reached for it. Zel took it out of his hand and instead produced a bottle of whisky as Ros placed four glasses down. Cross sipped the wine he had produced for me instead.

"Yup, that'll do it." I waited until I had a shot poured in mine, and downed it. The burn was everywhere. I wasn't really a shot girl, but I could neck Macallan like it was cheap tequila when it mattered as if I were a first-year student during freshers week.

"It was utter devastation," I told them. "Buildings were rubble, cars blown up or burnt out, complete emptiness, except for…" I couldn't go on.

"For?" Sam's voice was quiet.

"Him." I felt a tear slip over and nodded my thanks when Ros poured me more whisky. "He was…" My eyes closed. "Beautiful." I downed my whisky. "And so cold. So empty and cold."

"The Nephilim are like that," Sam told me as he reached for me.

"But he was *mine*, he was *ours*. We're not cold. We're *not* empty," I protested wildly, and I saw his sympathy. Rubbing my hands over my face, I stood abruptly from my chair. "You were going to attack him, you and the angels working together."

Someone scoffed, and I ignored them as I paced. "He knew you were there, called you out. Called you Dad." My breath caught as I stilled and stared at the ground. My feet were bare. How odd that I would be in jeans and a T-shirt with no shoes.

"Star?" Zel prompted.

"And then I saw them. In the shadows, laughing. Watching." My voice was a low whisper. "Why would they be laughing? Why were they even there? And I saw it, behind them, the movement." My head was back in the war zone, seeing the hundreds of demons behind the two princes. Climbing.

Climbing over a fallen Tree.

"I'm a distraction," I said as I looked up at Sam. "The pregnancy, the child, it was all a lie. I was never pregnant; he was never real. It's all an elaborate distraction."

I gestured to the opening of the tent where Gabriel now stood. "This war, this battle against each other, is for nothing. I am not pregnant. I never was."

"How?" Ros asked in confusion. "We all saw it."

"One moment," Cross spoke for the first time in a while. He winked out of there, and when he came back, he had Naomie. Zel's face turned stony, but she took it in her stride. "Star was not pregnant, and the Tree showed her and us the truth. How were we fooled?" he asked her. "How was *I* fooled?" His tone was sharp, and I was kind of pleased Cross was pissed.

"Nothing?" Naomie asked me as she crossed the floor to me and placed her hand on my stomach. Her eyes closed, and her lips moved as she mumbled words I didn't know. Stepping back, her eyes were full of sorrow. "I'm so sorry that I didn't see it, Star." She turned to them all. "It's true, her womb is empty."

The words were like physical blows, but I pushed it all down. My pain I would deal with later. My loss...I had lost nothing, I reminded myself. Drawing in a deep breath, I straightened.

"I felt pregnant." I saw them all look at me, some with pity, but I didn't want pity. "Why would I feel that?"

"The vitamins." Zel's voice was tight with anger. "I made you take a prenatal vitamin every day."

Naomie was nodding. "That could be it," she agreed. "They could have enhanced your body, as if it was prepping you for gestation."

"And I made you drink your daily tonic when you were with me," Cross said bitterly. "Which was basically a syrup of what Zel gave you in tablet form."

"And my bump?" I demanded.

"Illusion." Sam stood angrily, kicking his chair back. "While we have been running around fighting him"—his head jerked to Gabriel—"the princes have been preparing for the Return, unhindered."

"It was all a lie." My voice was flat. Hollow.

"It's a very elaborate lie," Gabriel spoke for the first time. "The power to fool us all? Quite something." His stare was hard and unyielding as he looked at Cross. "Where would Satan know to get that power?"

"If you're looking at me for an answer, I can try to assist you." Cross reached forward and picked up the glass of wine, taking a sip. "If you're looking at me in accusation, I suggest you look away before I take your eyes."

"How do we know it wasn't you?" I accused Gabriel. "You hate the Watchers. You've shown no interest in anything on this earth. How do we know you're happy up there in your ivory tower?"

Gabriel laughed so loudly it jarred my nerves. "Fool." He looked at us all. "Well, now that the threat to his creation is over, we are no longer needed."

"The Tree falls," I told him. "When I went back to the scene on the path a second time, to see what I had seen, while Satan and Lucifer pull my strings and make me dance to their tune, the demons are climbing over a fallen tree." Gabriel's jaw clenched as he looked at me. There was no love lost between us. He may have felt a smidgen of regret over what Michael had done to my gran, but that was long gone. He didn't like me, and I sure as shit didn't like him. "In the scene, in the war zone, you fight beside each other." I turned to look at Sam. "The scene shows me what was real and what is a lie. My son? Not true. The Return? True. The Watchers and angels working together against a common enemy, also true."

Zel looked like he wanted to gag me.

"The threat to the world is still there," I told them all tiredly as I sank back down into the seat. "The threat just isn't me. It was never me."

There was silence in the tent, and I eyed the whisky bottle. Could I just take it, find a bed, and drink myself into oblivion? Would anyone notice?

Sam lifted me out of my seat and onto his lap, and I sighed as I curled into him, my face burrowing into his neck, breathing him in. Letting him hold me as I pushed away my grief. I didn't listen as they spoke, I didn't hear what they said, I simply closed it all off and hung onto my demon.

When he lifted me later and laid me down on a bed, climbing in behind me, I didn't protest. I didn't tell him he should be with the angels, planning, strategising. I didn't tell him he should be somewhere where it mattered. I clung to his arm as he spooned me, and I cried.

I cried for what I lost. For what I never had. For the promise of something that I could never have.

I cried for the son who would never be mine.

I cried for the loss of a possibility that I had believed so much in. Eventually, I cried myself to sleep.

In the morning when I woke up, I was alone, the tent empty. My head was clear. My heart was full of rage.

I was a weapon, and we were at war. I was going to kill the princes of hell, or I'd die trying. They'd have to burn my soul in the hellfire, because I would never stop until they were all dead.

I was their puppet no more.

CHAPTER 25

WHEN I CAME OUT OF MY TENT, I SAW ROS FIRST. HE WAS sitting halfway up a sand dune, watching the scene below him. Our tent was at the periphery of a camp, which seemed to have sprung up overnight, but knowing how effective these males were at conjuring, I reckoned it went from sand to war camp in about three minutes.

In bare feet, jeans and a T-shirt, I made my way up to meet Ros and then plopped down beside him.

"Hey," I greeted.

"Hey, Starlight." He gave me a smile, and the pang at the familiar term didn't hurt as much.

"My gran called me that. Dad did too when I was little, but as I got older, it was just Star. Or, you know, the reason he was getting grey hair." My head dropped naturally onto Ros's shoulder. "But Gran always called me Starlight."

"It bothers you when I call you it?" he asked me tentatively.

"At first," I admitted. "Because it reminds me that I won't hear her call me it again." I watched the angels move through the tents, and I wondered how they could cope with the heat and not suffocate under all that armour.

"I won't call you it again."

"Please, do." My voice was barely a whisper. "She's gone, but you're here, and I like the nickname; it reminds me of her."

"She isn't gone," Ros answered softly. "Not really. Yes, her soul has gone, but her memory remains. As long as she is in your memory, she lives."

I leaned off of him and looked up at the blond demon with the Viking hairstyle as he stared down at the camp. "I'm immortal. Or I will be."

Ros glanced at me, and he smiled. "Well, then she will always be here with you."

"I'm going to cry again," I warned him, and he chuckled.

"You're allowed." He handed me a water flask. "General caught me with the whisky. We're on water today."

"Spoilsport." I took a long drink and handed it back to him. "There's more than water in that flask, Ros."

"Yup."

"He's going to scold."

"Meh."

I laid my head back on his shoulder. "What is it?" I asked him as we both watched angels prepare for war. "You're my jovial, happy, wonderful Amaros. Why are you so sad?"

"I know enchantments," he said bitterly. "I can get through any ward, any spell, so why the fuck didn't I see it?"

"Because you believed it." I tilted my head back to look up at the sky. "Your faith was stronger than what your head was telling you."

"I believed in something that wasn't there." Ros spoke in disgust.

"Bit like religion."

"There *is* something there," Ros reminded me.

"Sure." I kept my eyes on the clouds. "But does he care?"

"A conversation for another day, little witch."

He was probably right. "Where's my hellhound?" I asked suddenly.

Ros chuckled and I knew I had to be worried. "What have you let him do?"

"Morax and the hellhounds have been terrorising hell." Ros nudged me to sit up. "The reapers have shown no mercy as they hunt, but I would warn you, between me and you, I think your Hound is pissed."

"I did ditch him," I said worriedly.

"Mm-hmm."

"You practically kidnapped me. Actually, you *did* kidnap me."

Ros was grinning as he took a swig from his flask. "You were my accomplice."

"Can I be an accomplice to my own kidnapping?" I asked as I took a drink off him.

"Who cares?" He slung his arm over my shoulder. "We okay, little witch?"

"Course we are," I said as I leaned against him again. "We were all tricked. We'll get the fuckers."

We sat for a while, and even though I saw Sam look up at us a few times, he didn't come for us, and we didn't go to him. Ros and I needed this. Or maybe I needed it, and Ros just didn't want to have to do any of the chores below.

Der joined us some time later and wordlessly held his hand out for the flask, and we simply sat on the dune, watching the camp, drinking from Ros's self-refilling flask.

"Remember the night you lot made fun of me for scolding Sam for calling my lady parts names? And you all then decided to suggest alternative slang?" I asked them both. I didn't need to look at them to know they were both grinning. "Could you imagine if we knew then that this shit would happen, should you just have dropped me in the sea and walked away from me then?"

"Never," Der growled as he pushed my arm in what I hope

he thought was a playful swat but felt like a whack from a baseball bat.

"I think you should have dropped me," I said quietly.

"I think you're feeling sorry for yourself," Ros chided. He stood. "Come on, little witch, let's go see what the bossman's planning."

Der sighed as he rose too. "Azazel and Gabriel are going to kill each other," he confided to Ros. "Chaz has already come between them three times."

"Chaz is here?" I asked them both as I looked between them.

"He is." Der held onto me as we made our way down the dune. "Pen and he are strengthening the Tree wards."

"Why can't the Tree strengthen itself?" I asked sourly.

"I'm sure it is," Ros snorted as we reached the bottom. "Fucking thing."

My hand caught Ros's. "Satan is who the Tree will save me from?" I asked him quietly. "Is that right?"

It didn't feel right.

Before Ros could answer, we heard hurried movement, and we both looked towards Gabriel as he marched towards us as his fellow angels scrambled out of his way. "Oh, so you've decided to rejoin the war," he snarled at the two Watchers. "Finished drinking?"

"We were discussing things," Ros answered with derision.

"Like what? Incompetence? Failure? A complete disregard for authority?"

"Dick." They all looked at me, Gabriel with narrowed eyes, Ros with glee, and Der in warning.

"What did you call me?" Gabriel asked me in a low voice.

Fuck. "I didn't call you anything."

"I heard you—"

"We were discussing dicks." Was there a hole I could be swallowed up in? "You know, penises."

"Penises?"

I nodded. "Yup. Dicks, they come in all shapes and sizes. Big dicks, small dicks, thick dicks, all sorts. But I'm sure you know that."

I wished I had a camera because I thought he was going to implode.

"You were up there, all morning, talking dicks?" The scorn in his voice would have scared me shitless a few months ago, but now, well, now he just pissed me off.

"Yup."

"Dicks."

"Meatpoles," Ros added, and I pressed my lips together to stop the laughter from escaping.

"Cocks," Der suggested. "If you prefer cocks?"

Gabriel looked at all three of us, and I was pretty sure I was about to get detention. He started to speak, but Ros cut him off.

"Purple-headed yogurt slinger." He was completely straight-faced.

Der was shaking with laughter beside me, and I knew I was about to lose it completely.

Gabriel's eyes were on me, and he was furious. He knew we were mocking him, but he couldn't do anything about it. His eyes scanned over me with contempt. "Are you done?" he asked me quietly.

"Womb ferret," I blurted.

Ros burst into laughter as did Der, and Gabriel turned and

stormed away as the three of us laughed hysterically in the middle of the camp that was preparing for war.

I HAD SEEN little of Sam all day, my time spent with Cross as he resumed his training of my poor skills. He had arrived at the camp not long after our encounter with Gabriel and taken me into a tent, away from prying eyes.

Cross didn't like to be involved. Well, that wasn't entirely true. He didn't like to be seen to be taking sides.

He was Death.

Impartiality was his thing.

"You should not provoke the angel," he had told me as he changed my clothes to soft yoga pants and a clean, fresh T-shirt.

"He makes it so easy."

"You should rise above it," he reprimanded me. "He is on your side."

I cast a look over at my friend. "He really isn't."

Cross pursed his lips together. "In this, he is on your side," he conceded.

"Why are you helping?" I asked him as he got himself ready to spar. "I'm not the threat they thought I was."

"You still plan to go to battle; therefore, you must still know how to defend yourself."

We spent several hours training. In the desert, in a tent with no air-conditioning. There was a lot to be said for hell.

I was back in our tent, wondering if I could wink somewhere for a shower before anyone noticed, when Sam ducked through the tent flap.

"You're here," he said with a warm smile.

"I am." His hair was pushed back, his jaw had a light scruff across it, his tunic was dusty from the desert, and his leather trousers looked unbearably suffocating. "You look tired," I said as I approached him.

"I feel filthy," he replied as he pulled his tunic off, revealing his broad chest, his tattoos catching my attention as normal and his wonderfully lickable abs. "You're drooling, witch."

"I can't help it, demon."

Firm hands pulled me into his body. "What do you want?" he asked as he nipped my bottom lip.

"Honestly?" I asked, and he nodded. "A shower."

Sam's rumble of laughter caused me to smile as he hugged me tight and winked us to a very opulent bathroom. Turning in his arms, I saw the open double shower, the deep sunken bathtub, the twin basins.

"Where are we?" I asked as I began pulling off my T-shirt.

"Does it matter?" he asked as he watched me.

"Nope, not in the slightest," I admitted, kicking my yoga pants off and crossing to the open shower and staring at it in confusion as I considered how to switch it on. After a few moments' perusal, I found the switch and then the corresponding settings for the showerhead. Stripping off my underwear, I stepped under the water.

"Oh, that's good," I moaned in appreciation as the first jets hit me. The water flowed over me as I tipped my head back and wet my long hair. Opening my eyes, I saw him staring at me as he leaned naked against one of the sink basins, his ankles crossed, his heavy length lay soft along his thigh, tight abs, wide pecs, muscled forearms crossed against his chest as his eyes ran over me. He had to belong to hell, I decided; there was no way his sinful good looks belonged above with the likes of Gabriel. Licking my lips when I saw him stir, I quickly turned, giving him my back as I looked for shampoo.

I didn't know why I was suddenly nervous. I'd been naked in front of him so many times. He had touched, licked, and kissed every part of my body. With a shaky hand, I reached for a shampoo bottle. It was a make I didn't know, in a language I couldn't read. Sniffing it, I decided it was better than nothing and squirted some in my hand. Lathering my hair, my breath caught when firm, deft fingers began to massage my scalp, and my hands dropped to my sides.

Sam worked the shampoo through the lengths of my hair and, tugging slightly, tilted my head back as he used the shower to rinse it away. Pressing into him, I felt him thicken against me.

"I want to fuck you," he said quietly as he kissed the back of my neck and trailed light kisses along my shoulder. "Do you want that?"

"Yes." I was a throaty mess.

"Here? In the shower?"

"Yes," I moaned as his fingers dipped between my legs.

"And then in the bed?"

"Everywhere." I breathed out as a finger slid inside me and his thumb teased my nub, and his finger slowly moving inside me curled towards that secret spot. "Oh shit," I gasped as I lifted onto my tiptoes.

"Spread your legs." I did as I was told. "Wider."

Again I did as he commanded and lost my balance, my hands slapping against the wall tiles as I caught myself from falling.

Sam withdrew his hand from between my legs, and taking my wet hair, he wrapped it around his fist, tugging me backwards. "Keep them spread," he told me gruffly as his other hand reached between us. I felt him guiding himself to my entrance, and there he paused.

"How much do you want it?"

"Sam." My voice was needy and pleading. I almost didn't recognise it.

"Tell me, witch, how much do you want my dick inside you?"

"Give it to me." I tried to turn my head to look at him, but his hand squeezed my hip in warning as his other hand tightened in my hair, forcing my head to stay straight.

"You kissed Cross."

A hard wet slap stung across my butt cheek, and I yelped in surprise.

"You straddled him, naked." Another slap against the other cheek, and I cried out as my bum smarted.

"It wasn't really me!" I protested. Another slap, and I jerked forward, but Sam followed.

"It is a version of you, and that version of you wants to fuck Cross."

"No! It wasn't real!"

Another slap.

"Ow!" I yelled. "It may be another me, or another version of me, but *this* me is the one who matters, and I want you. Only you." I cried out when I got another smack, and then I screamed in pleasure as he filled me in a single thrust. "Shit," I hissed as my body struggled to take him all at once.

"You're mine." His low growl at my ear was in complete contrast to the deep steady strokes he was giving me. "You belong to me."

"I know." Gone were the days of me not being a possession. Here in some stranger's bathroom, getting fucked in their shower by my demon, I was happy to accept how possessive he was.

Teeth sank into my shoulder, his tongue quickly soothing the sharp sting of his bite. "You feel so fucking good," he groaned as his hips picked up pace.

My hands were slipping on the wall with the force of him driving into me. The water was running in my eyes and into my mouth, making it so hard to breathe without choking.

Sam powered into me from behind, and I stumbled forward, my breasts flattening against the tile, my head jerking to the side as he let go of my hair, and his hand rested against the back of my neck, pressing me into the wall, holding me there. The whole time, his rhythm didn't slow. Opening my eyes, I looked at him, and his smirk as he fucked me made me only want more.

Sam's hand slipped between me and the wall, and he started to circle my nub. Blindly I reached for him, bringing his mouth to mine as I screamed my release into his mouth, his tongue sinking in, stroking against mine as he caught my moans of pleasure. He gave a few more deep strokes before his hips jerked erratically, and he finally stilled within me, our heavy breathing loud over the sound of the running water.

"Fuck," I hissed as he withdrew and turned me to face him. He kissed me deeply as his hands tangled in my wet hair.

"I love you," he whispered against my lips. "Nobody else touches what's mine."

"I know." I kissed him long and slow. "I'm yours, only yours."

"And I'm yours."

We kissed again and then washed each other, our heated

lovemaking turning into playful kisses and gentle caresses. Later, we curled up in each other in a big bed after a lot more lovemaking and a few more showers.

Sleepily, I lay in Sam's arms, drifting off to sleep, when he nudged me gently.

"Star?"

"Hmm?"

"Who the fuck says womb ferret?"

I fell asleep smiling.

CHAPTER 26

DESPITE PREPARING FOR WAR, AND BOTH ANGELS AND Watchers scouring earth and hell for Satan and Lucifer, I was in a better place than I had been. I wouldn't say I was over what they had done to me, because it was cruel, malicious and made me want to bathe in their blood as I tossed their souls in hellfire, but I had accepted that I had never been pregnant.

I had been scared for the entirety of my phantom pregnancy—that's what Chaz was calling it, a phantom pregnancy. Between the illusion, the vitamins Zel gave me, and whatever I drank with Cross, my body had tricked itself into believing the lie that Satan and Lucifer had placed there.

I'd heard of a phantom pregnancy in dogs. And every time Chaz referred to it, I had the insane urge to bark at him. Even I was questioning my sanity, but at this point, I decided this was my weird way of working through things until I fully accepted that I had lost nothing except an idea.

Which hurt like hell.

Loss was loss, wasn't it? No one person or demon in this world or the next should be able to tell you how to cope with grief. Grief was personal, and I was grieving.

My sweet, dear Chaz was also avoiding me a lot. And I needed to get that shit sorted. Which is where I was heading to this morning when all my plans went sideways, because sitting in the middle of the camp, head high, eyes narrowed on me was the one demon *I* had been avoiding.

Hound.

I saw Zel nearby, sitting alone at one of the table benches, eating from a bowl, and I wondered which demon was my better option.

"He's already seen you," Zel said without looking at me.

Shit. Ruled out Zel. Squaring my shoulders, I approached Hound. "Hi."

Hound morphed and I was in the Void. My Void.

"Pissed?" I guessed.

"I fail to understand why you keep thinking I do not matter."

My bravado disintegrated in a heartbeat. "No! Of course you matter!" I cried as I stepped forward.

"Then why am I constantly left behind, why am I left behind and then you shield yourself from me?"

"It's not from you, it's from everyone else." We stared at each other in the Void, and I felt shitty. "And they keep popping up and coming for me; it's not like I ask!" Which was true. Cross appeared; zap, I was in his domain. Ros appeared; zap, I was in the desert.

"They may come for you, but you can *call* for me."

"But you could be hurt," I told him as I turned away from him.

He turned me back to face him, his brow furrowed. "You protect me?"

Did I? Yes, I tried to. "I don't want you getting hurt."

"I am immortal. Truly immortal. There is no end for me, Star. Just this."

"What if it isn't though, what if they lied?"

"Who?" Hound asked me in confusion.

"Whoever told you this. It could be another illusion, for you to think you're infallible."

"I am immortal," Hound told me gently. "Doesn't mean I

cannot get hurt, but I am very, *very* good at being a hellhound."

"They could cut you into pieces and torture you daily!" I protested. "Eternal pain!"

He started to laugh. "Little witch," he said fondly. "Stop being so…silly. I am with you, really with you. Stop leaving me behind. We fight this war, together. We serve Death, together. Understand?"

"Well, we don't serve Death, do we?" I hedged as I gave him a small smile.

"We carry out some work for him now and again," Hound offered.

Throwing my arms around him, I hugged him tightly. "I'm sorry."

"I know," he grumbled as he extracted himself from me.

"Did we not just discuss you and nakedness with demons who are not me?" Sam grumped from behind me.

"I'm not naked!" I protested.

Sam stormed towards me and looked at Hound. "Find the fucker yet?"

"No." Hound didn't seem to care that he was still naked, and I had never been distracted by Hound being naked. The others, I had accidentally drooled over, but Hound, I never looked down. He morphed into his humanoid form to protect me or shout at me or train me or talk to Sam. His sexuality was…irrelevant.

"You've been looking for Satan?" I asked him, not knowing why I was surprised.

"Of course," he answered before he looked at Sam and continued talking. "I think I know how the spell was cast, but I need Amaros."

Sam nodded and then Ros was there with Pen.

"What did you find?" Ros asked immediately as he joined us.

"We thought the pregnancy was shielded by Araqiel," Hound began, and I felt Sam's hand slip into mine, giving it a gentle squeeze. "But if there was no pregnancy, there was nothing to shield." Hound looked at me briefly. "When Cross rid Star of Araqiel's soul, nothing of his soul was left behind."

Ros drew his breath in through his teeth as he looked at me. "Shit."

Sam was crushing my hand.

"What's happening? Why are my bones being shattered?" I asked them as I stood waiting for an explanation.

"Should we go?" Pen asked quietly.

"Go?" I looked at them all, and they were all looking at me with intense sadness. "Why are you all so sad, what's happening?"

"We can't let anyone know," Ros suddenly said. He looked at Sam, his eyes wild. "Gabriel finds out, it's a game changer."

"Sam!" I asked desperately as I wrenched my hand free.

"You *were* pregnant." Sam walked away from me before stopping and looking down at the ground. "You were actually pregnant. Araqiel shielded it, and his soul fused to yours, knowing when he was discovered, he would lose his soul forever."

"Actually pregnant?" I asked as I looked at them all. Only Hound would look at me.

"When Cross expelled him from your body, he said he could hear two heartbeats," Hound said quietly. "I know illusion, but to fool Death, it's a skill I have never managed. It's annoyed me ever since you learned of the illusion, that he heard both."

"When did I lose my son?" I asked in a hoarse whisper.

Hound cleared his throat. "I think, and I may be wrong, but I think when Satan killed Mammon, he may have cast the spell then."

But the world was spinning. Hands steadied me as I screamed internally.

Cross was in front of me, and my power lashed out at him. "You! You offered him a Watcher's soul," I screamed as I advanced upon Death, who stood unmoving. "You gave him my baby!"

And Cross, who was always calm and collected, was suddenly the male who had fought Sam before. A long black scythe was in his hand, his shoulders squared, and his eyes burned with blue fire.

"You will control her, Morax, or I will take her now."

Hound stood in front of me, facing Cross. "She is emotional. She just learned she was pregnant and she lost her child." Hound's hands were raised, and he looked to be holding Cross back. "Please, she is distraught. She needs to listen."

"Explain," Cross ordered sharply. As he listened to what the others had just realised and as I now knew what they had been saying, I watched Cross closely as his eyes became brighter with the burning blue flames that were the same as my power. When Hound was finished, Cross was looking right at me.

"I offered Mammon the soul of a *Watcher*." His voice was clinical. Cold. Detached. "Your child was never a Watcher. It was half human. I did not *feed* your child to a prince of hell."

The derision with which he spoke to me broke my fury. "I kept you, I fed your soul, I fed that body you still have because I teach you how to train it." Death cast a disdainful eye over us all. "You think I would do this?" he asked me.

"I don't know." I knew I was crying again. "How did it happen if not for trickery?"

"There are four princes of hell that can answer that question. I suggest you find them. *All* of them." Cross was gone.

We stayed in silence for a long moment before Ros let out a breath. "Fucking hell, Star, you can't accuse Death like that!" he protested. "I think I may have shit myself."

"Did you think him innocent?" I asked them all, but I looked at Sam. Sam, whose head had not yet risen.

"When Satan killed Mammon, was there blood?" Pen asked me as he paced.

"He ripped his head off his body like it was tissue paper."

"How many bites of his heart did he take?" Ros asked as he and Pen shared a look.

"Three." I would never unsee Satan tearing into the black heart of Mammon.

"The second bite was for the child, the third to cast the illusion." Pen suddenly yelled out his frustration. "Why did we not see it? Why have we been so blind?"

"It would need blood to keep the truth hidden," Ros said as he too paced, his face screwed up in concentration. "The bite of the heart would not be enough."

"He kissed me." I remembered. "He forced me to kiss him, and I bit him. I bit his lip, and it bled."

Pen and Ros both stilled. "After he had eaten the heart?" Ros asked me, and I nodded, and I saw them both looking at me, white-faced. "Did I do this?" I asked them. "Is it my fault?"

"No, Star, no." Pen was in front of me, consoling me. "He tricked you. He needed to get his blood into you. He was always clever. Forcing a kiss, he knew you'd bite." Pen tried for humour. "Literally. He used his blood, Mammon's blood and blood magic, ancient forbidden magic. The spell requires the heart of a prince of hell and the blood of another. It is the only way that the child could still be removed from the womb."

"Sam." It was Ros who spoke. "Samyaza, you cannot react. If Gabriel finds out, she's still in danger."

Pen's finger tilted my chin towards him. "Star, listen to me. I know it's hard, I know, I'm so sorry, but you cannot let them know it was real. You cannot. Gabriel will kill you."

"Because I can get pregnant by a Watcher," I said dully.

"Yes," Pen confirmed as he hugged me tightly.

"But I've seen the destruction my son causes," I told him as I stepped back. "I know what I would bring into this world." Pushing my hair back, I looked at them all. "I won't do it." It was clear they didn't believe me. "Sam?"

Finally, his head lifted, and he looked at me, and my heart stuttered as I took in his rage.

"Get Zel," I said quickly. "Sam." I took a step forward. My Void lit up to a brilliant white. "Sam?"

"Samyaza!" Azazel strode through my Void, his blue eyes pulsing with their own power. I knew Zel had no fucking idea what was happening, but he was reacting to his General in a fury. "General!" he snapped. "You're needed at camp, General. The Guard are getting restless."

Sam cocked his head as he listened, but his eyes were on me.

Hound had morphed back into hellhound form, and he and the two others surrounded me. Protecting me.

"Samyaza," Zel's voice was low. "To the ether, and then we will return." Sam took a step forward, towards me, but Zel's hand on his arm stopped him. "You may hurt her. To the ether first. Then the Guard. Your duty calls."

Confused, I watched as Sam winked away, and Zel looked my way once before he was gone too.

"What the fuck just happened?" I demanded.

IN MY TENT, I sat on my bed, my knees drawn up in front of me, my chin resting on top of them. Hound sat ramrod straight, smack bang in front of the entrance. The tent had been warded so many times I was surprised I was still able to sit within it.

The only way anything was getting in was through Hound. And no angel or demon was getting through Hound.

"He is grieving," I told Hound for the hundredth time since we returned to the desert and to the camp near the Tree. "When Satan spoke to me in Mammon's rooms, he told me, he actually told me I was nothing but a puppet."

He is what you call, a wanker.

I truly appreciated the effort from Hound, but my heart still hurt. Satan had killed my son. All my grief that I had felt silly for feeling had been real. Well, that wasn't right, my grief had been real even when my child was merely an illusion. Now I knew it hadn't been, it had been real once, and I no longer knew what was real and what wasn't.

"Why did he leave?"

The General had been strong for you, but it is hard to be strong all the time.

"He went to grieve."

Yes. I think they thought it best if you did not witness it.

"He witnessed mine," I objected slightly.

He loves you.

"Are you questioning my love for Sam?" I asked in surprise.

You do seem to leave him as easily as you leave me.

Wow.

"Wow."

Hound turned to fix me with a deep red eye. *I will never lie to you.*

"Sometimes you don't always need to be so honest."

We sat in silence for a while longer before I had to ask. "How pissed off is Cross?"

I doubt he will return.

"Seriously?" I was on my feet. "I was angry."

You were. As is he.

"I've fucked up with Cross?" I couldn't believe it, then I thought of what I accused him of. I would leave me too.

You have eternity to work out your differences.

"If Gabriel doesn't kill me first."

Keep it down. He glared at me again, and I got back on my bed to mope.

"When I confronted the angels, and Lucifer and Satan turned up, was that real?"

Yes, you are not insane.

"And in the pit?"

I was not there, but I do not doubt you.

"They were enhancing the illusion," I whispered. "They were playing me."

Hound turned completely to look at me. *Yes, I see it now.*

"How do I kill them?" I asked him. "You said before, we could kill them all. Tell me how."

The Tree.

"What?"

The Tree is the answer.

"How?"

What were you shown? Tell me all three, in detail.

Quickly I rattled through the three scenes, then I ran through them again as Hound asked me every question under the sun. When I was done, he sat back and studied me.

"I'm not felling the Tree of Life," I warned him as I waited for his thoughts.

Too easy. And it upsets the Balance.

My eyes were saucers as I stared at the hellhound.

They watched?

"Yes."

The Tree and the demons for the Return were behind them?

"Yes! I told you this."

Hound looked at me, and we reached the same conclusion.

"They aren't interested in the Return?" I asked as I jumped to my feet. "I mean, Satan told me he wasn't, he said he didn't care, he's only interested in taking over hell."

I headed to the tent entrance before I turned back and looked at Hound. "Am I right? This time?"

Hound nodded, but I could feel his hesitance.

I think so, but there is one thing for certain. There is another prince of hell in play.

CHAPTER 27

THE TWO OF US WALKED THROUGH THE CAMP QUICKLY. I DIDN'T really have any interaction with the angels because they were, after all, angels. Which freaked me out. I had always accepted the demons and hell thing. I'd even kissed Death, but the idea of upstairs, nope. Not happening. Blinding Michael and stabbing him in the neck made me give them a wide berth now that they were grounded.

The angels also had no interest in me. They simply no longer cared about me because I was no longer carrying the end of days in my womb. I was no longer carrying anything in my womb.

I found Chaz first. He was at the Tree. Or as close to the Tree as you could be without the Tree breaking you down.

"I need to talk to you all," I told him as he stood and looked between me and Hound. Chaz gave a simple nod and went to move away when I grabbed his arm. "Actually, you need to talk to me, now."

"Star, I..."

"You know damn well you're avoiding me, Chazaquel. I thought we were past this bullshit?"

A smile teased at his mouth before he simply embraced me. Chaz gave good hugs, and I took the hug for what it was, an apology from a friend.

"I'm sorry," he whispered softly in my ear. "That I didn't come for you like Zel did. I'm sorry that I thought you would ever bring destruction to this world. You are good, Star, and I doubted."

Drawing back, I looked up at him, and then rising up, I kissed him on the cheek. "Everyone doubts everyone at some time. It's what makes us human." His eyes widened fractionally, and then he beamed at me.

We picked Pen up in a discussion with Der about something to do with tridents. I am sure there was more to it than that, and it most definitely didn't involve the sea since we were in a desert, but I heard *trident*, and my mind entertained the possibility of Neptune appearing. But then, considering there were angels behind me, was thinking of Neptune, the sea god, blasphemy?

Yes.

"Hound," I scolded as we walked, and I heard him chuckle.

"Where is Ros?" I asked as we gathered closer to the other Watchers' area. I had not interacted with the others. Knowing the six I knew, was enough. I knew little of military lifestyle, but Sam was basically the top guy, Zel his second, and I still hadn't figured out if it was Chaz who was third, or was it Pen? I had noticed throughout the short time I did watch the others that they all moved in threes. Pen, Der and Ros were a three, Chaz, Zel and Sam the other. They were the six that came for me the very first night, the night that changed my life forever.

"He went hunting," Der answered as he cast a casual eye over the camp. "What brings you out, Star?" Der glanced up at the sun and then my loose camisole top and shorts. "You'll burn."

"Pen made me a lotion that doesn't make my skin greasy and is like factor a hundred and something." I grinned at Pen. "I'm in the desert, and I get to tan."

"Weirder every day," Der muttered to Chaz, who chuckled. "Did Pen dress you?"

I looked down at my top and shorts. "No, these are mine. One of the hellhounds got them for me."

"It's quite a lot of leg," Pen commented. "I can give you robes if you prefer."

"You mean you would prefer." I glanced down at my milky white legs. "Nope, I'm good like this." Shoving my hands in my back pockets, I scanned the area. "I need them here."

"All of them?" Pen asked, and Hound nodded.

"Then we should go to the ether," Der said.

"No," I cut in. "I can feel Gabriel glaring at me all the way from here. They need to come here, to avoid suspicion."

Ros came back first, covered in blood from head to foot. He had blood sprayed over his face and in his hair. He had never looked more Viking to me.

Zel came next, careful, watchful. He glanced at me once and then frowned at Ros. "Who?" he asked him.

"One of Lucifer's. Fucker needed to learn manners."

Warm hands slipped around my waist, and I automatically leaned back into Sam. His teeth nipped at my neck, and I turned my head to gaze up at him.

"I'm sorry," he whispered against my lips before he caught them in a kiss. Breaking away once he kissed me hello, I understood. We could talk later when the time was right, but right now, I understood he needed time. I'd disappeared on him so many times now, who was I to be a hypocrite? I knew he would return to me when he had taken the time that *he* needed to come to terms with it all.

"Why are you half-naked?" Sam asked as he moved around me, and I felt my clothes change.

Looking down, I was in a strappy yellow sundress that fell mid-calf. Staring up at him, he handed me a straw hat. "Really?"

"Your father says you are susceptible to heat stroke and will refuse to wear a hat unless I make you." He grinned. "This is me making you."

Gritting my teeth, I plopped the hat on my head and snatched the sunglasses off of him with a low growl. "When did you see Dad?"

"Earlier. He sends his love."

I squinted as I watched him, and I knew he couldn't see me behind the shades, but that didn't mean he didn't know I was having words with him later.

"You called us?" Zel asked.

"I need a ward," I said to Hound, who nodded, and I felt the ripple in the air. Then another, and I eyed Ros, who was rubbing demon blood off his face.

Unnecessary.

I turned away to hide my smile at Hound's grumpiness at Ros enhancing his ward.

"They can't hear?" I asked.

"No."

"I don't think it's Lucifer and Satan behind the Return. The illusion of my child was for a reason, but I don't think the Return is them," I blurted and saw a few of them raise their eyebrows in surprise. "When I was in the Tree, I saw the scene twice, but the"—I swallowed—"the shock of what I was being shown made me blind to some of the details."

"How so?" Sam asked me thoughtfully.

"When I focused on them, especially the second time, I

could see Satan literally pulling strings, and the demons and the Tree were behind him."

"You told us this," Der said.

"They were *behind* him."

"Behind his back," Chaz mused. "Lucifer's too?"

"Yes, there is another prince working on the Return. Satan told me he hates Bumblebee, but is there another? Cross said *four* princes."

"Beelzebub," Pen corrected me. "Prince of Envy."

"That was it." I nodded in agreement. "Who else is there?" They exchanged a look, which was really impressive for six males to do and not once meet my stare.

"Abbadon." Ros looked grim as he turned to Sam. "If sloth or envy have joined in, we need to tell Gabriel."

Sam was staring over at the camp. Gabriel glowed in the afternoon sun in his armour as he stood watching us. "We do." He held his hand out to me. "Witch."

Taking his hand, I squeezed. "Demon."

Sam and I walked to meet Gabriel hand in hand. Sam had once been one of them, once stood like they did, once believed what they had. I wondered if he regretted it. He never looked at the angels with scorn, he never mocked them. He may not always be respectful to Gabriel, but he was courteous to the others.

Sam understood soldiers. He understood war.

"It's not Satan that would have been the Angel of War, it's you," I realised as we walked over the sand. "That's why you're the General. You would have been next."

"Different life." Sam smiled down at me.

"If we defeat Satan, do you become the Prince of Wrath?"

"Fuck no, I'd rather fuck myself with something sharp and

pointed." My cheeks flushed, and he noticed. "Don't get kinky on me now, witch, we have bigger issues to focus on."

Gabriel waited for us with intolerance for our hand holding clear on his face. "What is it?"

"We need to take this inside," Sam told him pleasantly. Which was a shock for Sam to be pleasant to Gabriel, and it showed when Gabriel jerked his head in surprise.

In his tent, he turned on us and raised an eyebrow.

"Abbadon or Beelzebub may have joined the Return," Sam told him brusquely. "Potentially Abbadon, but I'm more inclined to believe it's Beelzebub."

"Working with Lucifer?" Gabriel asked thoughtfully.

I went to correct him, but Sam squeezed my hand in warning. "Yes, the princes all need to be apprehended and dealt with," Sam spoke calmly.

And I understood what he had just done. He was going to let the angels kill them all.

"We should clear all of hell," Gabriel told him bitterly as he sat down. "Rebellions should be ground to dust so they can never rise again."

Whoa, hateful much?

Sam smirked but remained calm. "My Watchers are not part of this."

"That you know of," Gabriel replied just as calmly. "All need to be interrogated."

It was me that squeezed Sam's hand this time. "You should go into the Tree." Both of them looked at me. "What's the big deal? If you truly doubt them, then enter the Tree. You'll see for yourself. It shows you what is true."

"You know nothing of what the *Tree* is and *I* do not need to be tested," Gabriel snapped at me. "My Father reveals all that is true to me," he added on.

"Really? When was the last time you spoke to him?"

"Heathen."

"Heathen? How?" I challenged him. "I sleep with a fallen angel, I'm speaking to an angel, I eat lunch with Death. I've seen the pit of hell. Trust me, angel, I'm a believer." I drew a breath. "My faith in your Father was never in question, well… until I met his sons."

Sam choked on a laugh, and within moments, we were walking back out of Gabriel's tent, the angel fuming behind us.

"Think that tipped him over?" I asked quietly.

"Pretty much." Sam grinned. When we reached the Watchers' camp, his smile was dimming as he looked around. "Go to the tent," he told me as he pressed a quick kiss to my lips. "Don't come out until I come in."

"Sam?"

"Run quick," he encouraged me as Hound came running towards us. "Morax, no one in, no one out."

"Sam!" I demanded.

"They're here."

Turning, I saw what he saw. A swathe of blackness across the golden sand, four riders on horses leading the way.

Holy crap.

WHEN WE HAD SPOKEN about the war between heaven and hell, I never for one moment thought they would keep me out of it. But out of it I was.

I blamed myself. When Sam told me to run, I had panicked and done exactly that, and with Hound beside me, I hadn't thought about my blind obedience until I was in the tent.

And I couldn't get out.

Because they had spelled me in.

Hound would not be persuaded to let me out, so I stayed in the tent, listening to the sounds of war outside, and had no knowledge if my friends were okay. I had stopped talking to Hound about a day ago and had meticulously and methodically tried to coax my power to do what I needed it to. Which was let me out of the tent.

But they had blocked me.

And I knew exactly how. I had been betrayed with a kiss.

Sam had kissed me and apologised. He hadn't been apologising for taking his anger and loss away from me and dealing with it on his own. No, the motherfucking backstabbing demon had been apologising for blocking my powers. He wanted me safe, so he spelled me to stay in this tent. Out of danger.

When I got out and if he was still alive, I was going to kick his arse so badly and rip his balls off so hard they were going to have to call him Samantha.

Hound snorted and I knew he could hear me. "Don't laugh at me," I warned him. "It's not funny."

Sorry.

"I told you not to talk to me," I reminded him.

Of course.

"Then stop talking to me!"

I paced the floor of the tent. I was never going into a tent ever again, and the desert could go fuck itself.

"Quite the pickle you're in." Cross smiled as he took a seat.

Hound glanced at me when I stopped walking but resumed his position facing forward.

"I thought you weren't allowed to let anyone in?" I demanded of him.

Is this a trick? If I answer, do you tell me I'm not to talk?

I gave up. "How did you get past the wards?" I asked Cross.

"Magic."

"Let me out."

"No." He gave me that smile that made me want to knife him.

"Your energy is very violent," he observed. "Why?"

"They locked me in."

"You cannot fight in a war," Cross scoffed. "You can hardly fight yourself." He looked me over clinically. "What are you wearing?"

Looking down, I took in the torn sundress I had tried to rip off myself in fury and didn't succeed. With my shorts on and a cardigan tied around my waist because it got cold in the desert at night.

"I don't know."

Cross dressed me in leggings and a long T-shirt. Simple, comfy, completely me.

"Thanks." I looked at him and then the tent flap. "Why aren't you out there reaping?"

"I was asked to bring you." He stood and fixed his black suit jacket.

"Bring me where?"

"The Tree." As he walked over to me, I hadn't realised I had backed away. "Come, Star, it's time to end this."

"You're working with the bad guys?" I asked him in disbelief and I saw Hound had stilled completely, as if he had been frozen.

"I am Death."

"My death?" My heart was pumping so hard I thought it was going to explode.

"Everyone's death."

Horror flooded me. "Oh, my fucking Lord." I recalled what I had seen. "You were on one of the horses. *You're* going to bring about the fucking apocalypse. It was never me."

Cross grinned. "He rode a pale horse, and his name was Death."

CHAPTER 28

I wasn't sure what shook me more, that Cross was part of it all, or that Hound was powerless to stop him. Death walked through the camp casually. No one turned to confront us, no one glanced our way, and then I saw them, shimmering in the sunlight.

Souls.

Thousands and thousands of souls shielding us.

Twisting in Cross's hold, I searched for Sam. I needed to see that he was alright. I needed to see him one more time, because I was almost certain that I would never see him again.

I caught sight of a long braid swinging as the wearer ducked and cut curved blades of fire upwards to its attacker. Ros spun on his heel, his eyes meeting mine but looking right past me. He was bleeding, a cut above his eye, his arms streamed with blood, his tunic cut and torn. But he was still alive.

If Ros was there, Der would be close. Sure enough, I saw him, wielding his axe as he waded through demons like a lumberjack on speed. I now understood his crisscrossing of scars on his arms. He used them like blockers for attacks, and I felt bile rise as he simply lobbed a head off of a demon.

Where was he? Why couldn't I see him? As I turned again, Cross sighed in frustration, and I was hoisted over his shoulder. Flattening my palms against his back, I propped myself up and saw the fury that was Azazel fighting beside his General. I had seen them fight before, I had seen them fight together and apart, and I had seen them tear through scavengers like a hot knife through butter. Seeing them fight demons? I had the irrational wish that Cross would slow down so I could watch them, which was quickly overridden by a scream for help.

But they never heard me, because the souls were my personal soundproofing as Cross carried me through a war zone to the Tree. The Tree pulsed with power, but Cross did not falter. He strode up to it like he was walking up the garden path. When he got to where he wanted, he dropped me like a sack of potatoes. I looked up and saw the other three.

Satan stood with his hands on his hips, watching the battle, his lip curled with disgust or hunger, I wasn't sure which. His eyes were their snake slits, and the back of his hands showed scales. He didn't look at me, too fixated on the battle.

Lucifer stood beside him. His dark trousers and white shirt looked pristine. He glanced at me once and gave me a cursory nod. Like I was here at my own will. He too returned to watch the battle.

The third one, I didn't know. Dark brown skin, long flowing dark hair, eyes that burned red. He looked a lot like Hound, only his hair was long.

I was going to throw up.

"Who are you?" I asked him.

When he smiled at me, I saw his teeth were sharp and pointed. With legs trembling, I raised myself to stand. They were all facing the battle, except Cross, who watched me the whole time.

"Why are you doing this?" I asked him, not caring that the others could hear me.

"Come, it is time to enter." He turned his back on me, and I rushed to tackle him. The prince I didn't know grabbed me, and I screamed as he tossed me over his shoulder and followed Cross.

I saw Lucifer reluctantly turn and walk behind us, but Satan did not move. His attention stayed riveted to the battle. He looked up sharply and I did too, as golden streaks lit the sky, and Satan started to laugh.

He turned and saw me watching him. "Little morsel, it's been so long." He looked amused. "Think you're going to miss the finale, but hey, maybe you'll catch the highlights."

We were inside the Tree, and I didn't know why it opened for them. The woman from before was nowhere to be seen. The Tree still throbbed with power, but as the long-haired demon set me down, I saw that there were no longer three paths, there were twelve.

"I go first," the long-haired one spoke.

"We've spoken about this, Beel, and we agreed, remember? We don't enter." Satan spoke to the demon, who I now knew was Beelzebub, in a calm, placatory manner.

Which Prince was Beelzebub? Envy? Satan told me he hated envy. Why were they all together? Why was I still thinking that everything that Satan had told me was the truth?

"You're going to walk the paths?" I asked as I turned slowly to look around the chamber.

"No, we are not interested in what is true and untrue." Lucifer spoke crisply and calmly. "We only seek one thing."

I waited. They were all looking at a separate path. "Well?" I snapped.

"To bring the Tree down," Beelzebub rumbled.

"You will walk the path," Cross said as if he suddenly remembered I was there.

"Me?"

"You are human, and you seek the truth," Cross explained. "Walk one or walk them all, you will find the one that leads to how it ends." His dark stare held mine unblinkingly.

"Fuck you."

"She is not pleasing," Lucifer suddenly declared. "To look at or to listen to. The accent is jarring."

"I bet she fucks well," Satan answered him. "Samyaza, the prick that he is, his scent is all over her." Satan looked me over. "She good?" he asked as he turned to Cross.

I scowled at Satan. "Pig. Shut the fuck up."

"I don't like her," Beelzebub declared. "Where is the Watcher?"

Suriel must have been hovering on a path, because he stepped into the chamber, and I knew I was definitely in trouble. *This* Watcher definitely wanted me dead.

"They are falling?" he asked the four of them.

"Yup." Satan beamed. "Just like we knew they would. Father empties heaven to deal with the rising of hell." He cast me a victorious look. "And you know what they say, while the cat's away, the mice come out to—"

"Die." I cut him off. "In mousetraps. Because the cat's not fucking stupid and plans ahead for rodents who think they're clever."

The blow from Suriel knocked me down. But I didn't care. I got myself back to my feet and stood as I looked at them all.

"Why am I here?"

"Choose the path," Cross told me firmly. "Tell us what it shows you."

"No."

Suriel hit me again, and again I fell. With my hand to my

cheek, I stood. I'd sparred with Ros, Der, Hound and Cross. I could take a hit.

"Pick one," Cross spoke as if I wasn't facing the biggest betrayal of my life.

"Go fuck yourself."

Although I was ready for it, I still fell hard when the punch knocked me down. The follow up kick to my ribs cracked something, but holding Cross's stare, I got back to my feet.

"Star," Cross admonished with a slight shake of his head.

"Dickface," I mocked with a shake of mine. I saw him grit his teeth as he looked away.

When Suriel went to strike me again, Lucifer stopped him. "You kill her, she is no use to us."

"And after?" Suriel asked as he flexed his fists.

Lucifer looked at me. "Break her."

Suriel's feral grin made my throat close up, but I kept my head high.

"Little tasty witch," Satan walked around me, tutting. I tensed but tried not to react. "I've been watching you."

"Should I be flattered?" I asked him as I dabbed at my lip, which was bleeding from Suriel's blow.

"No," Satan snickered. "You think you're strong, you're not strong. You think you are equal to a Watcher," he scoffed. "You are nothing compared to them." His hand ran over my head before he gripped my hair and yanked my head back. "You think you can beat me, Star?"

Snake eyes stared down at me, and my eyes watered when he wrenched my head back further.

"No," my voice was hoarse. "But Samyaza will, and he will rip your spine from your body."

Satan thrust me at Cross, who caught me as I stumbled and quickly let go of me.

"Just tell her," Beelzebub said. "Tell her so she goes in."

Lucifer grinned, Satan laughed, and Cross looked momentarily confused before he schooled his features.

"Tell me what?"

"You," Satan crooned in my ear, "are going to walk the path, all of them if you have to, and when you find the path that brings this all down, and the path opens back to my Father's house, I will go up there and I will kill them all and we will have both heaven and hell. If you do that, find the path, I won't kill you."

I snorted. "Do you want gratitude?"

A sharp piercing in my side made me scream as he stabbed me. "I didn't hit anything major," he assured me calmly as he slipped the knife back into his pocket.

The pain was nauseating, and I staggered, but I yelped when hands reached out to steady me.

"I said no." I was going to die here, in this Tree, with these lunatics, and I would never see Sam again, because I had no doubt these fuckers would throw me in the hellfire.

"Staaaar," Satan sang beside me. "Guess what I have?"

"A limp dick?"

He was in my face, snake eyes glowing amber. His tongue darted out, exactly like a snake's, and licked the blood from my lip, causing me to jerk backwards, but he caught me and he brought my face up to meet his.

"No, little morsel, my dick is just fine." He grinned. "I heard about your loss."

"Don't." I knew better than to plead as he pushed me away from him.

"Such a shame. I mean, it wasn't, not really, Nephilim? After all my hard work here? *All* the planning, and you were going to birth a fucking Nephilim? Fuck that."

The blood from my side was trickling over my hip and down my leg. I felt faint. I had to be stronger.

"Pick a path," Satan ordered me as he steadied me. Pushing my hair behind my ear, he brought his lips close, and I hated myself for the whimper I let out. "Pick a path, or I burn the soul of your son in the hellfire." My head whipped around to meet his, and he nodded with a big shit-eating grin. "That's right, I have his soul."

My eyes flew to Cross, who remained expressionless.

"You're not a reaper."

"Fallen angel, sweet cheeks, fallen...*angel*. And I'm hungry for a bite."

My head bowed as my face throbbed, and my hand pressed into my side. When he killed his fellow princes previously, he ingested their power. How much power would the soul of my son give him? "Oh fuck, I hate you so much right now."

I heard their laughter, and I didn't care.

Willing myself to not be the weakest one in the room and break down and cry, I raised my head. "When they come for you, I hope they leave you until last," I told Suriel. "I hope they make your death nice and long and slow." I smiled at him, splitting my lip further. "I hope you feel every single cut as they take your head, and I hope, *desperately* hope, they dip you in hellfire, slowly. So you can feel every last lick of the flame as it consumes your soul and you are erased from this world."

"You'll be dead," he snarled at me.

"I'm counting on it." I jabbed the knife that I'd stolen from Satan's pocket when he taunted me, right into my jugular.

Cross's eyes widened in horror, and I almost faltered when I saw it, but with a final thrust of energy, I jumped onto a path.

Stumbling, I banged off the walls as I ran, my blood draining from me, and before I was ready, I was on my hands and knees, panting. "Don't let me die here," I begged the Tree. "Please, not on the path. Take me to the scene, let me see how it turns out."

My hands clutched at my neck, trying to stem the flow as I tried to stand. The flash happened, and I was on my back under a million stars, and all around me, a scene played. Like one of those cinemas that were round, so you could see it all in a three hundred and sixty degree visual.

The blood ebbed slowly from my neck, and I coughed, the sound wet and gargled as more blood poured from me. "Damn, I bleed a lot," I muttered in disgust.

"They say an average human holds eight pints of blood."

Turning my head, I looked at her as she lay in the grass beside me, long hair loose as she turned her attention to the scenes playing around us.

"Where the fuck have you been?" I asked her.

"I am not allowed to interfere."

"If you say balance, I will stab you too."

Rising up on her elbow, she cupped the side of my neck. "I can't heal you," she told me, "but I can slow it down."

Tears spilled over, and I nodded my thanks. "Show me how it ends," I begged her.

She lay back down, her hand in mine, and I looked to the stars. "Look left," she whispered, and I turned my head.

They were fighting. I saw them clearly. They had formed together, battling. Sam was covered in blood and grime, his eyes glowing green, his shadows dipping into his enemies. Zel, fierce and furious beside him, had nicks and cuts, but he seemed okay. Pen, Chaz, Der were all fighting, all bleeding but alive. Ros had been fighting too, lethal and true until he stopped short, blood all down one side of him, as Hound burst from the tent.

With a cry, Ros ran after him, screaming at Sam.

They were all running to the Tree.

I saw Gabriel see them run and think they were attacking the Tree, not knowing I was inside it. Streaks of gold fell across the sky, and Gabriel turned his attention from the battle—the distraction that it was—to the real danger at the Tree.

Only, the Watchers were not the danger. The danger lay within. But Gabriel didn't know that, and he struck out at them from where he stood, as Sam struck the Tree.

"No, they'll bring it down," I whispered as I realised. They were *both* attacking the Tree to get inside.

Gabriel and Sam.

Heaven and hell.

Satan's plan was working. It was never about me picking a path, it was about me as bait, a focus for their combined attack, and they didn't know. The Tree would never show how to fell it. Would Cross know that? But the combined power of heaven and hell striking it, in the wild hope to break inside? Would the Tree stand? I feared that it would fall. Their power was immense. The Tree shook.

Samyaza, in his love for me, was going to do what he said. He would burn it all down, and he *didn't even know* he was playing into their hands.

"No." I struggled to sit up. "No."

She caught me, and gently but firmly, she pressed me back into the grass.

"Watch."

Hound threw himself at the Tree again and again, howling his fury.

Sam struck the Tree trunk again, and I felt it shudder.

Gabriel reached them, and I watched as he leaped for Sam, the sword aimed at his back, and I cried out when Zel's sword stopped the blow.

Ros raced forward, shouting words I couldn't hear, and I saw Gabriel's eyes widen in understanding and then narrow in realisation. He now knew that he hadn't been deceived, that the Watchers weren't double-crossing them, but Sam was still going to bring the Tree down.

Because he knew I was inside.

"I have to get out." I tried to move, but my blood loss was too much, my energy was gone. "*Please*, I need out."

"No, little Star, you don't." Her voice was so gentle. Her fingers smoothed my hair back as I lay dying on the grass.

"Please." My voice was no more than a whisper, and she kissed my head gently.

"Let go."

With every ounce of remaining strength I had, I caught her hand. "Please, let me...see."

Her hand rested across my forehead, and I saw him. Eyes wild, shadows dancing around him, fury in every particle of his body. Sam stepped back and looked up at the Tree.

Grimly, he tore his shirt off, and I could feel my confusion until I saw the tattoos on his shoulders. The tribal ink he wore, that ended in pointed tips over his shoulders, in my head, I saw the tattoos move.

Huge wings of shadow sprouted from him, and he stood there with his swords of fire in his hands and his wings spread out behind him. I saw but did not pay attention to the Watchers behind him, who were poised and ready to fight.

All I saw was him.

How could I look at anything else?

He was breathtaking.

He was really going to end it all.

Please no, stop him. Not this. Not for me.

She heard me. I felt cool lips brush against my forehead, and then she was in front of Sam.

She was small. So slight. He could knock her over with one of his pointed glares.

I couldn't hear what she said, but I saw Ros turn away in pain, I saw Chaz cry out, I saw Zel flinch, and I saw Sam bow his head, and I felt the pain like it was my own.

It probably was. I was in a shitload of agony. But I needed to hang on.

I watched them turn from the Tree and look at the army of demons before them, and then I watched Sam beat his wings of shadow and the demon army started to scream as the Watchers advanced with the angels by their side, and they unleashed their fury.

The scene stopped in my head suddenly, and I knew I had been allowed to see all I needed to see. I lay there struggling when I realised breathing hurt. I felt her come back and lie beside me.

Did you know he had wings made of shadows?

"Yes."

Coolest shit I ever saw.

My eyes dipped closed, but I forced them open again.

I'm going to die inside the Tree of Life. Can you see the irony there?

"Yes."

Dying sucks.

"It does."

Will you make sure Hound is okay?

"I can't move far from the Tree. I am bound to it."

Ever? Fuck, that may be worse than Hound's curse. He can't die.

A cough caught in my throat, and I choked on my own blood and saliva for what felt like eternity.

Okay, you slowed it down, speed it up. I'm ready.

"Are you sure?"

Yeah, I'm done. My fight is over. They stopped the Return, right?

I opened my eyes and saw the sky. The stars were fading, and the dawn was rising, ready to blaze across the sky and chase the darkness away for another day.

"Star?"

Mm-hmm.

"Choose."

Epilogue

The water splashed into the pool below it, and I looked up at the pale blue sky as I relished in the quiet of the Waterfall of Solitude.

The Land of the Souls was peaceful. It had always been peaceful to me. Well, apart from that time I burned all the souls. But in my defence, that was the Watchers' fault. Kind of.

Climbing out of the pool, I shook my wet hair as I picked up a cover-up. Yup, even dead, I was self-conscious. Hound lay watching the water as it spilled into the pool below, and I wondered if he was fighting the urge to jump in and splash around.

You insult me.

"I could really insult you if you like?" I teased him.

You swear enough as it is.

"What can I say, my friend, I'm just a foul-mouthed, sarcastic ray of sunshine."

He grunted but didn't reply.

Kicking back on the wall, I looked upwards. I would never tire of looking at the sky. Even if it was here.

You have a lot to do today.

"I know." I sighed. There was a lot to do every day.

You made this choice.

"I know, you remind me daily."

I *had* made the choice, as I lay dying in the Tree of Life, the irony, I had been given three choices.

I could become a soul, like Naomie, which would then be hauled into the hellfire by my enemies before I could say boo.

I could die and become just another sad soul waiting to be processed by the elevator repairman, who was currently missing.

I could die, become a full necromancer, and I would be able to reside in the Land of the Souls and learn my craft, be the necromancer I was meant to be, but to gain that chance there is always a catch. *Balance.* My sacrifice was the Watchers, I would never see them again. I would be erased from their memories as if I never was.

I chose option three.

One was, well, one wasn't an option. Two, the complete paradox of the option broke my brain every time I thought about it. I *was* the elevator repairman, so was I simply waiting for myself? Three, well, three offered me peace and afterlife, if not afterlove. In all of the choices, I died. My human body was not permitted to go on, because I could bear the child of a Watcher.

The Tree of Life wasn't a fan of the apocalypse. In my death I realised that the Tree was *the* balance, the neutral between heaven and hell. Me being able to carry a Nephilim that would command every soul, ever? The Tree wasn't taking chances.

There was to be no miraculous save for me from my hero. I was the only one who could save me, so I chose option three, and I knew it was more than I could have hoped for. The Tree gave me the chance to find my son's soul, I hadn't ruled out Satan had told me another lie, but I also couldn't say it wasn't the truth. I was determined to learn my calling.

I hadn't expected Hound to arrive the very next day. Or… whenever it was, but it was soon. Because the Tree was kind of groovy. Yes, I did make the terrible dad joke, and the Tree let me have one fallen angel who did not forget me, and who would quite honestly take my secret to his grave, and since he couldn't die, I was safe.

I had cried out my loss until I had no more tears, and then Hound had filled me in on the events after I snuffed it.

Sam had gone full fallen angel apocalypse on the demons' asses. Between him and Gabriel, the wrath for their duplicity had been, for all accounts, epic. I felt a tiny bit sorry for the demons in the battle; I think they were ignorant of their role as a decoy, while their leaders played their own game inside the Tree. But still, those demons wanted to return from whence they fell, screw them.

Lucifer, Beelzebub, and Satan did not escape Sam's wrath either. You wanted to fuck with the General of the Watchers? You should have had a plan B.

The three princes didn't, as they were so confident that Lucifer's plan would work. The Prince of Pride's head had rolled first. The Prince of Envy had not been envious of his brother's death but had also met his demise in the hellfire.

Satan, Sam had taken himself, to kill personally. Hound had not shared details, but I think it was long, painful, torturous, and I really hoped someone had recorded it, because when I could figure out how to get electricity here—that wasn't coming from me—I would watch that on repeat.

Cross had vanished. There was no sign. He was Death, and even though I was not really clear on his complete involvement or how they talked Sam out of his revenge, I don't think the world would cope without the true balance of life and death. I was already dealing with a backlog in his absence.

But for me, right now, the shady motherfucker could walk

himself right off his white sand beach into his sea and keep walking for all I cared.

His betrayal hurt. But in my weaker moments, I tried to convince myself he was playing both sides for some special reason only he knew, and it wasn't to break my trust and watch me get beat up or kill myself, but something *more*. Had he known I would never let the princes win? Possibly. But those weaker moments were very few and far between.

Hound did delight in telling me, in glorious detail, how Azazel killed Suriel. Again, lots of torture, burning in the pit, salt, melting of eyeballs, all really bloodthirsty stuff, and I was so pleased that Zel never let me down. The Lady in the Tree had told them what I had said to Suriel before I killed myself, and my Watchers had delivered.

And when they had struck the last blow, she had already spelled them to wipe their very long memories clean of Star Elizabeth Archer. The naïve witch who they found in a village in Slate wasn't even the echo of a memory for them.

I was gone, as if I had never been.

Standing up, I called for my Wind. He came hurtling towards me, joyously twisting in all his cyclone glory. Stepping into him, I directed him to the Plains of the Dead.

Naomie sat on the edge of a cliff, watching the sea below her. It was a training day for Star the Inept Witch. She had found me by complete accident, weeks after I died. She had come looking for Hound as she sought Death. Instead, she caught Hound mid tirade about my inability to control my powers as a necromancer. I had been arguing back that they weren't as effective since I had, after all, died.

Once Naomie had overcome her shock, we had sworn her to secrecy, and slowly she had introduced training. Because I may reside in the Land of the Souls, but clearly hell still waited for me in the afterlife.

"Yo, Grandmother, no point jumping, you're already dead, love."

She turned to look at me, rolling her eyes as she stood. "Did I not tell you that you can't call me grandmother, especially as I'm technically the same age as you?"

"You did, but I'm really disobedient."

"I ought not to teach you today," she snarked as she walked over to me.

"I don't know why it has to be so hard," I complained. "I'm going to drown in this pool of knowledge you insist I immerse myself in."

"You won't drown, and I've told you before, all you need to do is tread water. I'm not asking you to rise from it."

"Fine, fine, whatever, but not too long today, I have a heap of new ones to process." I ignored Naomie's wince. She didn't like some of my terminology about my processing souls any more than Cross had. *Arsehole.*

Hours later, I was walking back to the Waterfall of Solitude, but as usual, my feet pulled me to the Grove. I'd discovered it a few months after the Lady in the Tree sent me here. It was a cluster of trees, a low stone wall, and in the centre of a concrete patio was a birdbath.

For a dimension that didn't cater too much to the death of animals, it had confused the hell out of me. Until I looked in.

And I saw him. I had stayed and watched him for hours, maybe more. With some difficulty but a whole lot of perseverance, I had eventually seen them all.

My Watchers. Again with the irony: *I* was watching the Watchers.

I tried not to come here all the time. I knew it wasn't healthy. It hurt only me, and in my weird brain, that therefore meant it was okay because I wasn't hurting anyone else. I had named it the Grove of Reflection and thought I was the shit until I told Hound and he had laughed and told me that I was incredibly basic. I didn't care. It showed me them, and that's all I needed.

Tonight, they were at dinner, eating, laughing and drinking. Relaxed, being them, being free.

Naomie and I ate, but as I clung to the memory of my human life, food still lacked flavour. It seemed in death I answered my own question to Ros all those weeks ago. I hadn't lost my humanity when I died, it was what made me, *me*. However, I think if I was honest, I was holding myself back, which hindered my learning. But Naomie assured me it would get better in time, which hurt, because time was all I had.

Deciding that was enough for tonight, I headed back to my small house that I had built with my own hands and then some power, and then Naomie had fixed it. I would like my full powers back, but I understood, I had lost a lot when I died.

So much.

My parents…lost their daughter, and Hound checked on them periodically to ensure they were okay as they processed their grief. Until I could control my powers as a necromancer, I was bound to the Land of the Souls. Another requirement of the Lady in the Tree.

Stopping on the path, I looked up at the sky. It was dark in the Land of the Souls, and somehow I knew that was me. I was slowly changing it; how, I wasn't sure. My mind was niggling on something I said when I spoke to Naomie. *Pool of knowledge.*

Pool.

Wetting my lips, I looked around as if I was scared that I was going to be caught. My mind flashed back to Zel, warning me that all he wanted me to do was dip my toe in, and all I had wanted to do was sink beneath the surface of the water.

The pool was *inside* me.

Dropping to sit on the path, I assumed the pose they used to make me do when we were meditating. Instead of searching externally for the Void, I looked within myself. The small cavern that Zel and I had entered waited for me. The pool was dark. Taking a deep breath, that I did not need, I walked into the water.

I walked into the water until it covered my chest. With a quick prayer to whoever listened to a soul, I sank under the water.

Flashes of colour raced around me as hands tugged me downwards. Kicking at them, I swam for the surface. When my head broke free, I scrambled for the cavern floor, dragging myself out. I lay like a drowned rat at the side of the pool. After a while, I pushed myself to my feet and opened my eyes in the Land of the Souls. Getting up, I resumed my walk to the house.

Did I feel any different? Not really. Had I thought I would burst out of the water reborn? I laughed at my own false hope. Maybe next time I wouldn't panic as much and let the hands take me.

"You have been watching us," he said behind me.

Holy shit, he wasn't supposed to be here.

"That's rich coming from a Watcher." *Shut up, you aren't allowed to talk to him!*

I heard his snort and knew he would have that arrogant smirk on his lips. *"You've* been watching. Why?"

I knew that tone, that was pissed off and angry Sam. "I observe only," I answered.

"Turn."

Absolutely not.

"You should go." I resumed walking.

"I said *turn.*"

I tilted my head to look at the sky. Arrogant bastard. I see *that* hadn't changed. He always was and he always would be. "I said you should *go.*"

I felt his power reach for me, and I wondered how I could make him show me his wings without looking at him. My own power flared to life, and I stumbled when I felt it rise. I swatted his power away. "Go home," I ordered as I kept walking.

With a tug and a jerk, I was rotated, and he was in front of me.

Dear delicious doughnuts, he looked amazing, the mirror in the birdbath hadn't done him justice. His hair was long, too long, and he had it swept to the side. His green eyes held a low pulse of power, and his brow was furrowed as he looked at me. His huge arms folded across his chest as he studied me.

"You?"

"No. Not me." I turned my back, my phantom heart pumping with excitement.

Again, I was turned, and I flung my hands up in frustration. "Go *away.*"

"Witch?"

"Demon?" *Shit.*

Sam stepped backwards in shock, his eyes scanning every inch of me before his eyes met mine.

"Witch," he said again as he started to smile, that slow lazy smile that melted my heart.

"Demon." I shook my head as he stepped closer, my hand raised to ward him off. "You should not be here."

Hands grabbed me, arms crushed me, lips tasted me. "I know you," he breathed against me. "Star." Green eyes searched my face in wonder before that smirk appeared, and his hand slipped around to cup the back of my neck, bringing his lips closer to me. "You're mine."

Heaven help me, but I was. I would *always* be. "I am."

I was a soul, and he was my mate.

I can't believe it's finished! I loved this series so much, I could happily spend my days here, learning Stars craft with her. Now I've been told that e-readers and/or tablets were in danger during the reading of this book, so if yours was, I dunno…thrown?…Star apologises. *I* would apologise, but I think you learned a long time ago, my characters are in control and I'm just here to take notes.

As always, if you enjoyed this book, it would mean so much if you considered writing a short review. Reader reviews are so important to a book's success and they help other readers discover new books and you can help with this, by writing just a couple of sentences. It's really appreciated.

Review a A Blaze of Stars & Dawn on your favourite book retailers site.

Thank you!

Eve L. Mitchell

ACKNOWLEDGMENTS

I would like to thank the people who help me get this piece of my imagination into your hands.

Anna, the cover is beautiful. I love it. Thank you. I screamed with excitement when I saw it and I loved that you said there were options and I was all "GIVE ME THIS ONE!"

Helayna, thank you for your perseverance through this book. I kept tweaking and you were your gracious and patient self throughout.

Thank you to Ashley, Shauna and Wildfire Marketing for the promo tours, the sign up and the management.

To the bloggers, reviewers, and bookstagrammers out there who have supported this launch, thank you so much. I appreciate each and every one of you.

To my beta girls and ARC team, thank you as always for being my support team.

Mr M, you are, as always, the reason I get my books published. Your love, support and patience keeps me sane, even when I know my focus drives you nuts. I know my levels of anxiety hit a new high during the writing of this book, because I love to give myself more challenges and each and every time you tell me I can do it, so…I think it's my turn to make the coffee.

To my readers, thank you from the bottom of my heart for continuing to pick up my books and lose yourself in the pages of a world I have created, it's an amazing gift that you give me each and every time you read my words.

Love Eve x

Eve L. Mitchell is a USA Today Bestselling author who writes contemporary romance and urban fantasy books.

Being an avid reader from a young age, Eve still considers herself to be a reader first. She believes there is nothing better than getting that new book either on your e-reader or in your hands, and the fact she may bring that excitement to a fellow reader, fills her with wonder. She writes under a pen name because otherwise her Secret Agent status will be revoked.

Eve lives in the North East of Scotland, with her three coffee machines and her significant other, Mr. M. She enjoys NFL Football, music and having long conversations with the voices in her head, which sometimes turn into the stories she writes.

If you want to keep up to date with all things Eve, to be the first to hear about updates from Eve sign up for her newsletter.

All the books; both fantasy and contemporary:
https://bit.ly/Evesnewsletter
Just contemporary romance book news:
https://bit.ly/Evesromancenewsletter
Just Fantasy books news:
https://bit.ly/Evesfantasynewsletter

Connect with all things Eve here: https://bit.ly/Eveslinks

Creatures of evil roam the shadows - the Drakhyn. They may look like humans, but their taloned hands and razor-sharp teeth serve one purpose only; killing.

A Sentinel's purpose is to patrol and protect. They are highly trained soldiers with superior skills and abilities. Whether they be Vampyres, Lycan, Castors or gifted Akrhyn, their purpose is the same; hunt the Drakhyn and rid the world of their evil presence.

GET THE SERIES
WWW.EVELMITCHELL.COM

FROM BOOK 1:

I am a typical, though admittedly anti-social, woman who lives alone in the rural Highlands of Scotland. I also happen to be a clairvoyant who can summon the dead. It's a pity the souls I see didn't give me a heads-up, nor did I glimpse my own future on the night six demons came hunting for me.

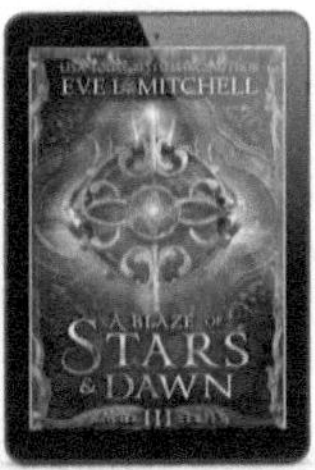

GET THE SERIES
WWW.EVELMITCHELL.COM

319

FROM BOOK 1: I knew the moment I saw Aiden that he was the kind of man who would break a woman's heart. With his looks he could grace the cover of any book or magazine.

Even as I got to know him, his hard no nonsense attitude was alluring. He was as captivating as he was intense. My pulse raced and my stomach fluttered when I was near him. Having his attention was as intoxicating as it was overwhelming.

Yes, Aiden would break a woman's heart. If she let him.

Maybe, even if she didn't.

GET THE SERIES

WWW.EVELMITCHELL.COM